# INNIS HARBOR

## By the Author

McCall

London

Innis Harbor

The First Kiss

Wild Wales

Laying of Hands

Return to McCall

Windswept

Undercurrent

**Visit us at www.boldstrokesbooks.com**

# INNIS HARBOR

by
Patricia Evans

2024

**INNIS HARBOR**
© 2024 By Patricia Evans. All Rights Reserved.

ISBN 13: 978-1-63679-781-6

This Trade Paperback Original Is Published By
Bold Strokes Books, Inc.
P.O. Box 249
Valley Falls, NY 12185

First Edition: December 2024

THIS IS A WORK OF FICTION. NAMES, CHARACTERS, PLACES, AND INCIDENTS ARE THE PRODUCT OF THE AUTHOR'S IMAGINATION OR ARE USED FICTITIOUSLY. ANY RESEMBLANCE TO ACTUAL PERSONS, LIVING OR DEAD, BUSINESS ESTABLISHMENTS, EVENTS, OR LOCALES IS ENTIRELY COINCIDENTAL.

THIS BOOK, OR PARTS THEREOF, MAY NOT BE REPRODUCED IN ANY FORM WITHOUT PERMISSION.

---

Credits
Editor: Stacia Seaman
Production Design: Stacia Seaman
Cover Design by Tammy Seidick

# Innis Harbor

## Chapter One

Loch Battersby spotted the journalist in a corner booth as she opened the glass door to the diner. He was already looking at his watch. The waitress behind the counter reached for a coffee cup as Loch rushed past and slid into the booth across from him, raking a hand through her hair. She took her sunglasses off, folded them with one hand, and glanced back at the waitress with a silent thank you as she saw her rounding the counter with her coffee.

"Sorry I'm late," she said, shrugging the black leather jacket off her shoulders and laying it beside her in the booth. "I was at a shoot for Madewell in Chelsea, and the photographer got there two hours after we were supposed to start."

The journalist, Colin Harper, was from *Avant Garde*, a well-known fashion magazine based in Manhattan, and today's appointment had already been pushed back twice due to her schedule. When he looked at his watch yet again before he spoke, Loch knew the interview wasn't going to go well.

"It's fine." He reached for the phone in his jacket pocket. "Let's just get started."

He set his phone to record and set it on the table between them, and Loch studied his face while he dug into his bag for a pen. He looked too young to have an attitude or the beard that took up half his face. It was unkempt in a hipster way, which meant it probably contained designer beard oil that cost more than her phone. She watched as he finally found his pen and checked the phone to be sure it was recording.

"So, I'm Colin Harper with *Avant Garde* magazine, and we're talking to Loch Battersby." He angled the phone slightly toward Loch.

He shuffled his notes, then dug into his bag again until he found the first page of questions.

"Okay. Most of our readers know you've spent the majority of your career working as a male model."

Loch nodded and waited for him to go on.

"What most people don't realize is that you started in the industry modeling as a girl."

Loch's favorite waitress, Roma, arrived just in time to catch what he was saying as the coffee cup and saucer clattered softly to rest on the worn Formica tabletop. Loch smiled as Roma turned to leave without a word, rolling her eyes as she went. Manhattan reporters usually wanted to meet in a bar for interviews, but Loch had always insisted on the diner on Thirty-seventh, one block over from her apartment. She'd been in the business long enough to know that martinis and recording devices didn't mix, and the waitresses had seen enough of the interviews over the years to be almost as tired of the stupid questions as she was.

"I did start as a girl booking traditional jobs, but after about a year, they started putting me into men's campaigns, and it just grew from there," Loch said. "Although in the last year, I've been booking more feminine jobs, just to mix it up a bit."

Colin nodded and took a delicate sip of the over-foamed cappuccino in front of him.

"So, you've been modeling for…?"

"Eleven years," Loch said. "An agent scouted me when I was fifteen at a music festival."

"And you'd say your look was more 'mainstream' when you started?"

"It was," Loch said, "but I still didn't book much the first year. I don't think they knew what to do with me."

❖

The agency Loch had initially signed with was one of the top three in the industry, but her look was hard to confine to a single category and even harder to book, as it turned out. She was tall, like most of the other models, but she also had broad shoulders and narrow hips, with a brooding, masculine edge to her features that stood out more on camera than in real life. The agent who'd scouted her, Harvey Goldberg, had always believed in her "unique" look, but unique didn't book shows or spreads in major magazines.

Almost a year after she'd started, one of the better-known photographers saw a test shot from a past job and asked her to shoot as a male model for Guess denim. From that point, her career blazed to life like a desert fire, and she started booking major men's campaigns, from Balenciaga to Burberry. She'd walked her first runway for Prada menswear in Paris the day she turned seventeen.

Loch was one of the first women in the industry to model almost exclusively as male, so she became instantly recognizable, but after a few years, she'd started to feel boxed in. She grew her hair out a bit and softened her look enough to shoot as both sexes, even within the same ad campaign, which had kept her current enough to stay on top. As the years passed, she became successful enough to choose the campaigns she modeled in and photographers she worked with and eventually became known for only choosing projects that promoted gender equality.

Colin cleared his throat and tapped his pen against the tabletop. "So, is that why you dye your hair?" He tilted his head to the side, studying her. "To look more masculine?"

Loch was known for her vivid, deep blue eyes and natural silver hair that had started to grow in the summer she turned ten. The trait ran in her family. Her great-grandmother had silver hair as a teenager, and it had become one of the characteristics that set her apart in the modeling industry.

"No." Loch ran her hand through her hair and tucked a stray lock behind one ear. "My hair is natural."

"Is it really?" He leaned across the table, bringing the faded scent of cigar smoke with him, and lowered his voice. "You can tell me. I won't put it in the article."

Loch looked again at Roma, who just shook her head and went back to filling the sugar containers. He waited for a moment, one eyebrow raised, but finally gave up when Loch didn't change her answer.

"Okay, whatever." Colin rolled up one sleeve of his button-up and turned to a new page in his notebook. "So really, you've come full circle, right?"

Loch raised an eyebrow and waited for him to go on. Hopefully, he wasn't headed where she suspected with this subject.

"You started in the business as a girl doing male modeling, and now after your sex change, you've gone back to booking more feminine shoots." He tapped his pen on the table with a blank look. "Why is that?"

The concept that she'd never had a sex change, that she might just be a woman with a more masculine look in photographs hadn't even occurred to him. Loch didn't answer, just pulled a five out of her pocket as she got up and left it on the counter for Roma. She felt the world turn under her foot as she stepped out of the building into the sheer gold sunlight. She'd just crossed West Thirty-seventh Street toward her apartment when she heard her phone ring.

It was her mom, calling to tell her that her aunt Samia had died in a car accident that morning. Loch stopped where she was on the sidewalk, clicked off her phone, and held it to her heart, the world streaming past her on both sides as if nothing had happened.

❖

Two weeks later, Loch slung her bag over her shoulder as she headed toward the exit in the Bar Harbor, Maine, airport. She hadn't flown into Bar Harbor for almost ten years, but the dark path of stains on the carpet still pointed like arrows toward the exit, and the same nicked plastic chairs with chrome legs lined the walls. She ran a hand through her hair and winced at the drift of stale cigarette smoke that still clung to it from the shoot she'd left that morning in Manhattan.

It seemed like every photographer in the world smoked, and

they all did it about five inches from her face, holding the cigarette and camera together as if they put either one down they'd cease to exist. The shoot that morning for Yves St. Laurent had started at five a.m. and finally finished seven hours later, three hours past schedule. She'd barely had time to jump in a cab to the airport and had almost missed her flight. One of the TSA agents recognized her at the last minute and rushed her through security in time to catch the last call at the gate.

Loch climbed into the only waiting taxi outside the airport, and after she'd woken up the driver, he managed to get her to the docks just in time to catch the rusted yellow ferry over to Innis Harbor. Her dad's sister Samia, Loch's favorite aunt, had lived there all her life, and it was also where Loch had spent most of her summers until she'd started modeling. If there was a place in the world that felt like home to her other than Manhattan, the tiny coastal town of Innis Harbor was it.

She stopped at the café bar in the ferry lobby for a large black coffee, then walked outside to the ferry deck as it left the docks and leaned against the rail, feeling the wind whip underneath her jacket. She zipped it up and dug her beanie out of her pocket, pulling it low on her head and squinting into the sun. Even in May, the wind coming off the water and wrapping itself around her had a sharp edge.

She hadn't had a minute since her aunt died to miss her, but now the ache was settling into her chest. She'd spent so many summers in Maine, watching Samia sketch for hours in her art studio and wandering down every empty dock she found, regardless of who it belonged to. Samia and her partner, Colleen, had pretty much let her do her own thing, which worked out until she was old enough to catch the ferry to Bar Harbor and get drunk with her friends. But even then, they were willing to watch her make her own mistakes; Samia had always listened a lot more than she talked, and that made all the difference.

After about twenty-five minutes, the ferry pulled into the community docks in Innis Harbor at the Marine Center. Loch shaded her eyes and looked toward town, a five-minute walk from the ferry. She stepped onto the dock, still swaying from the wake of the boat. Loch closed her eyes, letting the sun melt warmth onto her face. The water lapped at the side of the creaking gray boards, and seagulls swooped overhead before they came to rest on the wooden pillars supporting the docks, the breeze ruffling their feathers as they settled into noisy groups. The air was infused with salt, a texture she felt with every breath, and the lobster traps lined up in the water shifted and jostled like children. Loch stood there for a moment before she opened her eyes to find that for the first time in forever, no one was looking at her.

The last time she was here, the population had been under a thousand people, and it looked to be the same now, as Loch headed from the docks to the steps leading up into town. Innis Harbor did get some tourists in the summer, mostly to watch the lobster boats dock and line up their traps. But it was a working fishing village, and lobstering was the primary source of income, so the tourists had to be content to watch from a safe distance. Occasionally, one of them asked if there was a boat that provided scenic cruises or something similar, and the locals in chest-high yellow rubber waders just pointed their gutting knives toward the commercial ferry back to Bar Harbor.

As she walked up Main Street she stopped into Gerrish Market, where a striped blue and white awning flapped in the breeze across the front of the building. Long risers by the front door held crates of early season fresh blueberries, and the blueberry farms dotted the landscape in every direction like a handful of scattered rocks. The salt in the local soil gave a deep softness to the flavor. Loch had always been able to tell which blueberries came from the Innis Harbor farms and which were farmed farther inland from the scent alone. She ran her fingertips across the surface of the silvery blueberries as she went into the shop, and the handmade cardboard open sign fluttered against the glass door as it shut behind her.

It had been two weeks since Samia died. Loch hadn't gone to the funeral. She'd had back-to-back shoots scheduled in London, and it had been too late to cancel. Before she left, her agent asked when she was coming back to New York, but she didn't answer.

For the first time in her life, she didn't know what she was going to do next. Fashion had always collided with celebrity, and celebrity required constant exposure, but for the past few months, Loch had started to wish no one knew her name.

She bought some wine and a baguette at the market and slowly climbed the long slope up from the town center to Samia's house, the late afternoon sun warm and heavy on her shoulders. It finally came into view as she crested the hill—a two-story classic Cape Cod–style clad in cedar shingles and held together with white trim. The door was cherry red, and bright white Adirondack chairs dotted the length of the front porch. As she got closer, she noticed that it looked much older than she remembered. The paint on the trim had peeled, revealing the graying boards underneath, and one of the navy blue shutters on the second level hung from one hinge. Weeds choked the base of the front steps, and the lawn looked like it hadn't been mowed since the previous year.

The porch steps creaked under her boots, and she slung her bag onto one of the chairs with a *thunk*. Loch stood in front of the door, seagulls screeching behind her as they glided past on the way to the docks. She wanted to just go inside but couldn't make herself touch the doorknob.

Her eyes shut tight against the memories that swept across her mind in a dark storm. A vivid picture flashed through her mind as if projected onto the door by an old film reel, and she watched, her eyes still shut. It was her, running through the same front door as a child. It slammed shut behind her as she raced into the kitchen to grab the salami sandwich Samia held out to her with one hand while she filled the bright yellow farmhouse sink with the other. The lemon-scented steam rose past the chipped enamel as ten-year-old Loch pulled herself up on the counter to watch. Bubbles slowly covered the pile of paintbrushes at the bottom, each smeared with a different color and piled up like pieces of a broken rainbow. Samia handed her the brushes when they were clean, one by one, and mustard dripped slowly from the sandwich onto her frayed denim shorts as Loch laid them out in a neat row to dry.

The scene refused to fade until Loch shook her head to clear it.

Her feet were still frozen on the peeling white planks of the porch, unwilling to take her closer to the door. She finally gave up and sank down where she was, watching twilight darken and fade into the surface of the sea at the bottom of the hill, pierced by the amber lights of the boats gliding into the harbor for the night.

    She sat there until black night fell and the only light came from the moon, but when she finally stood to unlock the door, she realized she didn't have a key. Loch rubbed her forehead with the heel of her hand and fought the tears burning behind her eyelids. She reached into the backpack she'd tossed into one of the chairs and unscrewed the cap from the bottle of cabernet. She sank down the porch railing to the steps, the wood rails scraping her spine, relishing the burn of the alcohol and counting the seconds until it blurred the edges of her memory.

## Chapter Two

Amir Farzaneh lifted the last of the paint cans into the back of her truck and shut the tailgate behind them. She'd spent the last seven hours repainting the trim on Cal Horton's cottage, barely finishing the final upstairs window with the last of the twilight. The air had grown sharper as the temperature dropped, and she pulled on her Carhartt jacket from the front seat before she climbed in.

Amir had owned her own business now for seven years. She'd started with small carpentry jobs when she was twenty-three, then trained to be a locksmith and combined that with the odd jobs she was already doing. After a few years, the business had grown, and she was known in town as the one to call for pretty much anything. In a town as small as Innis Harbor, there wasn't enough business for specialized tradespeople, so she'd learned to do everything from plumbing to roofing over the years, as well as marine repair and maintenance.

She had just started the truck when her phone rang. Someone was locked out of their house on White Street. She knew the house—it was three blocks from the Horton cottage—but she also knew the owner had died, and as far as she knew, no one had been there since. Her headlights illuminated the house as she pulled up and cut the engine. Someone was standing in the shadows beside the door, and Amir saw as she came up the walkway that the woman definitely wasn't from the area. She wore an expensive black leather jacket, a beanie pulled low on her head, black jeans, and a white T-shirt. She had her hands shoved all the way down in her pockets and barely looked at Amir as she climbed the steps; she just kept her gaze fixed on the door.

"You need a key cut?"

The woman finally looked her way and nodded, and when she did, Amir was startled. She was beautiful, in a spare, angular way, with deep blue eyes and the palest wash of freckles across her nose. Amir watched her pull off her beanie and run her hand through her hair. She looked tired, and there were fine lines around her eyes that she rubbed away with the heel of her hand.

"Yeah," she said. "I need to get into my aunt's house, and I don't have the key. I didn't realize until I got here."

Amir looked at the bag Loch had dropped onto the chair by the door. "You're Samia's niece?"

She nodded. "She died a few weeks ago and left me the house. I just flew in today."

Amir waited until the woman met her gaze. "I can do that for you," she said. "But I need to see something that lets me know you have the right to be in the house."

The woman just shook her head, closing her eyes for a moment, before she looked back at Amir.

"As far as I know, criminals don't usually call a local locksmith to let them into a house before they rob it." Loch stopped, took a deep breath, and let it out slowly. "Look, it's been a long day, and I just need the key. I guess I can find something in there to prove it to you if you really have to have it."

Amir leaned over to switch on the porch light, then looked her up and down. "I'm not trying to be difficult here, but I can't just let some random person into a locked house." She paused. "And you don't exactly look like a local."

Loch zipped up her jacket and held Amir's gaze as she spoke. "I'm not a fucking local. That's kind of the point."

Amir shook her head, pulled her truck keys out of her pocket, and started back down the stairs. Whoever she was, she wasn't the only one who'd had a long day.

"I'm the only locksmith in town," she said as she walked down the hill to her truck. "So, good luck with that door."

The seagulls called overhead as they glided down to the harbor to pick over the remnants of the day's catch left on the dock after the crews finished unloading the boats. The truck door slammed shut as Amir started the engine, and she looked back over her shoulder as she shifted into gear. The woman was sitting on the porch steps, but her head was in her hands now, her hair falling forward and covering her face. Amir leaned her head back against the seat for a moment, then cut the engine, looking out to the stars barely visible through the tops of the trees.

"Congrats, Amir," she said to herself. "You've managed to make a random woman cry in the space of thirty seconds. That may be a new record."

Amir sighed, reached over to the cooler on the floorboard, pulled out the Friday afternoon beers she'd been too busy to drink, and shifted her truck back into park. As she walked back up to the porch, Samia's niece looked up and turned her head away to swipe at her cheek with the heel of her hand.

"Let's try this again." Amir held out a beer. "I'm Amir Farzaneh."

The woman paused, then took it and looked over at her in the yellowed porch light. "Loch Battersby."

They both popped the tops on the cans and drank, looking out over the sea. Amir looked at her and smiled, nodding toward the step. "So, you've been here for five minutes, and you're already copying my style?"

Loch looked down. They were both wearing black high-top Chuck Taylors, scuffed and unlaced at the top. It was enough to make her smile, and when she did, Amir saw the flash of resemblance to Samia.

Night sounds fell around them. The silence was surprisingly comfortable, and Loch pulled her beanie back on as she glanced at Amir. She was taller than Loch, rare outside the modeling world, with defined arms and square hands crisscrossed with scars. Her skin was dark olive, with black hair cut close and streaked with white paint at the tips. When Amir finally looked back at her, her eyes were the color of honey, like backlit amber.

Amir glanced at the door. "I'm sorry about your aunt."

Loch looked down, tightening the laces on her shoes while she tried to stop the tears threatening to gather in her eyes. "Thanks. Did you know her?"

"I did," Amir said. "I did some work for her last year."

"I haven't been here in a long time." Loch ran a hand through her hair. She stared out toward the sea, then shook her head and glanced back at the house. "And to tell you the truth, I don't know what I'm doing here now."

Amir studied the sharp lines of Loch's shoulders as she spoke. She looked fragile, as if she might break if someone touched her. "I'd better get going and leave you to it."

Amir stood and offered a hand to Loch, who looked surprised, but let her pull her to her feet. She stopped briefly at the front door before she started walking back down the steps, handing Loch a key as she passed.

"Your aunt was always locking herself out of the house. I finally just put a spare on top of the doorframe."

Loch watched Amir climb into her truck and pull out, the red glow of her taillights finally disappearing around the bend in the road.

❖

Loch woke the next morning to the sounds of the fishing boats leaving the harbor, the horns clashing and echoing over the surface of the water. She rolled over in the sleeping bag, her back dotted with what felt like bruises after sleeping on the porch. She'd finally walked into the house the night before after Amir left, turning on a single lamp by the door, but the memories hung dense and layered in the air. She'd stood there for a few minutes, but in the end, she just pulled a sleeping bag out of the hall closet, eyes straight ahead, and switched the lamp off on her way out the door.

But now it was a new day, and as Loch rolled the sleeping bag back up, she told herself to stop being such a baby. *People die. It happens all the time. It just shouldn't be this big a goddamn deal to walk into the house.*

She left her jacket and the sleeping bag on the nearest chair and opened the door. The screen door creaked behind her as she turned the handle and stepped inside. The curtains were all pulled shut, and dust particles hung in the air, suspended in the slivers of sunlight that had managed to edge in. There was a magazine and a mug beside the chair Colleen used to sit in, as if she'd been there yesterday, and a deep imprint on one side of the couch where Samia had always sat beside her. The ashtray Loch had made them when she was eight sat in the center of the coffee table, the sides covered in glued-on seashells. Two of the shells were missing now, leaving wide gaps showing only the rough edges of the hardened glue.

Loch pulled the curtains back one by one and opened the windows halfway to let in some fresh air. She gathered the pile of mail that littered the entryway, dropping it into the trash without looking at it as she picked up the magazine by Colleen's chair to do the same. As she folded it into her hand, she noticed the date. September 2012. The month and year Colleen had died.

Loch's phone rang just then, and she jumped, startled back into the present. She carefully smoothed out the magazine and set it back in place on the end table before she looked at the name on her phone and answered.

"Hi, Mom."

"Hi, baby," she said. "Are you at the house?"

Her mom's voice broke the spell, and Loch walked back outside into the sunshine and sank into one of the porch chairs.

"Because I remembered this morning that I forgot to send the key."

Loch nodded, then remembered she was on the phone and cleared her throat. "Yeah, I got here last night just before dark."

"Don't push yourself, okay? Just give yourself some time for everything to settle, and then you can decide what you want to do."

Loch took a deep breath, her gaze locked onto the ferry gliding sideways into the docks below. "I know," she said. "I will."

After they hung up, Loch grabbed her wallet and locked up the house. While she was on the phone, she'd gotten a good look at how badly the wooden porch stairs were peeling. The overgrown grass around them was littered with paint flakes still clinging to the fragments of wood they'd taken with them as they fell. The sun seemed unnaturally bright, so she slipped on her sunglasses and let the breeze play with her hair as she walked toward town. She stopped at the hardware store and bought some white paint and a paintbrush, then picked up a sandwich and a few groceries before she climbed the hill to the house. Not one person gave her a second glance. It felt luxuriously strange to be able to wander through shops and back out onto the sidewalk without flashbulbs going off in her face every two seconds.

By the time she got around to painting the steps, it was late afternoon. It turned out to be trickier than she thought it would be; the peeling edges of the old paint wouldn't stay down no matter how hard she pressed them with the wet paintbrush. She'd only gotten through half of the lower step when a truck rumbled up to the curb at the base of the hill and parked. The locksmith from the night before got out and slammed the door shut behind her. Loch went back to her painting until she heard Amir's voice beside her.

"Your aunt had me change the locks on the back door last summer and gave me a key in case she locked herself out again." She pulled the key out of her pocket and held it out to Loch. "I thought if you didn't have the front key, you might not have the back one, either."

Loch nodded and slipped it into her pocket as Amir leaned down to study the can of paint.

She looked up at Loch with a raised eyebrow. "What the hell are you doing with this?"

"What does it look like I'm doing?" Loch held a hand to her forehead to shield her eyes from the afternoon sun. "I'm painting the steps."

She picked up her brush again and went to dip it in the paint, but Amir lifted the can swiftly just out of her reach.

"Do you know what kind of paint you're using?"

Loch closed her eyes and took a deep breath. Why the fuck did it matter? "White," she said, her eyes still closed. "It's white paint." She sat back on her heels and nodded toward the half-painted step. "Coincidentally, you'll see the steps are also white."

She moved to dip her brush back in the paint, but Amir got the lid on the can before she got there.

"You don't want to do that," Amir said, setting it back on the step. "Trust me."

She walked to her truck and dug around in the back, then headed back to the steps carrying a different paint can, along with two brushes and some tools.

"I know you think I'm just busting your chops here, but you can't paint exterior stairs with"—she paused, clearly trying not to laugh—"interior semi-gloss."

Loch looked up, squinting into the sun behind her. "What are you—the paint police?"

"Yes." Amir pried the top off her can and handed Loch a tool that looked like a metal spatula. "Yes, I am."

Loch watched as Amir used the same tool she'd handed her to start chipping the old paint from the unpainted side of the stair, so she started on the one above, scraping the loose pieces onto the grass. Maybe removing the old paint shards first was a good idea, but Amir didn't have to be a jerk about it.

They worked together in silence for the next few minutes until the old paint was almost completely gone, then Amir pulled some sandpaper out of her pocket and sanded down the edges of what was left, smoothing her hand over the dust, testing for stray chips. Loch sat on the grass to the side of the steps.

"So, you paint, too? I thought you were a locksmith."

"I am." Amir scraped the last of the wet paint off the first step and wiped it on a towel. "But people in town call me for everything."

She was wearing khaki work pants and a black T-shirt rolled up at the cuffs with black work boots. She was nowhere close to Loch's type, but it was hard not to notice the sharp definition in her arms that flexed as she worked, which almost made up for the attitude. Almost.

Amir looked over at Loch, shielding her eyes from the last of the afternoon sun. "So, what do you do?"

Loch looked down at the steps, now smooth and ready for paint. "Nothing this useful."

Amir handed her a brush. "We're going to use marine paint on these," she said. "It's waterproof and designed for ship decks, so it holds up much longer outside under a snow load."

They painted the steps from top to bottom, which went quickly with two of them working. Amir painted three steps to Loch's one, then touched up the corners on Loch's stair before she put her brush down. Loch stepped back. Not surprisingly, it looked great.

"How much do I owe you?"

Amir put the top back on the paint can and gathered her tools. "Nothing," she said, glancing up at the house. "But I could use a sink to clean these brushes before I toss them back in the truck."

Loch pulled herself up on the porch beside the wet steps and turned to help Amir, but she'd lifted herself up before Loch could put out her hand. Loch opened the screen door, led Amir into the kitchen, and turned on the hot water in the sink.

"Sorry about all the dust. I don't think my aunt was much of a housekeeper after her partner died."

Amir worked the brushes with her fingers, paint flowing in a translucent white river into the drain below.

"Wow." She glanced over at Loch. "She was gay?"

Loch nodded. "She and her partner, Colleen, were together for forty-two years."

"I never knew that," Amir said. "I must have met Samia after her partner passed away." She nodded toward the back door. "Which reminds me, that deck is going to need another coat of polyurethane before the snow hits this fall."

Loch's eyes followed hers. "What deck?"

Amir shook the water from the brushes and laid them on the counter. "You haven't been outside yet?"

Loch rubbed her temples, trying to stave off the headache forming like a murky cloud behind her eyes. "I haven't really been past the front room and the kitchen."

Amir nodded, then turned the water off and dried her hands on the kitchen towel. "It's a lot to deal with, isn't it?"

"Yeah." Loch let out a long breath. "It's like she's still here."

"I get it." Amir paused and looked over at the door. "Come out back with me."

She opened the door for Loch, who reluctantly walked through it, only to stop in her tracks once she did. The backyard had always been just a fenced plot of patchy grass, but now curved cedar steps led to an expansive, glossy deck with a sunken rock-lined firepit in the center, surrounded by built-in cedar risers. Globe lights crisscrossed above more white Adirondack chairs along the upper deck, surrounded by handmade bird feeders mounted on the railing.

"This is amazing." Loch turned to Amir. "How did you even know this was here?"

Amir leaned back through the door and flipped a switch on the inside wall. "Because I built it."

The lights sparkled against the falling dusk and scattered amber light across the deck. Loch spotted the firewood rack next to the door, pulled two split pine logs off the top, then walked over and dropped them in the center of the firepit with a resonant clatter.

"Hang on." Amir smiled and lifted the lid of the wood box beside the firewood rack, pulling out some smaller kindling and a stack of newspaper. "You're going to need these."

She walked over, picked up the logs Loch had dropped in the firepit, and crumpled the paper at the bottom, adding the smaller pieces of kindling in a vertical grid over that.

"Wait," Loch said, looking back toward the door. "I have no idea where she'd keep a lighter." Amir pulled a chrome lighter out of her pocket and clicked it under the edge of the newspaper. It caught quickly in a burst of blue flame and ignited the dry kindling. Loch watched it for a moment, then walked back into the kitchen and pulled two beers from the refrigerator. When she got back, she sat back on the bench seat, zipping her hoodie and pulling the sleeves down over her hands. She handed one of the bottles to Amir.

"Thanks for this," Loch said, her gaze following the first sparks from the fire up into the navy blue evening sky. "I feel like I can breathe out here."

Amir sat and looked over at Loch. "So, where are you from?"

"Manhattan. The last time I was here was about nine years ago when I was seventeen."

The logs caught fire suddenly from the kindling and shifted, sending flames toward the sky.

"But I wish I'd come back sooner." Loch's voice was suddenly softer, and Amir watched her eyes fall as she peeled the label from her bottle. "I wanted to. I was just always working."

"You never told me what you do."

Loch ran her hand through her hair, wishing she could say something other than the truth. "I'm a model."

Amir went to the woodpile for another log and set it a few feet from the fire as she sat back down. "Do you like it?"

Loch paused before she answered. "I used to."

Amir brushed a sliver of wood off her shirt with the back of her hand. "So, if you could do anything, what would it be?"

"I don't know." Loch looked at her. "No one's ever asked me that." She watched the flames engulf one of the logs, and it slipped off the pile, crushing the smaller sticks into ash and coals. "What would you do?"

"I'd probably do what I do now." Amir paused, then smiled as she looked over at Loch. "Someone's got to save exterior steps from interior paint."

"Well, it wouldn't have been me." Loch leaned against the back of the riser and smiled back in spite of herself. "I've never actually painted anything before."

Amir raised an eyebrow. "You're kidding, right?"

"No," Loch said. "I started working when I was fifteen and never stopped. I had tutors that helped me finish high school between jobs, so I never went back after my freshman year."

"Wow," Amir said. "Now that I wouldn't have minded. I hated high school."

Loch looked over at her. "Why? What was it like for you?"

"Rough." She threw the other log on the fire, sending a spray of sparks into the black night toward the treetops. "I think the guys took it personally that I looked a little too much like them."

"Did they know you were gay?"

Amir laughed and raised an eyebrow. "Are you kidding? Blind and deaf people know I'm gay."

Loch smiled. She wasn't wrong, but only if you didn't look at her mouth as she spoke. She had a guy's walk and a low scrape to her voice, but her lips had a soft fullness to them, and she bit the bottom one sometimes as she listened.

"I might have had it easier in that respect," Loch said. "It seems like everyone's queer in fashion. I never even had to come out."

"I'm not sure I would have known if you hadn't told me."

Loch smiled. "I probably threw off your gaydar because I couldn't figure out which end of the paintbrush to use."

"Well," Amir said, standing and searching for her keys in her jacket pocket. "If you forget again, you know who to ask. My card is on the memo board in the hardware store." She flashed a smile at Loch, then walked toward the door.

"Wait, what's the name of your business?"

"Lock Up Your Daughters," she said, dropping her empty bottle in the recycling container before she disappeared through the door.

## Chapter Three

Amir's mother called her before she'd even pulled into her driveway.

"Hi, Ma." Amir tried to keep the phone pressed to her face as she juggled her jacket and keys at the same time. "How was your day?"

She listened as she unzipped her jacket, dropping her keys in the process.

"No, I can't come over for dinner, I have to draw up the plans for the Nelsons' greenhouse project."

She tossed her jacket onto the couch and opened the fridge, pulling out the leftover jeweled rice her mother had sent her home with the previous night. It was her favorite, and she'd made it the same way since Amir was little, with basmati rice, orange blossom water, saffron, currants, and pistachios.

By the time she'd gotten her first bite, her mother had launched into a story about a bathroom faucet Amir's father hadn't fixed to her liking. Amir smiled and pulled herself up on the counter to eat as she listened. Within five minutes, she knew every detail of how long it had taken him, the unholy mess he'd left in the bathroom, and that her mother had told him afterward that if she wanted something done right she clearly had to call her daughter. Her father had told her once he'd been trying for years to screw up the home repairs in hopes that someday her mother might actually call Amir first. Amir finally stopped her when she started talking about trying to fix it herself.

"Mom," she said. "Just leave the wrench where it is on the faucet and don't touch it. I'll drop by tomorrow and look at it. It's probably just a leaky gasket."

That seemed to placate her, and Amir put her empty bowl in the sink.

"I've got to go now, though. I need to get started on these plans." She ran hot water into the bowl and dried her hands on the kitchen towel. "I promise I'll come by after work and take a look."

After she'd managed to get off the phone, Amir opened her laptop and pulled up the specs for the greenhouse. This was her favorite part of the job, designing structures from the ground up, like the deck she'd built for Samia. That reminded her suddenly of the conversation she'd had with Loch. She paused, then typed two words into the search bar of her computer.

*Loch Battersby.*

Instantly, her screen exploded with hundreds of images, but it wasn't until Amir looked closer that she even recognized Loch. Most of the photos featured her as a male model, and it was easy to see why. In person, Loch had something delicate, almost vulnerable about her, but through the lens of the camera, that was definitely not the case. Her height and broad shoulders gave her a similar frame to the guys, and the angles of her face stood out even more through the lens and gave her a masculine edge. Her look was intense—she was almost unrecognizable with her brows pushed together in what looked to be her trademark brooding stare, eyes focused somewhere out beyond the camera.

Beyond the advertising campaigns, there were thousands of other photos of Loch on the red carpet at award shows or at parties with celebrities, and she'd been featured in countless magazine and newspaper articles over the years, both queer and straight publications. Amir glanced over an article in last year's *New York Times* that described her as the first model to "shatter gender stereotypes." The piece included a video link, which Amir clicked. It was a runway show in Paris for the fall collection of some French menswear designer she'd never heard of. For the first minute or so, lanky male models walked the runway in long coats, sweaters, and scarves, then Loch strode out wearing green tweed trousers gathered slightly above her waist with a leather belt. Her face was set in an intense gaze, and she was naked from the waist up. She paused at the end of the runway, looked directly into the cameras, then turned on the ball of her foot and walked back as the next models stepped onto the runway toward her.

Amir paused the video and sat back in her chair. It was hard to recognize her as the woman she'd just shared a beer with, the same one who went right for the logs and dropped them into the firepit but clearly couldn't start a fire in a burning barn. Through a lens, she was mesmerizing, powerful, and impossible to look away from. There was something inspired about her, the contrast of masculine and feminine, fabric against bare skin, vulnerability layered with rock-solid confidence. It was beautiful, and so was she.

Amir closed her computer slowly, startled by her own voice in the empty room. "Holy shit."

That night, Loch decided to stay in the small guest room off the hall at the back of the house. She didn't feel right staying in Samia's room. In fact, she hadn't even gone into it or the art studio yet. The studio had decades of Samia's art hanging on the walls and stacked in frames on the floor below. She'd taught art in Bar Harbor schools her entire career, but when Colleen died, she finished out the school year and never went back. Loch knew the studio was the closest place to Samia's heart, and she just couldn't face walking in and seeing the piece she was working on when she died. She knew she had to do it eventually, but what she really needed to do right now was figure out what the hell she was doing with the house. It was solid, full of light, and built in a classic coastal style; it would sell in a heartbeat with a few cosmetic repairs. Loch knew every quirk and corner of it, so the thought of selling it to someone else who would erase the last traces of her aunt seemed wrong, but it didn't make sense to keep it when she went back to Manhattan, either.

❖

When she woke the next morning, Loch pulled on a pair of jeans and walked into the kitchen, where she quickly remembered Samia had never owned a coffeemaker. She drank tea. Loch had never been able to wrap her head around that concept, and this morning was no exception.

*God*, she heard herself say to the empty house, *who drinks tea?*

Loch found her hoodie and raked her hand through her hair. If she was going to stay here for even a few days, a coffeemaker of some sort had to be found. She pulled the door shut behind her and walked out into the sunshine, digging her sunglasses out of the pocket as she walked. It was strange to be out so early. She'd traveled so much in the last decade she'd forgotten how it felt to go to sleep and wake on her own in the morning.

She walked down the hill toward Main Street, watching the sunlight sparkle off the surface of the water in the distance. Some of the lobster boats were still leaving the harbor, so it had to be early. Too early to be without coffee. She stopped into Gerrish Café, where it seemed everyone was over the age of sixty and reading some sort of newspaper. In fairness, there were only five people in the place, but that was still quite a coincidence.

She walked to the counter and almost ordered a cappuccino before she remembered where she was. "Just a coffee, please."

The waitress nodded and started to hand her a laminated menu. "Nothing to eat?"

Loch shook her head and picked up the classified section of the local paper, the only pages left in the pile. The waitress filled her coffee cup from a scratched glass pitcher and nodded at the set of powdered creamer and white sugar on the counter before she walked back toward the cash register.

"If you're trying to blend with the locals, you may want to lose the sunglasses."

Loch turned to find Amir at the register beside her and realized she was still wearing her sunglasses. Great.

"What do you think?" She took them off and blinked against the light. "Am I pulling it off?"

Amir raised an eyebrow, and Loch saw the waitress smile out of the corner of her eye. "It may take a little more practice, but you do pour that powdered creamer like a diner pro already, so you're halfway there." She stepped closer to Loch and lowered her voice. "They have half-and-half in the fridge. Just ask for it."

The waitress handed Amir her coffee to go and the half-and-half without a word.

Loch smiled. "Or just be a local?"

"Yeah," Amir said. "That never hurts." She put a five on the counter and poured the cream into her cup. "What are you doing up so early, anyway? You don't strike me as the morning type."

"I have no idea if I am or not," Loch said, rubbing an eye with the heel of her hand. "I honestly can't remember the last time I was awake to see it if I didn't have to be up for a job."

As she talked, she dropped her gaze just long enough to take in the strong lines of Amir's shoulders and arms under her shirt, her hair still wet from the shower. She wasn't her type—Loch tended to date other models—although Amir's muscles flexed into defined cuts even lifting a coffee cup, so she'd pretty much have to be straight not to notice.

"I actually just walked down from the house to buy a coffeemaker," Loch said, folding the paper and putting it back onto the stack. "Where do I get one of those around here?"

Amir looked at the waitress, and they answered together. "Bar Harbor."

Loch looked at them, waiting for them to tell her they were joking. Surely, she didn't have to spend an hour on a ferry and go to a different city just to get her hands on a French press and some decent dark roast.

Loch asked for a to-go cup and poured her coffee into it. "Well then, it looks like I've got a ferry to catch," she said. "How much do I owe you?"

The waitress topped off her coffee from the pot and glanced at the five on the counter. "Nothing," she said. "Amir already got it."

Loch hesitated, then grabbed her sunglasses, and they walked out together. "Thanks for the coffee." Loch squinted into the sun and looked over at Amir. "Random women don't often pay for my drinks."

Amir paused, resisting the urge to look her up and down. "Then you're hanging out with the wrong women." She started to walk toward the docks but stopped to look back at Loch. "I'm going into Bar Harbor before long to get some lumber. I can give you a ride unless you're dying to catch that ferry."

"I may take you up on that," Loch said, sliding her sunglasses back onto her face. "If it isn't any trouble."

Amir turned back and started walking toward the docks. "I'll pick you up in an hour."

Loch showered and pushed the long front layers of her hair back with some product. She never wore makeup and hadn't owned a hair dryer since she was sixteen; she got enough of that at work. She dug around in her bag for her gray skinny jeans and paired them with black boots and a long-sleeved white thermal. She was still getting used to the cold here. It was a good fifteen degrees cooler than Manhattan with the wind coming in off the water, even in the summer. She remembered her wallet and sunglasses at the last second and stepped out on the porch to lock the door just as Amir pulled up.

It wasn't far to Bar Harbor, and when they got there, Amir stopped first at a kitchen store downtown to let Loch buy a French press, then headed to the lumberyard where she loaded her wood order into the back of her truck.

When they pulled out of the parking lot to head back to town about twenty minutes later, every street between them and the road to Innis Harbor seemed to be blocked off, and traffic had come to a standstill.

"Shit," Amir said, looking at her phone for the date. "It's Friday. I think they're setting up for the Fat Tire Triathlon tomorrow."

"What does that mean?"

"It means these roads are all going to be closed for a while until they get everything set up and taped off." She tapped her thumb on the steering wheel, then looked over at Loch as she pulled back into the lumberyard. "Do you have anything you need to be doing for the next couple of hours?"

"Actually," Loch took off her sunglasses and looked at Amir, "for once, I don't have to be anywhere."

Amir got out and walked around the truck, opening Loch's door. "Good," she said. "Then let's eat. I'm starving."

They walked back into downtown, which was only a half mile or so. Amir led her through a few brick alleys until they came to what Loch assumed had to be a restaurant, despite the absence of a sign. Bright flowers and dewy green ivy dripped over the doorway of the old brick building, and a narrow path led to a crumbling courtyard with a white marble fountain in the center and a collection of tables surrounding it. They got the last available table, clearly because everyone in the restaurant seemed to know Amir.

"This is beautiful," Loch said after Amir finished greeting most of the waitstaff and a few of the customers with a kiss on both cheeks. "How do you know everyone?"

Amir unfolded her napkin and put it on her lap, looking over and smiling at two older women in aprons peering at them from what looked like the kitchen entrance to the main building.

"My family is Persian, and there are a few other Persian and Iranian families here in Bar Harbor." She leaned into the table and smiled. "In fact, I'd be willing to bet in about three minutes, one of those two ladies will be on the phone to my mother wanting to know who I just brought to the restaurant."

Loch smiled and leaned back in her chair. "And what are you going to tell her when she asks?"

"That's a good question," Amir said with a raise of her eyebrow. "I'll let you know how that goes."

A carafe of white wine appeared on the table with two glasses, followed by a platter of grilled crostini drizzled with olive oil and a small bowl of dip topped with bright ruby pomegranate seeds.

"What is this?"

"It's borani, with yogurt and pomegranate." Amir spooned it onto the bread and handed it to Loch. "It's basically eggplant dip, but there are some sneaky ingredients in there like pomegranate molasses and mint."

Loch bit into it and closed her eyes, breathing in the scent. Sunlight shifted across her face, illuminating delicate silver lashes scattered through thicker black ones.

"Oh, my God, that's amazing," Loch said, opening her eyes. "I could literally lie around in bed and eat this all day."

"A model who eats." Amir scooped the extra pomegranate seeds off the top of the bowl and dropped them onto the borani on her bread. "I'm impressed."

Loch looked down and set the crostini on her plate. "I wish that was true. I love food, but I don't get to eat that much of it."

More dishes arrived then, covering every available space on the table with bright color and intense, layered fragrances. Amir went through each one for Loch, letting her taste it before going on to the next. Loch tried one bite of everything, closing her eyes as if memorizing the textures and flavors, more relaxed than Amir thought she might be given that everyone she knew was still watching them.

Amir spooned some ghormeh sabzi into Loch's bowl and leaned back in her chair.

"Wait." Loch looked around at the rest of the dishes on the table. "Which one is this?"

"Loosely translated, it's called green herb stew. My mom makes it every Sunday, but I actually like this one slightly better, not that I'd ever tell her that." She dished more into her own bowl, as well, and looked up at Loch. "So, what's your family like?"

Loch put her spoon down and ran a hand through her hair.

"I don't remember much about my father, he died of a heart attack when I was six," she said. "Then my mom started sending me here to spend summers with Samia every year so I'd stay close to his side of the family." She paused, then went on. "I have a younger sister, Skye, who's a competitive swimmer at Columbia. She was always at swim camp in the summers, so she never really got to spend time here."

"How old is she?"

"She's twenty, and everyone says we look like twins, although we've never thought so." Loch put her napkin beside her plate and scooped up the last of the pomegranate seeds. "We're both tall with a similar build, but she's got blond hair like a normal person and a good twenty pounds of muscle on me."

"Are you close?"

"Since day one." Loch smiled, then paused for a moment, turning her head toward the music in the background. "That's Hamad Homayoun playing, isn't it?"

Amir looked at her and raised an eyebrow, a slow smile spreading across her face. "Yes," she said. "But how does a white girl from Manhattan know that?"

"I'm pretty sure I should be offended by that," Loch said, laughing and tossing her napkin at Amir. "But that should teach you something about appearances." She laid her silverware on her plate and took a sip of her wine. "I love his music. I saw him just outside London a few years ago. He was doing a midnight concert in an old stone church when I was on my way back to my hotel from some marketing event. It was raining, but I still heard his music from the next street over and followed it until I found where it was coming from. The doors were open to the street, and the church was lit entirely by candlelight. I was soaked by that time but sat in the back of the church until it was over. It was the most beautiful music I've ever heard. I never forgot it."

"Wow, I did not see that coming." Amir bowed her head slightly and laid her hand across her chest. "I stand corrected."

Loch smiled. "That's better, Farzaneh."

Somehow, the waitstaff managed to fit dessert onto the table, and Loch leaned back in her chair and looked at Amir.

"I can't eat any more," she said, her eyes soft. "But thank you for bringing me here. I loved it."

Amir held her gaze, then reached over and chose a rose petal from a saucer at the edge of the table. "Come here."

Loch leaned closer, and Amir brushed her lower lip with her thumb as she put it in Loch's mouth. Loch closed her eyes and forgot to breathe as the sugared petal melted on her tongue.

❖

It was late afternoon by the time they finally pulled back up to Loch's house. The seagulls wove a tight pattern against the blue sky, calling loudly to one another on their way down to the water. Loch rolled her window down as the breeze lifted the hair at the back of her neck, brushing across her skin like fingertips. Amir pulled something out of her pocket and handed it to her.

"I don't remember your aunt ever actually building a fire, so I thought you might not have a lighter in the house."

Loch took it and looked at Amir. "So you brought me one?"

"Don't look so shocked." Amir smiled. "It's like you're some jaded New Yorker or something."

Loch traced the edge of the lighter with her fingers as she climbed the hill to her house and watched Amir's truck disappear around the corner.

## Chapter Four

After Loch went into town for groceries the next day, she let herself into the house and almost slipped on the mail that had been dropped through the door slot. Under the advertisements, junk mail, and an electric bill, there was a small manila envelope. It was addressed to her in her mother's handwriting, which seemed odd because she'd talked to her mom that morning, and she hadn't mentioned it.

She slid her finger under the seal and popped it open, then pulled out another white envelope with a note attached.

*Loch*, the note said in her mother's loopy feminine script, *I promised your aunt that if anything ever happened to her, I'd send you this letter.*

Loch opened the envelope slowly, tears forming behind her lashes when she saw Samia's handwriting. She'd always written in tiny block letters almost too small to read.

*Dearest Loch,*

*If you're reading this I've already kicked the bucket, and I don't want you moping around about it. Your mom has the number of my lawyer in town, and he'll have all the paperwork you need. I've left everything I care about to you, including all my art and my truck in the garage out back. If you can learn to drive, you can have it.*

> *Learn to drive, kiddo.*
> *Now, I know you, so listen to me here. Don't get all sentimental about the stuff in the house. It's just stuff, and I was tired of most of it anyway. Clear it out and get some fresh energy in the place, make it your own, whether you decide to keep it or sell it. It's yours now, as it should be.*
> *And take this letter right now and walk down to the docks. Crumple it up and throw it as far off the end as you can. I don't want you keeping stuff that doesn't matter.*
> *The day you were born, I held you and you wrapped that little fist around my thumb. From that day on, you were my whole heart. Nothing's different today, except that now I'm still alive in yours.*
> *I'm sure as hell not in that stuff lying around.*
> *I know you don't want to, but cut it the fuck loose.*
> *All I ever wanted was to be back with your dad and Colleen, so just be happy for me.*
> *I love you. I always will.*
>
> *Samia*

Loch slid down the wall and dropped her head into her hands, the tears falling hot and fast into her palms and sliding down her wrists. Her aunt was the only person in her life who never gave a shit what she looked like, and the world seemed colder the second she'd found out Samia died while she was standing on that Manhattan sidewalk. But now for the first time, she felt Samia's energy around her, pushing her toward the door and down to the docks.

"Okay, Jesus, I'm going," Loch muttered, dragging the sleeve of her flannel across her eyes and getting to her feet, grabbing her leather jacket as she headed for the door. She folded the letter back into the envelope as she walked back to town in the sunlight that suddenly seemed too bright. She stopped twice before she got to the docks, barely resisting the urge to put it into her pocket and run back to the house. As she resealed the letter, she saw a small line of script near the bottom edge of the envelope.

*PS. You've got enough money. Stop working so damn hard.*

Loch laughed out loud. Samia never did mince words.

❖

She reached the dock just as the sun was setting over the water, the gulls dipping and diving around her, waiting for the shrimping boats to come into the harbor. She'd been there for almost a half hour, unwilling to let the letter fall from her fingers, sink slowly under the dark water, and slip away from her. She knew that if she sat there until the sun rose, until people started to stare, she wouldn't be ready to let Samia go. But her aunt had known that, and now she had to do it whether she felt like it or not.

She stood, holding the crumpled ball of paper as tightly as she could for one last second, then threw it into the setting sun, watching it hit the water without a sound and sink slowly out of sight. As Loch sat back down on the dock, her heart was raw, but she knew she'd done the right thing. The thing she'd never have done without a letter from the aunt who knew her heart.

"Hey," a voice said from behind her. "I thought that was you."

Amir sat beside her on the end of the dock as Loch dragged her sleeve across her cheek. After a moment, Amir reached over and tipped Loch's head onto her shoulder, fingers soft around her neck. They sat there until darkness fell and the wind picked up, then Amir stood, picked up Loch's jacket, and held out her hand.

"Ready?"

It was just one word, but it was the one Loch needed to hear.

Amir walked her to the end of the dock where her truck was parked, then opened the door and asked her where she wanted to go.

"Anywhere."

Amir just nodded, shutting her door and walking around to the driver's side. Loch rolled down her window as Amir started the truck, letting the wind dry the last of her tears as she looked out one last time over the water where the letter had disappeared. Amir took the road that led into the woods and out of town, and just a few minutes later, they pulled up a winding drive to a two-story log cabin tucked into the woods at the edge of the water. It was small but beautifully built with a slate roof and a redwood deck to one side that wound around to the back of the cabin. Amir got out and walked around the truck to open Loch's door.

"This is your house?"

"It is." Amir offered her hand as Loch stepped out of the truck. "My family buys and maintains rental properties, and I bought this one from my dad when I was twenty-two."

"Wow," Loch said as they stepped onto the hand-laid stone path leading to the door. "This is amazing."

The door was heavy, textured wood, painted a deep emerald green with hammered iron hinges. Amir let them in and turned on the lamps in the main room, which was open to the kitchen on the left. A massive stone fireplace took up most of the back wall, rising past the loft tucked behind it. The house had a masculine look, with etched glass windows and mission-style lamps, but there was an unexpected softness to it as well. Gray and white herringbone pillows lined the couches, with tweed wool throws draped over the back.

Loch slid her jacket off and draped it over a kitchen chair, then wandered over to the hearth and picked up the ash-coated iron poker leaning against it. It was heavier than she thought it would be, and it slipped out of her fingers with a sudden heavy clatter.

Amir looked over at her and smiled. "Fire?"

"Um," Loch stammered, "only if you want one." Her face gave her away before the words were even out of her mouth, and Amir just managed to look away before she laughed.

She joined Loch at the fireplace and crumpled up some newspaper onto the grate, placing the twigs and kindling Loch handed her from the brass bucket beside the hearth. Amir stood and found the matches on top of the mantel, but by the time she'd gotten back to the grate, Loch had pulled the lighter she'd given her out of her pocket and was holding it to the pile of sticks, trying to get them to catch.

"Here." Amir covered Loch's hand with hers and lowered it

to the newspaper. "You might have more luck getting this to light first."

She sat back on the hearth and let Loch start the fire, watching her as the flames took hold and slipped across the logs like liquid light. The angles of her face were sharp, her eyes intensely blue against the pale lock of silver hair swept across her forehead.

"Have you eaten today?" Amir asked. "I'm going to make a sandwich. Do you want one?"

Loch started to say something, then caught herself. "I'm okay, I don't need anything."

Amir paused, then went to the kitchen and made a cheese sandwich, tucking two Heinekens under her arm on the way back. She sat on the floor in front of the fire with Loch and held out one of the halves. Loch just looked at her and shook her head, and Amir set it slowly back on the plate.

"So," she said. "What have you had to eat today?"

Loch raised an eyebrow in Amir's direction and looked back into the fire.

Amir smiled. "And yes, I do realize it's none of my damn business."

Loch took a breath, but it was a long few seconds before she spoke. "Coffee and a banana."

Amir didn't say anything, just put the plate behind her on the hearth and listened. Loch hesitated before she spoke, and when she did, the words fell out in a rush.

"Everyone thinks models are anorexic, but that's not always true." She pulled her beanie off her head and raked her fingers through her hair. "I want to eat. I'm sick of being hungry. Actually, I've been sick of it since I was fifteen."

Amir handed her a beer and settled against the hearth, facing her. She wanted to say a thousand things, but it wasn't the time.

"It's just part of the job," Loch said finally, rubbing the back of her neck with her thumb. "Designers want the world to see their designs, not the model, so basically, you're a clothes hanger. The thinner you are, the better the clothes look, and that's all they care about." She paused, glancing into the fire. "And they're right. It's my job to make their work look as good as possible without getting in the way."

Amir nodded, taking her bottle back and flipping off the top she'd forgotten to open before, then handed it back.

"I know some girls go too far, but they start so young, it's easy to lose perspective." Loch dropped her gaze as she set the bottle back down. "Gaining five pounds is like quitting your job, and there are literally hundreds of girls in line to take your place at any moment."

Loch pulled her knees up to her chin and wrapped her arms around them.

Amir waited a moment before she spoke. "What else?"

Loch looked up, surprised, but didn't answer for so long that Amir thought she might not. "Honestly?"

Amir nodded, watching the gold reflection of the fire against the deep sea blue of Loch's eyes.

"I'm sick to death of people looking at me. When your face is everywhere, people start to assume they know you." She paused, and the muscles in her jaw tensed. "And they don't."

Amir reached back onto the hearth and handed Loch half of the sandwich. This time, she reached for it and took two bites before she went on.

"I know I sound ungrateful, but I'm really not. I feel so lucky I ever got to do it in the first place. Some people never get a chance like that." She looked down again and rubbed her forehead with the heel of her hand. "I guess I'm just tired."

Amir watched her put the last bite of the sandwich half in her mouth and glance over at the plate, so she handed her the other half.

"Okay." Amir leaned back and tossed another log onto the fire, the coals crumpling into layers of brilliant orange with a hiss. "If you're going to eat my half, you're going to have to tell me more."

"Why do you want to know all this?" Loch pulled the pickle slice out of the sandwich and popped it in her mouth. "You're just going to find out I'm not that interesting."

"Bullshit." Amir paused and held her gaze, her voice gentler than her words. "There's a lot more to you than how you look."

Loch smiled as she pulled her sleeves down over her hands. "Well, you may be alone in that opinion."

Amir got up and threw a log on the fire, sending a spray of sparks up the chimney. Night had fallen dense and black against the windows, and Loch reached over and turned out the lamp next to the couch.

Amir smiled. "You did that so you can see the fire better, didn't you?"

"Maybe."

Amir laughed and sank down on the couch. "So, what is it with you and fire?"

"I loved it when I was a kid, and I just miss it, I think. No one has a fireplace in Manhattan, and I never have time to go out to the Catskills and sit around in a cabin like this." She paused, running her palm across the arm of the couch. "I've never even been camping." She curled her legs underneath her on the couch and looked at Amir. "Now that you've somehow managed to charm some secrets out of me, tell me something about you."

"There's nothing exciting to tell," Amir said, then took a swig of her beer. "I'm thirty, good with a paintbrush, extensive collection of floral dresses."

"Now I'm calling bullshit. At least the part where you said there's nothing exciting to tell." Loch smiled and raised an eyebrow. "The dress collection thing may be true."

"Okay, how about this?" Amir said, twisting the mariner's watch on her wrist. "My dad's gotten it in his head lately that it's time for me to settle down, so he's trying to find a *man* for me to marry."

Loch started to laugh but stopped when she realized Amir was serious. "Oh, wow, you're not kidding, are you?"

"I came out when I was sixteen, and he never said anything about it, just pretended it didn't happen." Amir's hand tightened around the beer bottle. "My older brother is already married with two kids, so it's not about grandchildren. And he won't talk to me about it. I've tried."

"How does your mom feel about it?"

"She thinks he's being ridiculous. She doesn't care who I'm with as long as she's Persian."

Loch tried not to laugh. "I'm guessing that dating pool is pretty small."

"Are you kidding? It's nonexistent. Mom will have to just get over it if I bring someone home eventually."

"You've never brought anyone home?"

"So far, I've liked my girlfriends too much to do that to them." Amir smiled and looked over at Loch. "Okay, it's your turn, although it may be hard to top a homophobic dad who wants his butch daughter to marry a dude. Good luck with that."

"Okay," Loch said, biting the edge of her lip. "I might have something."

"All right, let's hear it."

Loch paused, looking into the fire for a moment before she spoke. "I look pretty masculine in most of my photos, so everyone I've ever slept with has just assumed I'm a top in bed."

Amir held her gaze. "And are you?"

"What do you think?"

Amir's voice was gentle. "Do you really want me to answer that?"

She nodded, and Amir reached over and tucked Loch's hair behind her ear. "I think that you haven't gotten the chance to find out."

Loch stared into the fire, watching as a log gave way and dropped into the coals. "It's like everyone has all these expectations based on how I look in pictures, and if I don't fit into them, they're disappointed or something." She picked at a thread on her sleeve. "Either that or they just assume I want to be a man."

"I understand that," Amir said. "I think some of the older ladies in town think I actually am a man."

Loch smiled. "You'd think the floral dresses would be a clue."

"Cute."

Amir tossed a pillow in her direction as she got up to put another log on the fire.

Loch looked at her watch and then the door. "It's late. I should get back to the house." Loch looked like she had something else to say. Amir waited for her to go on, but she didn't, so she took a guess.

"But you don't want to?"

Loch paused, then looked over at the window to the branches swaying in the wind outside the slick black glass. "Not tonight, I guess."

"Then stay here," Amir said, dropping her gaze to Loch's mouth. "I'll sleep on the couch."

Loch looked up at the loft, then back at Amir as she ran a hand through her hair. "What if I want you upstairs with me?"

Amir hesitated, then walked over to Loch and slid her hand around the back of her neck, gaze locked onto hers. "I'll be fine down here."

Loch stepped slowly closer, her mouth nearly touching Amir's. The warmth of her breath hovered between them. Amir closed her eyes.

"Please?"

A few minutes later, Amir pulled Loch into her arms in bed, Loch's hair sifting and falling through her fingers like snow until she heard her breath drop gently into sleep.

## Chapter Five

The next morning, Loch woke before Amir and walked the two miles back to Samia's house. She unlocked the door hurriedly, dropped the keys on the table, and didn't even bother to take off her jacket before she dug her Nikon camera and lenses out of the bag she'd brought from New York. She walked into the living room, opened all the curtains to let in the natural light, and started shooting. She shot every angle of the living room, then went on to the next, looking at everything only through the lens. She knew she had to let go of all the things in the house that were holding her in the past, but she didn't want to forget, either.

When she was sure she had pictures of everything just as it was, Loch spent the rest of the day packing up everything she wanted to keep, which, in the end, filled one small box. Afterward, as she sank down the kitchen wall and opened a bottle of water from the fridge, she remembered a sign she'd seen about a new women's shelter being set up in Bar Harbor.

It took some calling around, but she finally got in touch with the director, Shelley Hart, who told her that someone had donated the house they were currently using for the shelter, but they'd been there for weeks and it still had almost no furniture; there was nothing to make it feel comfortable for the women who had just lost their homes. Loch liked Shelley right away, and by the end of the conversation, they'd arranged for her to send a truck and movers to Innis Harbor the following Sunday for Samia's things.

When Loch hung up, she sat where she was in the middle of the living room, the breeze from the open window washing over her, lifting just the edge of the curtain like a nod.

❖

The next morning, Loch showered and decided to walk downtown instead of using her French press. The diner coffee was growing on her, but this time, she left her sunglasses at home in the hopes it would up her chances of getting some actual cream.

The bell clanged on the door as she walked in, and she instinctively reached into the pocket where her sunglasses usually were, but no one turned to look at her. Even the waitress, the same girl she'd seen working last time, just asked her what she wanted and turned to pour the coffee. As Loch chose a stool and unfolded the classifieds, the only section left once again, she realized that for once, nobody cared who she was.

The waitress set a cup in front of her and filled it from the pot. She was slender with dark glossy hair, and when she looked up, Loch noticed a smattering of freckles across her nose.

"You buying the Cape Cod on the hill?" She glanced down at her name tag. "I'm Cara, by the way."

Another customer walked up to the register just then, so she turned to ring up the ticket before she turned back to Loch.

"No, not really," Loch said, refolding the paper into a crumpled square and setting it back on the counter. "Samia was my aunt. She left the house to me."

Cara nodded, her face softening. "Ms. Battersby taught my high school art class, and I still draw sometimes. She was a great teacher."

Loch nodded, looking down at her coffee. "I miss her. I haven't even gone into her studio yet, but I'm going to have to at some point."

Cara didn't answer, but the next time she passed Loch at the counter, she set the pitcher of cream next to Loch's cup.

"Can I have a coffee to go, Cara?"

Loch heard the voice and put her coffee cup down on the paper placemat. It was Amir. Loch turned toward her and smiled.

"Ah, the vanishing Loch." A slow smile spread across Amir's face. "I was starting to wonder if I was going to see you again."

Loch smiled, and as Cara turned away to get the coffee cup, she ran her fingertips up the back of Amir's thigh.

"Jesus." Amir looked at her, then leaned close to Loch's ear. "What is it going to take to get you out of here and into my truck?"

Loch whispered back, her lips just touching Amir's ear. "A to-go cup."

Amir put a five on the counter and asked Cara for the cup, her hand warm at the small of Loch's back as they left.

❖

"So, where are you taking me?" Loch watched the steering wheel slide through Amir's hands as she turned out of town and up the hill toward the house.

Amir smiled. "Anywhere you want to go."

"Are you not working today?"

Amir shook her head. "Not really. I have a major project starting Sunday, the Nelson greenhouse, but I cleared my schedule this week to try to get some decent photos of some of my past work."

"Why the photos?"

"I want to expand into Bar Harbor and hire more crew," Amir said. "But to do that, I have to step up my game a bit. My brother said he'd build my website, but I have to come up with pictures of my work for him to use."

"That sounds fairly easy."

"Yeah, you'd think," Amir said, turning onto Loch's street, steering wheel slipping under her hands like water. "But the first two times, I crashed and burned. I was out all day, but nothing looked remotely right when I tried to use them later. It turns out getting good pictures is a lot harder than it seems."

"Maybe it's the camera," Loch said, glancing around the inside of the truck for it. "What are you using?"

Amir pulled up to the curb at Loch's house, shifted the truck into park, and pulled her phone out of her back pocket.

Loch looked at her blankly, then realized she was serious. "You're kidding me, right?"

"No." Amir turned it over in her hand. "What else would I use?"

Loch got out of the truck and shut the door, leaning in through the open window. "Give me a minute. I'll be right back."

Loch unlocked the door of the house and grabbed her jacket, camera, and lens bag from the front room. Amir watched her as she locked the house and walked back to the truck and slid in, running her hand through her hair.

"You're seriously going to help me with this?"

"Yep," Loch said, shutting the door and reaching for her seat belt. "This is kind of my area. But don't get too excited. I need something from you that's guaranteed to be a pain in your ass, so I'm just trying to butter you up before I ask."

"Well," Amir started the engine and slid the truck into gear, "it's working."

❖

Thirty minutes later, they pulled up a long, winding drive on the outskirts of Bar Harbor. A summer home appeared at the end of the road, framed by the calm blue water behind it and into the horizon. It was made of traditional white clapboard, with a bright blue door and brilliant yellow zinnias spilling out of the flower boxes under the windows.

"Good God," Loch said. "This is beautiful. It's like every New Yorker's dream."

"It belongs to a client I've had for years." Amir pulled into the driveway and shifted into park. "Last fall, he needed his dock rebuilt, but he only lives here in the summer, so he wanted someone he knew to do the work. I contracted a company here in town to put in the flotation system, then I laid the dock surface."

As they walked down to the water, a red cypress dock came into view, the wood polished and gleaming in the sunlight over the deep blue surface of the water. It extended about twenty-five yards out, but instead of the severe square angles of most docks, this one was designed with sections that curved smoothly out from the main length in three different directions. From land, it looked more like a sculpture of an ancient tree, framed by the sea and sky.

"You designed this?"

"I did," Amir said. "His wife wanted something unique, not a traditional dock design. She wanted it to look more organic, like part of the water, with the same movement and shape as the sea."

As they approached, Loch stopped and handed the camera to Amir while she chose a lens from her bag. When she had it snapped on, she took a series of photos from the left side of the house with the sunlight glinting against the surface of the water and white-capped waves crashing onto a rocky point in the distance. When Loch was done, they continued down the dock, the boards shifting slightly under their feet, water lapping gently against both sides as they walked.

"This is amazing, Amir," Loch said, shading her eyes and looking out over the surface. "I can't imagine having the talent it takes to design this, let alone build it." She paused and looked back at the house. "Are we the only ones here?"

"They left yesterday." Amir zipped up her jacket and looked out over the water. "They're in Boston this week but gave me permission to come take whatever pictures I needed."

Loch set the camera on the dock and pulled her shirt over her head, dropping it at her feet. A smile swept across Amir's face in a sudden flash.

"I'd ask what the hell you're doing," she said, biting her lip, trying to keep her eyes on Loch's face, "but I'm afraid you'll stop."

Loch laughed, stepping out of her boots and jeans, leaving her in just a black racerback bra and underwear.

"It's not that exciting," she said, smiling at Amir. "We're just going to get an action shot, and what I'm wearing should look like a bikini in the pictures. If all your photos are static, the site won't be as interesting."

She looked around to find the direction of the sun, then picked up the camera, standing close to Amir and showing her the button to push.

"Click it right after you see my feet leave the dock, okay? Then keep clicking until I disappear into the water."

"I don't know if I should let you do this." Amir held her gaze and nodded toward the water. "Do you know how cold that water is?"

Loch nodded and walked to the end of the dock, dipping her hands in the water and scraping her hair away from her face for the photo. "About twenty degrees warmer than the water at the swimsuit photoshoots every February."

Amir just shook her head and lifted the camera. "I'm ready when you are, crazy girl."

Loch dove toward the sun, her body rising into a perfect high arch, then slipped silently below the dark surface of the water. As she broke the surface and swam toward the ladder on the side of the dock, Amir lowered the camera.

"God, that was beautiful," she said. "Where did you learn to dive like that?"

"My sister's a competitive swimmer." Loch smiled at her and pulled herself up onto the dock, water streaming down her body in rivulets that caught and held the sunlight. "I've been in the water a couple of times."

She leaned in close to Amir to get a look at the camera as Amir clicked through the shots.

"I think you've already got what we need," she said. "But let's do it one more time and then get some photos as I come up the ladder. Just get me in the background, though. Walk back far enough that the dock is the main focus."

"The dock," Amir said, sweeping Loch with her eyes as she walked away, "is nowhere near my main focus right now."

After Loch dove again, she swam over to the ladder and stood so the water was at her thighs, then looked to the left, letting the sunlight fall across the angles of her face in a soft gold wash. Amir took a few shots from several yards down the dock, then walked slowly toward Loch, dropping to her knee a few feet away and taking one more photo as Loch looked directly into the camera, her eyes soft.

Amir stood and took off her jacket, handing it to Loch as she came out of the water, even though she tried to tell her she didn't need it.

"You may not, but I need you to put it on." Amir held it out for her, and Loch slipped into it. "People stare at you all damn day. I'm trying not to be one of them."

Loch turned around and looked into her eyes, wrapping the coat around herself and pulling the sleeves down over her hands. Amir felt the slow, wet warmth of her body as Loch leaned against her.

"It feels different when you do it."

Amir pulled Loch into her body, then looked into her eyes as she held Loch's face in her hands. "It is different."

❖

After getting the shots they needed at the dock, they went to three more properties. After the last one, Loch paused as she opened the truck door.

"Wait," she said, sliding into her seat. "Why haven't we taken any pictures of you?"

"Oh, no." Amir laughed as she slid the truck into gear. "That's definitely not going to happen."

"You need to show up somewhere on the website." Loch clicked through the shutter on the camera and pointed it at Amir. "Let me take a couple pictures, just in case."

Amir hesitated. "As long as I don't actually have to use them."

"Not at all." Loch slowly spun a dial on the top of her camera. "But you might want to. Your look is going to be way better for this business than mine."

Amir laughed, getting back out of the truck and slamming the door shut. "I can guarantee you, Ms. Battersby, that is not the case."

Loch walked a few steps toward her, then looked down at Amir's sweatshirt and tipped her head. "What do you have on under there?"

Amir laughed. "You get right to the point, don't you?"

"I meant that in a purely professional sense." Loch smiled, her gaze moving across Amir's broad shoulders.

"I think I've got on a white sports bra and a white T-shirt."

"Perfect," Loch said, stepping back and focusing the camera on her. "Lose everything but that."

Amir pulled her jacket and sweatshirt off, leaving her in just the T-shirt and jeans, with a worn black leather belt. Loch put the camera down in the truck bed and ran her hands through Amir's hair, leaving some of it standing slightly on end and disheveled as if she'd been working all day. Amir closed her eyes as Loch pulled pieces forward toward her face.

"Are you doing this to drive me crazy?" Amir asked, looking down at Loch's mouth, her voice a low scrape. "Because it's working."

"No." Loch smiled and swiped a bit of dirt from the ground across Amir's cheek with her thumb. "That's just a bonus."

Loch moved Amir until she was leaning against the tailgate, arms resting on the top edge on both sides.

"Okay," she said, her face disappearing behind the lens of the camera. "Eyes to the right. Look into the sun."

When Loch finally convinced Amir to stop laughing, she got a few great pictures, then suddenly, she put the camera down and let it hang from the strap around her neck.

"I'm starving. Feel like getting something to eat?"

Amir smiled. "Now, *that's* what I've been waiting to hear."

❖

It was almost evening when Loch finally got home and burst through the door just in time to pick up her phone, which she'd heard ringing as she got to the steps outside the house.

"Hey, Skye," she said, holding the phone to her ear and flopping her camera and lens bag on the couch as she passed. "I feel like I haven't talked to you forever."

"That's because you haven't," her sister said, her words falling out in a rush. "I was at that swim meet on the Connecticut meet tour, and Mom decided not to tell me what happened to Samia until I came back this morning. I could kill her."

"I had no idea you didn't know. I should have called you. How did you do at the meet?"

"I won," she said. "But that's not important. How are you doing about Samia? Mom said you left New York."

"Yeah." Loch sighed, the screen door slapping shut behind her as she walked back out onto the porch and sank down on the porch step. "She left me her house in Innis Harbor, and I'm trying to figure out what to do with it, but being here is actually not that bad. I needed to get out of the city for a while anyway."

"I miss you already, but I'm glad you did. I don't know how you're not completely burned out."

"I think I have been for a while, I just didn't realize it." Loch kicked her shoes off and pressed her bare feet against the sun-warmed porch step, looking out at the endless blue water on the other side of the harbor.

"When do you have to be back?"

"I don't know." Loch closed her eyes as the breeze brushed her hair away from her face. "I guess I need to call my agent at some point and find out."

Skye was quiet for a moment, and Loch knew she was winding her hair around her finger, something she'd always done when she thought, even as a toddler. "You're thinking about staying there, aren't you?"

"What? I couldn't even if I wanted to," Loch said. "I can't just walk away from everything."

"Why the fuck not?"

"I'm supposed to be at London Fashion Week next month, and I'm still under contract with Hermès for the fall show at the Grande

Palais before the Cannes Film Festival." Loch suddenly felt like crying for some stupid reason and stopped for a second to take a breath. "I'll be fine, I just need to get my head around it again."

"Let me let you in on a little secret," Skye said.

Loch smiled. She knew what was coming.

"You don't have to do *shit*. Get that agent of yours to call them and get you the hell out of it."

"It's not that simple."

"Only because you haven't picked up the phone yet."

"I'll think about it." Loch smiled and rubbed her temples. "I promise."

"Are you still staying up till all hours?"

"Actually, I'm sleeping like a normal person these days."

"If you ask me, you need to stay there long enough to catch up on a few years of shuteye, then find some hot girl to keep you awake at night." Skye paused for effect, and Loch heard her smile. "I'm just saying."

Loch laughed, watching the bats fly out from under the eaves and scatter, stirring streaks of lavender dusk into the night falling around her. "I can't believe my little sister is lecturing me about my sex life."

"That's where you're wrong," Skye said. "I'm lecturing you about your *lack* of a sex life. Totally different."

Loch smiled and watched a seagull land on the porch railing, then seem to think better of it, darting off toward the harbor as quickly as she came.

"How's Danny, by the way?"

Skye had been seeing a New York University med student for the last few months, and she'd brought him to dinner in the city once so Loch could meet him. He was nice. In the same way unflavored oatmeal was nice. The only thing she'd liked about him was that he had no idea who she was.

"God, I don't know. I mean, I'm still seeing him, but I swear, I'm only with him because I'm in love with his family. In fact, I might have a thing for his sister."

"I can't say I'm faint with shock over here." Loch's voice was teasing as she went inside to get a beer and brought it back out to the porch, propping her feet on the railing. "So, how's the sex? Is that good at least?"

"It's actually great." Skye paused. "As long as he's not in the room."

Loch laughed, and they chatted for a few more minutes before Skye had to run to swim practice.

"But call me tomorrow, okay?"

Loch promised she would and clicked off the phone, only to pick it up and dial a minute later. It rang twice before Amir answered.

"Yes, Ms. Battersby?"

"I've heard you're the one to call for everything here," Loch said. "I know it's after hours, but I have a problem."

"And what's that?"

Loch smiled and leaned on the porch railing, looking up at the crescent moon just visible over the now dark surface of the sea. "I just went out to the back deck, and there's no fire."

Amir laughed, reaching for her jacket on the way out the door. "I might be able to handle that for you. Don't touch anything. I'll be there in five minutes."

Loch smiled as she put the phone down and went inside to change.

❖

A few minutes later, Amir pulled up to the house and cut the engine. She gripped the steering wheel, watching her fingers turn white around it. It had been all she could do not to kiss Loch on the dock that morning when she was soaking wet and wrapped up in her jacket. She was trying like hell to be respectful of the fact that this was a vulnerable time for her, but Loch was making that more and more difficult.

Amir sighed as she got out of the truck and walked up the hill to the porch. All she had to do was not kiss her. *Sure*, Amir muttered to herself. *Just don't kiss the most gorgeous woman I've ever seen who just happens to be cool as hell and gay as fuck. Right.*

Loch opened the door wearing gray men's chinos that sat on her hips, barefoot, with a blue cashmere hoodie the color of her eyes zipped low enough to see she was bare underneath. It stopped at her waist, leaving a few inches of bare skin between the soft edge of it and the chinos.

"Come in," she said, raking her hand through her hair and leaning out to turn on the porch light. "But we have a problem."

Amir smiled and rubbed her forehead with the heel of her hand before she looked up and swept Loch with her gaze. "Well, I certainly do."

"Why?" Loch tilted her head to the side. "You forgot to bring it?"

Amir looked at her for a second before she realized they were talking about two different things. She pulled the lighter that Loch had left by her fireplace out of her jacket pocket and held it up. "Is this what you're talking about?"

"Yep." Loch took it from her and dropped it into her pocket. "And it turns out, you were right. I couldn't find another lighter anywhere in the house."

Loch stepped aside as Amir came in, bringing the cold air in on her jacket. "But what were you talking about?"

"Nothing," Amir said, then stopped and shook her head, smiling. "But you look beautiful."

Loch took her hand and led her out the back door to the deck. "Look, I have it all set up."

She stopped just past the door and pointed at the very tall and perilously balanced pile of logs and newspaper in the firepit, then tipped her head to the side.

"Although now that I'm looking at it, that doesn't look right."

Amir walked ahead to the firepit so Loch wouldn't be able to see her trying not to laugh. The contrast between Loch the wildly talented supermodel and her earnest inner Boy Scout made it hard to keep a straight face.

"Almost," Amir said, kneeling by the firepit and concentrating on the pile. "You have everything we need here, but we might have better luck taking it in a few stages."

She took the pile of logs off the top and set them aside, then switched the kindling from the bottom to a teepee shape over the newspaper. She handed the lighter to Loch.

"For this kind of fire at least, it's usually easiest to do it in three stages, and you have to be sure you have a solid flame with each one before you go on to the next."

Amir led her through the process until fire engulfed two of the logs, the flames shapeshifting into gold sparks that chased one another into the night sky. Amir stacked the rest of the logs a safe distance away and sat by Loch, leaning back on the riser behind them. The smoke curled into the crisp air, the sharp scent of cedar rising around them. The green sap in the wood popped and crackled, sending tiny pieces of delicate ash aloft, and one of them landed silently on Loch's cheek. Amir gently turned Loch's face toward her and brushed it away with her thumb.

"Thank you for teaching me to build a fire," Loch said, her gaze dropping slowly to Amir's mouth. "And for not laughing."

"Hey, it's just not something you've done before," Amir said. "If someone gave me a million dollars, I wouldn't be able to walk a runway without falling on my ass. Which, by the way, looks a hell of a lot more difficult than starting a fire."

Loch smiled. "It can be a little tricky."

"So," Amir said after a moment. "What are you doing the day after tomorrow?"

"Well." Loch looked up at the sky as she considered her options. "It's either walking down to the diner to read the paper or watching the tourists all stand on one side of the dock and sink it. I'll have to check my calendar."

Amir laughed out loud and ran a hand through her hair. "Why the hell do they *do* that? I've never understood it."

"I think they're scared of falling off, so they figure it's safer to just all huddle together and sink it instead."

"Well," Amir said, "I took this week off to try to get some decent pictures of my work, considering the disaster it turned out to be last time. You knocked it out in six hours, so I have some extra time on my hands." She got up and put another log on the fire, brushing an ember off the sleeve of her fleece as she sat back down. "Feel like going somewhere with me on Wednesday?"

"That depends," Loch said, smiling and pretending to consider her options. "Where are we going?"

"That's the catch," Amir said, looking over at her. "I'm not telling you. You'll just have to trust me."

"Not fair," Loch said. "You have to tell me something."

"Okay," Amir said. "Bring what you need for a night or two and some warm clothes."

"Ooh," Loch said, looking instantly thrilled and cute as hell. "Where are we going?"

"That's all you're getting, Battersby," Amir said. "You'll just have to wait for the rest."

Loch got up and sat on the riser below Amir, leaning back into her and pulling her knees up to wrap her arms around them. Amir let out a slow breath as she felt the warmth of Loch's body sink back against the inside of her thighs.

"Are you cold?"

"Kind of," Loch said. "I can go in and get a jacket. I just don't want to leave. I'm afraid the fire won't be like this when I come back."

Amir shrugged off her jacket and held it in front of Loch, who put her arms through the sleeves backward and held it to her like a blanket. It was a long time before she spoke.

"I'm thinking about taking some time off," she said finally. "Like a year."

Amir ran her fingers through Loch's hair and waited. She knew her well enough by now to know she had more to say.

"I don't even really know why. I just don't recognize what I'm doing anymore."

Loch started to go on and then hesitated, following a burning ember with her eyes as the wind picked it up and lifted it toward the black sky.

"When I started modeling, I loved challenging people's ideas about what's perceived as feminine or masculine. It was such a new concept then, and no one knew who I was yet, so that concept really stood out and I sort of faded into the background."

She watched as the last log finally caught fire, shifting sudden layers of light across them before it settled into a slow burn.

"But now I've gotten more recognizable, so the focus is constantly on me as a person, what I'm wearing, who I'm with…I don't feel like I'm changing anything anymore, I'm just being a celebrity. I didn't even realize it until I came here."

Amir squeezed her shoulders. "Want to know what I think?"

"Yeah." Loch turned around and looked at Amir. "I do."

"You're amazing at what you do." She brushed a stray lock of hair out of Loch's eyes before she went on. "I think the part you don't like about it is being famous."

Loch turned back around and pulled one of Amir's hands into both of hers, tracing the lines of her palm with her fingertip. "It's just started to bother me that I'm not putting anything meaningful into the world anymore."

"I wouldn't be so sure about that." Amir leaned in and dropped her voice to a whisper, her words warm against Loch's ear. "I promise you, there are hundreds of queer, trans, or even genderfluid straight kids out there right now in tiny hostile towns who had the courage to be themselves because they saw you do it first."

"I hope so." Loch turned around, her blue eyes as dark as the sky. Amir ran her hand through Loch's hair, then stood slowly and held out her hand.

"I should head home," Amir said. "Walk me out?"

Loch looked at her for a long moment, then took her hand and stood. "Only if you tell me why you're really leaving."

Amir pulled Loch's body into hers and closed her eyes. When she opened them, she held Loch's face in her hands and whispered against her lips, "Because if I don't leave now, I won't go."

She slid her hand slowly around the back of Loch's neck, holding her gaze before she kissed her. Loch melted against her as Amir slid her hands around her waist and down the curve of her back, pulling Loch's hips into hers as she kissed down her neck.

Loch's hands slipped under Amir's shirt and across the warm, bare skin of her back, the strong lines of her body tense under her fingertips. Amir brought her hands back up to Loch's neck and bit her lip gently, then kissed her until they were both breathless and Amir heard herself groan as she pulled Loch tighter against her. At the last possible second, she pulled away just enough to touch Loch's forehead to hers and whisper before she turned and walked back into the house.

## Chapter Six

The next morning, Amir was up early. She'd promised her brother, Hamid, she'd show him the pictures they'd taken the previous day before he had to go to work. His wife, Anna, answered the door with a cup of coffee for her, and Amir kissed her cheek on her way into the living room. Hamid was on the couch leaning over his laptop.

"I'm hard at work on your website already." He stared at the screen as Amir walked up behind him and set her computer beside his on the coffee table.

"Dude," she said, nodding toward his screen. "Those are the basketball scores from last night."

"Actually, you're right, we should get on it." He pulled up her website on his computer. "We'll need all the time we can get considering your last photos looked like rejects from *The Blair Witch Project*."

"Hey, you know I'm not a photographer, which is good since you seem to break shit in your house every two days."

He smiled and took a sip of her coffee. "Fair point."

Amir brought up the photos from the day before on her computer and clicked through them one by one. She got through three before Hamid stopped her and leaned in closer.

"Who is *that*?" He was looking at the first photo of Loch diving. "And I'm not complaining, but how did you get her in the picture? She looks like a model."

The close shot she'd taken of Loch came up next, water streaming down her body as she leaned into the camera and smiled. Amir clicked past it quickly, but Hamid nudged her laptop over so it was in front of him.

"Hang on. You know this girl, don't you?"

"Yeah," Loch said. "But what do you think of the pictures?"

"It looks like you got smart and hired a professional this time. They're amazing photos, which makes my job easy." He leaned back against the couch and smiled. "So, now that we've gotten that out of the way, you can spill it about this girl."

He looked at Amir, but she just shook her head and smiled. She and Hamid had always been close, but she wasn't ready to talk about it just yet. He scrolled through the next few photographs until he came to the one of Amir, arms across the tailgate of her truck, looking off into the distance.

"If you tell anyone I said this, I'll deny it, but that's a great picture. We should put it on the front page."

"Hell no." Amir tried to grab at her computer but failed. "There's no chance that's even going on the site, much less the front page."

Anna called just then from the kitchen to ask Amir if she wanted a muffin.

"Hey, baby," Hamid called back, looking at Amir. "Can you come here for a second?"

"Don't you dare show her that."

"Shut it, it's not like you're naked," he said. "Let's let Anna decide."

"Seriously, Hamid? Jesus."

Anna walked up behind them with a chocolate chip muffin just as Hamid was closing the computer.

"Okay," Hamid said. "You know how many rich housewives have summer homes on the coast, right? Especially Bar Harbor?"

"A lot," Anna said with a nod. "In fact, I think they may be solely responsible for keeping California's chardonnay vineyards in business."

"So, imagine you're one of them, and you're looking for

someone to come and fix something at the house or maybe install something on the boat."

Amir groaned and reached for the muffin. She knew him well enough to know there was no way he was going to let it go at this point, so she might as well eat something while he dragged it out to torture her.

"So, you're looking for someone to hire, and there's the couple of old guys that do marine repair at the Bar Harbor docks," he said, opening the laptop and turning it around to Anna. "Or there's her."

She leaned in to look at the screen, then looked slowly over at Amir. "Holy shit."

"Right?" Hamid said. "But she doesn't want me to use the picture."

"Look," Anna said. "If I was one of those women, I'd break a faucet or something just to get a closer look at those arms. And I'm straight."

"Oh, my God." Amir took another bite of muffin and sank farther down into the sofa. "I can't believe I'm having this conversation."

"You're not." Hamid clicked the picture into place on the front page of Amir's site. "We're using it."

He emailed himself the rest of the photos before he handed the laptop back to Amir. Anna winked and squeezed Amir's biceps as she left, and Amir threw one of the couch pillows at her as she disappeared around the corner.

"Hey," she said, looking at Hamid. "Are you guys grilling out tonight?"

"Yep," Hamid said. "It's Tuesday. The kids threaten to do it themselves if we even try to plan something else."

"Do you mind if I come over?"

"Hell no, I might actually get to have some adult conversation for a change." Hamid looked over at her and paused. "Why, are you bringing someone with you?"

"Maybe. Only if Mom and Dad aren't coming."

"Mom has that book club in town tonight that she never misses, and Dad's at that work thing in Portland."

"So, in Vegas with his buddies playing poker?"

"Exactly. Bring her over. I'll try to keep the kids from scaring her off completely."

They managed to work out a few more details about the website text before Hamid had to leave for work. He stood and wedged his computer into his bag.

"She must be special." He glanced over at Amir. "I've never met one of your girlfriends."

Amir pulled on her jacket and nodded. "She is."

"Well, let me know if you get serious about her. I'll try to work on Dad."

❖

Loch turned slowly around Samia's bedroom, double-checking she hadn't missed anything she wanted to put aside before the movers from the shelter arrived Sunday. She'd gone through the entire house in the last few days, with the exception of Samia's art studio, trying to keep in mind that her aunt had specifically told her to clear out the house. It was hard to think about letting it all go. Maybe she'd just leave them to it and sit at the dock until it was over.

Her phone pinged suddenly from across the room, and she jumped. It was Amir.

*Have any desire to have dinner tonight with my obnoxious brother and his family?*

She typed quickly and hit send before she changed her mind.

*I'd love to. I didn't bring any nice clothes, though. Do I need to dress up?*

Her phone pinged back a few seconds later.

*God no, we'll be lucky if my brother is wearing a shirt. Brace yourself. I'll pick you up at six.*

❖

That evening, Loch changed clothes three times before she decided on black skinny jeans, a white button-up, and black boots.

*Great*, she thought, unbuttoning the shirt and dropping it back in her bag. *I spend an hour deciding what to wear and end up looking like a waiter.*

In the end, she decided to go with a faded denim shirt and switched the boots out for her Chuck Taylors. She'd just pulled them on when she heard Amir's truck pulling up outside. She raked her hands through her hair and grabbed her jacket just as she heard the doorbell. On the way out, Loch remembered the six-pack she'd gotten to take with her as she passed the kitchen and finally stepped out on the porch, beer in hand. Amir took it from her and set it on one of the chairs, then pulled Loch into her arms and kissed her, hands sliding from her shoulders into her hair, holding her gaze as she finally let her go.

"Ready?"

"I was," Loch said, dropping her gaze to Amir's mouth. "But now I just want you to do that again."

Amir smiled, picking up the beer and taking her hand as they walked down the steps. "Hopefully, you'll still think that after you meet my family."

❖

Hamid's house was only five minutes away, an old Victorian at the north edge of town with a wraparound porch and kids' toys strewn across the yard. The scent of charcoal and burgers on the grill surrounded Loch as soon as she stepped out of the truck.

"Oh, no." Loch stopped in her tracks as she suddenly remembered what she'd meant to tell Amir.

"What's wrong?" Amir asked, coming around to her side and shutting the truck door behind her. "Changed your mind?"

"Not at all. I just forgot to tell you I'm a vegetarian. I usually try to tell people that before I come over, and I totally blanked."

"Thank God," Amir said as she reached into the paper grocery bag she was carrying and held up a package of veggie dogs. "Because I've been the only vegetarian in the family since I was eight."

She took Loch's hand, and they walked to the door, which opened dramatically the second they stepped onto the porch. A little girl in a fireman's hat and a pink tutu stood in the doorway and studied them. "Am I supposed to let you in?"

Amir matched her doubtful look. "Maybe. But you'd better ask your dad just in case."

She flounced back into the house and dragged Hamid back to the door a few seconds later. "They want to come in, Daddy."

Hamid paused, narrowing his eyes and studying Amir. "What do you think, Yasmin? Should we let them in?"

Yasmin threw open the screen door and ran down the hall. Hamid motioned them in, then sprinted to the kitchen to pull a pot off the stove, turning around and offering his hand to Loch when it was safely on the counter.

"Loch, this is my brother, Hamid," Amir said. "Hamid, this is Loch Battersby."

"It's nice to meet you." He glanced at Amir with a raised eyebrow before he turned back to Loch. "What can I get you to drink? We have white wine, I think, if Anna didn't get into it last night, or we definitely have beer."

Amir handed him the six-pack. "Loch brought this, so you can put it in the fridge with the rest."

"I like you already." Hamid pulled one out before he put them in the fridge. "I love Dogfish Head IPA. It's my favorite, and Anna never lets me have it."

"What are you saying about me, Hamid?" Anna walked into the kitchen and thumped him affectionately on the arm. "Telling lies again?"

She smiled at Amir, then froze. "Oh, my God," she said slowly. "You're Loch Battersby."

Loch smiled warmly and held out her hand. "I am, and thank you so much for having me over. I met your little girl when we got here. She's precious."

Anna nodded, still staring, then managed to pull herself

together enough to take Loch out to the back deck to meet Yasmin's little brother, Hameen. Hamid waited until they'd just rounded the corner to turn to Amir and set his beer on the counter with a *thunk*.

"Okay, obviously, that's the girl from the pictures, but explain to me how Anna knows her by name." He paused. "She's fucking gorgeous, by the way. What the hell is she doing with you?"

Amir laughed and punched at him, whispering for him to keep his voice down. "The last thing she needs is to have everyone make a big damn deal out of her being here. Just treat her like you would anyone else."

"So, she's famous or something?"

"She's a model. I'm sure Anna knows her from ads or beauty campaigns or something."

"Oh, shit," Hamid said suddenly, looking into the fridge. "I forgot to actually hand her a beer."

"Come on," Amir said, still laughing as she picked up a plate of burgers from the counter. "Let's get these on the grill before I starve to death."

"Not that the grill will do you much good." Hamid took the plate from her and headed through the living room and toward the back deck. "I know you're eating wheatgrass dogs or whatever you call them, don't try to pretend you're not."

"Every damn time." Amir shook her head as she followed him out the glass doors. "You just can't miss an opportunity to make fun of my grass dogs, can you?"

Once everything was ready, they all sat around the long farm table at the end of the deck to eat, the fireflies out in luminous force as evening fell around them. The kids raced back and forth from the deck to the wide expanse of green grass beyond, stopping to eat a hot dog only because Anna threatened to hide the ice cream if they didn't. Hameen was particularly displeased and stomped up the stairs, scowling until he saw Loch. He walked over to her, standing on his tiptoes to touch her hair with the flat of his hand when he was close enough.

"Hameen!" Anna said from the other side of the table. "You need to ask before you touch people."

"No, it's okay," Loch said, leaning toward Hameen so he could inspect it more closely. "He's just curious."

"Your hair is gray like old people," he said, lifting it with his fingers. "Why do you have grandpa hair?"

"That's such a good question," Loch said, smiling. "No one really knows. It just started growing in that way when I was about ten years old."

"Well, I like it," he said as she sat back up. "It's pretty."

He ran over to his spot at the table and poured a river of ketchup on his burger, chattering to his sister about Loch's hair and grabbing a handful of chips off her plate when she turned to look.

"Sorry about that," Anna said. "You never know what's going to come out of his mouth. He gets that from his dad."

"It was perfect." Loch smiled. "I wish everyone was that honest."

"My niece Kelly is actually a huge fan of yours," Anna said, handing Yasmin a napkin to wipe the mustard off her cheek. "She's a sophomore in high school, although she's threatening to drop out. She's been having a rough time lately."

"What do you mean?"

"She's gay and presents as masculine. She doesn't identify as trans, but she prefers to be called Kiran."

"Presents as masculine?" Hamid swiped at the relish on his lip with a thumb. "What the hell does that mean?"

He looked at Amir, who just smiled and shook her head in his direction. "Don't you worry your pretty little head about it."

Anna rolled her eyes at Hamid and went on. "Anyway, the kids in her school just can't get their heads around it, I guess."

Amir looked across the table at Loch. "Bar Harbor High is year-round, so she's in school now, even though it's summer."

Anna smoothly grabbed the butter knife Hameen had decided to pretend was a sword and put it on her plate. "Anyway, I think it's really starting to get to her."

"Are there any other gay kids at her school?" Loch asked, pushing her plate toward Amir, who just slid it back to her.

"So far, just some gay boys, and they're great. I've met some of them, but it's just not the same as having butch friends that get you."

"Okay," Hamid said. "Someone needs to start explaining this stuff to me."

Anna nodded toward Amir. "Butch."

He looked at her blankly, then nodded, his face lighting up. "Ah, got it."

"Does she live around here?" Loch said.

"Yep," Anna said. "Just a few blocks down. My sister Darlene is a single mom, so she works all the time, and Kelly's dad left when she was little." She glanced at Hamid before she went on. "She's not happy about her daughter being gay and kind of just avoids her, so Kelly's over here a lot."

"I like her," Hamid said. "She's a good kid in spite of Darlene being an idiot."

"Hamid!" Anna said, glancing at the kids, who were trying to catch the fireflies hovering above the table. She leaned closer to Loch and whispered, "She's my sister and I love her, but it's kind of true, actually."

She reached out and caught Yasmin's can of orange soda just as it was tipping over and set it back down on the table.

"You know, if you think it might help, I'd love to meet her," Loch said, then looked at her watch. "If it's not too late on a school night."

"Are you serious?" Anna said. "That would be amazing, but I'm sure you have better things to do than talk to my angsty niece."

"Actually, there's nothing more important than that," Loch said. "I was in that situation once, so I kind of get it."

Anna touched her hand, then pulled out her phone and stepped away from the table to call Darlene.

"That's really sweet of you," Amir said, pulling her close. "Thank you. I've been worried about her for months."

"So, what's going on?" Hamid asked Amir. "I know she's been down for a while, but Anna hasn't told me the whole story yet."

Hamid opened a bottle of water and handed it to Loch.

"She's been dating one of the cheerleaders for a while, and someone saw them kissing and outed them to the whole school. The jocks had never really noticed her before, but now they all think it's their job to put her in her place, like every cheerleader belongs to them or something."

"Great," Hamid said. "They sound like jackasses, not that I'm surprised."

"Yeah," Amir said. "They've been pretty relentless. She still hasn't decided if she's going to the summer dance coming up because she's intimidated by those guys, and I can't say I blame her."

Anna stepped back to the table and told Loch that Kelly was on her way as she scrolled through the pictures on her phone.

"Do you remember that beauty campaign you did last Christmas for Dior where you wore a tux?"

"God, yes," Loch said. "It was shot in Times Square in the middle of the night and I just about froze."

Anna held her phone out and showed her a picture of a girl in a black tuxedo, standing by a Christmas tree.

"That's Kelly. She wore a tux last year to a school Christmas party because she saw you in that commercial on TV."

"Wow." Loch glanced at Amir.

"When she said she wanted to do it, we looked everywhere for a tux that was small enough to tailor to her size, and we finally found one the night before the party. I stayed up all night taking it in."

"Didn't she meet her girlfriend that night?" Hamid said.

"Yep, that's the night she met Amy, the girl she's dating now."

Everyone turned to look as they heard the front door open, and a few seconds later, Kelly walked through the kitchen and out onto the deck, stopping dead in place when she saw Loch. Loch got up and walked over to her.

"Hi, Kiran," she said. "I'm so happy to meet you. I'm Loch Battersby."

Kiran just stood there, her hand covering her mouth, until she finally came to her senses and slowly shook Loch's hand.

"I can't believe it's you." Her voice rattled the words as they came out. "And you know my name."

"Hey," Loch said, walking back to the table and making a space for Kiran to sit beside her, "I just saw that picture of you in the tux last Christmas."

"You saw that?"

"Yep," Loch said. "And yours looked way better than mine when I did that commercial. You can't see it, but the back was gathered with a million pins so it fit me. Yours was perfect."

"Anna took it in for me," Kiran said, glancing over at her with a wide smile. "I loved it." Everyone else turned back to their own conversations then and let Loch and Kiran talk.

"If you don't grab that girl up, you're an idiot," Hamid said, his voice low, leaning into Amir. "She's a sweetheart. I can't believe she just offered to hang out with some high school kid she'd never met."

"Believe me," Amir said, watching the last of the fading sun glint off her hair as Loch threw her head back and laughed, "I know."

❖

Hours later, Kiran went home with a big hug from Loch, and Hamid walked Amir and Loch to the door.

"Thanks for hanging out with Kiran," he said, squeezing Loch's shoulder. "I want to help her, but I never know what to say."

"Thanks for the opportunity to meet her," Loch said, smiling. "She's a great kid."

Amir took Loch's hand as they walked to the truck, then opened the door for Loch before she went around to the driver's side.

"Just so you know," Loch leaned into Amir and whispered as she put the truck in gear and turned on the lights. "No one's ever opened doors for me like you do. I like it."

Amir leaned over and slipped a hand around the back of her head, pulling her gently forward to kiss her. "My pleasure, Ms. Battersby."

## Chapter Seven

The next morning, Amir finished loading the camping gear and filled the cooler with ice, remembering at the last minute to stack firewood in the back of the truck. The chances of Loch forgetting to start a campfire were slim to none.

She'd just pulled up to Loch's house when her phone rang. She picked it up and brushed a piece of bark off her shirt, then tossed it out the window. "Hey, Hamid, what's up?"

She listened, her fist tightening around the steering wheel. "What the fuck, how did that happen? Is she okay?"

Amir glanced up at the house and nodded, sliding the truck into park and killing the engine. "Of course I can. I'm leaving now, I'll be there as quick as I can."

She left her phone in the truck, clicking the lock as she climbed the hill to the door. Loch saw her through the window and opened the door.

"I might be running behind a little bit," Loch said, buttoning her shirt as she talked. "My bag is packed, but I don't know where we're going, so I can't decide what to wear."

Amir stepped in and ran a hand through her hair. "We may actually be getting a late start anyway. Hamid just called and said Kiran got into a fight at school."

"What?" Loch stopped in place, her eyes wide. "Is she okay?"

"He said she's got a black eye, but he doesn't know what happened. He wants me to go check on her. She doesn't want her mom or Anna to know about it, so she called him. He's leading a seminar at work today and can't leave."

Loch grabbed her jacket and opened the door. "Let's go. You can tell me the rest on the way."

Amir looked at her. "Wait, you're going with me?"

"Only if you want me to," Loch said, suddenly unsure. "Although I totally understand if you'd rather go by yourself."

Amir pulled Loch into her arms, breathing in the scent of her hair before she let her go. "I'd love for you to go with me. It just didn't occur to me that you'd want to."

"Well, what I really want to do is punch whoever hit her in the face, but I guess I'll have to settle for keeping you company."

"You may have to keep me from doing that." Amir picked up Loch's keys on the way out the door and locked it behind them. "Especially if she's really hurt."

Loch glanced over at her as they started down the hill. "How did you know what key to use to lock the door?"

"Because I cut it." Amir smiled and handed her the keys. "My initials are on the back of every key I make."

Loch turned the key over in her hand and climbed into the truck. Amir shut the door behind her and walked around, climbing in and checking the rearview mirror before she pulled out.

"I know this probably isn't the best time to say this, but something about your initials being on my house key is incredibly sexy."

Amir reached over and slid her hand up Loch's thigh, her gaze still on the road. "Good. Because I can cut you a thousand of them."

"Okay," Loch said, turning toward her in the seat. "Tell me what else you know about what happened."

"That's it, really," Amir said. "No one saw the fight, so she's not in trouble, and she doesn't know we're coming. Hamid just wants me to make sure she's really okay."

"Do you think it was the guys that have been harassing her?"

"Absolutely." Amir changed lanes and looked over at Loch. "As far as I know, they've never gotten physical with her before, though, and it worries me that it's escalating."

When they got to Bar Harbor, they pulled into the high school parking lot, and Amir texted Kiran to come out to her truck.

"I don't want to storm in there and embarrass her," she said. "She probably doesn't want anyone to know."

"Are we taking her back with us?"

"I'd like her to go home until we figure out what happened, but I don't know if she'll want to leave or not. She's pretty stubborn with this stuff."

"I can imagine. It's a tricky balance," Loch said. "You don't want to put yourself in danger, but you also don't want to back down from the bullies."

"I was never that smart about it." Amir tapped the steering wheel with her thumb as she watched Kiran walk toward the parking lot. "I got into fight after fight. The girls were just as awful to me when I was in school, or at least the popular ones were. And when I finally got a girlfriend, someone outed us, and all hell broke loose."

Loch and Amir got out and shut their doors as Kiran got to the truck.

"Uncle Hamid called you, didn't he?"

"Yep," Amir said. "And I'm not here to hassle you, I just want to get a look at that eye and make sure you're okay." Amir reached toward Kiran's face, but she stepped away.

"Look, I'm fine. It wasn't that big a deal."

Loch reached back into the cab of the truck and looked around. "Hey, you work from this truck, do you have a first aid kit in here?"

"Under the seat."

Loch found it and left the door open to shield them from view.

"Get over here, let me look at it." Loch smiled, and she was evidently hard to resist because Kiran stepped close enough for her to get a look at the cut across the top of her nose. Loch dabbed at a smear of blood along the side with an antiseptic wipe and looked closer at her eye.

"It looks worse than it is," Kiran said. "The football guys said they were just reminding me what locker room to use."

"Let me guess," Loch said, squinting at her. "By slamming your face into the door?"

"Good guess."

Loch turned Kiran's face toward Amir.

"It doesn't look broken," Amir said, leaning closer to look and squinting in the sunlight. "But that eye is going to look bad for a couple of days."

"How do you know?" Kiran said.

"What," Amir said, bumping Kiran's shoulder with hers. "You think you're the only butch to get into fights in high school?"

"Did you really?"

"Hell yeah," Amir said. "Ask Hamid, he jumped into one on the field one day and got suspended trying to protect me."

"What were you fighting about?"

Amir raised an eyebrow. "Same thing you were."

"Wow," Kiran said, smiling. "I never knew that."

"The good thing about this," Amir said, smiling and dropping her voice, "is that your girlfriend is going to be all over you making sure you're okay, which makes it almost worth it."

"I can't believe you just said that." Loch swatted her arm with the first aid kit.

Amir and Kiran thought that was hilarious, and pretty soon, Kiran was smiling again.

"You're totally right about that one," she said, glancing back toward the school. "Amy's pissed as hell and didn't even want to leave my side to go to class. It's not all bad."

"Do you have a picture of her?" Amir asked. "I've never seen her."

Kiran pulled up a picture of them on her phone with Amy standing behind her kissing her cheek, long blond hair falling over Kiran's shoulder.

"Damn, she's pretty," Amir said. "You guys look great together."

"She went nuts for you after you did that music video last year, by the way," Kiran said to Loch, sliding her phone back into the pocket of her jeans. "Half the girls in school were in love with you."

"What?" Amir leaned back on the truck and smiled at Loch. "What music video?"

"Oh, my God, you haven't seen it?" Kiran looked at Amir like she was crazy. "She transforms herself from a guy to a girl with just clothes and makeup in the same video, and you'd never know it's the same person."

"The artist was a friend." Loch looked at Amir and shrugged. "He had this idea for the video and wanted me to do it. It's totally his thing, though, I was just the visual. I had already heard the song and loved it, so I said I'd do it. He donated the profits to an LGBTQ youth charity in London."

"How do I not know this?" Amir said. "That's amazing."

Kiran looked back at the school again, biting her lip as she glanced down at her watch.

"I've got to go back in there. I can't just not show up at lunch like they hurt me and I ran home or something."

"So, you don't want to go home?" Loch asked.

"Hell no," Kiran said. "The last thing you want to do is look like you're scared."

Amir nodded. "I hate to say it, but you're right." She held Kiran's gaze. "But if you want to go, I'll take you."

"Hey, Kiran." Loch looked up at the front doors of the school. "Do you think many of the guys in there saw that video?"

"Actually, every one of them saw it because they showed it at a mandatory assembly during diversity week last month. They were all drooling over you as that girl."

Loch looked at Amir, then back at Kiran. "Feel free to say no to this, but how do you feel about some company for lunch?" She hesitated, thinking for a moment before she went on. "If you're sure it wouldn't make things worse."

Kiran stepped back. "Are you kidding me with this?"

Loch shook her head, smiling.

"I don't know why the hell you'd want to go in there," Kiran said. "But I'm not about to turn it down."

"Well, that's that," Amir said, a slow smile spreading across her face as she locked up her truck. "Let's go."

❖

Loch and Amir stopped at the office to sign in and get visitor passes, then Kiran directed them to the cafeteria. As they walked through the double doors into the dining area, the steamy, familiar smell of cafeteria food enveloped them, and Amir felt Kiran take a slow breath beside her. Heads swiveled toward them in a slow, surreal wave that started at the back of the room and moved like falling dominos to the front. Bar Harbor High wasn't a big school, and there were only about a hundred kids dotted in groups around the room, but within a few seconds, every single one of them was looking at Loch.

"Just pick a table with no varsity jackets," Kiran whispered. "I'll grab some drinks from the line."

Amir took Loch's hand and led her through the tables until she found a smaller one that was empty except for a forgotten algebra book. Amir looked around as they sat down.

"Yep," she said. "It's like I never left. They haven't changed a thing in here."

A petite redheaded girl with freckles approached the table then and tapped Loch on the shoulder.

"Sorry to bother you," she said, glancing back over her shoulder at a table of captivated girls a few yards away. "But you look like that model from that Ed Sheeran video." She hesitated. "The one where you go from a girl to a boy?"

"That's me," Loch said with a smile. "What's your name?"

"Oh, my God." She looked back and nodded at the table she'd come from. "It *is* her!"

That was all it took to start a flood. Every one of them came over to the table, all asking questions at once and asking Loch to sign their notebooks. Flashing camera phones were going off in every direction, and for the first time, Amir started to realize what it meant to be someone everyone recognized.

"Can you sign this for my little brother?" A heavier girl so shy she could barely get the words out thrust a sheet of notebook paper in Loch's direction. "He's gay, too, and you're like his idol."

"Sure," Loch said, smiling as if that girl was the only other person in the room. "What's his name?"

"Michael."

The girl studied Loch's face and hair as she signed the paper and added a short personal note to Michael.

"Here you go." Loch handed it back and looked up at her. "And you have really pretty eyes, you know. It's rare to see such a light green color."

"Thanks," the girl said, smiling for the first time.

Someone touched Loch's shoulder just then and pulled her into a new conversation as Kiran returned with three cans of soda.

"Geez," Amir said to her, nodding toward the rush of kids still piling deeper around Loch. "You weren't kidding."

Loch turned and whispered something in Kiran's ear, giving her a big smile as she went back to the throng of kids.

"What did she say?"

Kiran spoke quickly, her voice low and hushed. "She said the football guys are walking up behind us right now—don't you dare look, by the way—so she wanted to be sure they saw that she was here with us."

And that was it. That was the moment Amir knew she was falling in love with Loch. This wildly successful woman giving up an afternoon to hang out with a bullied teenager in some small-town high school cafeteria. The same one who was leaving any day to go the hell back to Manhattan.

Five athletic-looking guys in varsity jackets gathered around the outside edge of the group, and one of them pushed his way through to be close enough to get Loch's attention.

"So," he said, looking her up and down. "You're the chick from that video?"

Loch nodded, her gaze locked on his. "No woman is a 'chick,'" she said. "But if you're asking my name, it's Loch Battersby."

"What are you doing at Harbor High?" He looked back at the other guys and smiled, then swept her body with his eyes. "I can think of a few things I'd like you to teach me."

Amir stiffened and resisted the urge to step closer.

Loch turned and nodded toward Kiran. "Kiran's a friend of mine, and I was in town, so I stopped by to see her."

One of the other guys laughed, but someone elbowed him, and he stopped abruptly. Cameras were still going off in every direction, but the room now seemed suddenly quiet.

"That kid is your friend?" He nodded toward Kiran.

"Yep." Loch held his gaze. "And my girlfriend lives here, too, so I see her a lot."

"Yeah," he said finally, glancing back at his friends. "She's pretty cool."

One of the cheerleaders got Loch's attention and asked her about some other celebrity, and she turned away to talk to them. The guy stepped back to join his buddies, and they headed back to their table in a group, most of them still staring at Loch as they passed.

A few minutes later, he came back to where Kiran was standing and cleared his throat to get her attention.

"Hey, man," he said. "I'm sorry about today. I told them that shit wasn't cool."

"That's okay," Kiran said. "It was no big deal. You weren't even there."

"Yeah, but I heard about it." He glanced over his shoulder toward his table. "I'll make sure they don't bother you again. They were just being dicks."

Kiran nodded, and he bumped her fist with his as he left.

The bell rang, people started to scatter, and Loch signed the last of the autographs the students had time to ask for before the cafeteria was suddenly empty.

"Jesus *Christ*." Amir rubbed her temples and looked around in the thick sudden silence. "That was insane."

Kiran came over to Loch and hugged her hard. "Thank you for doing this for me."

Her voice was low, and it almost sounded like she was going to cry. Loch squeezed her back.

"It was no big deal. I think we got our point across."

Kiran just looked at her, then over at Amir. "It was a huge deal. And I won't forget it."

"Just do it for some other gay kid someday, although hopefully by then, you won't need to," Loch said. "Someone did something like this for me once and I never forgot it, either."

"I will," she said, brushing a cheek with the back of her hand. "I promise."

Amir handed Kiran her jacket. "Now get to class before I get called to the principal's office for keeping you out here."

They watched as Kiran disappeared through the swinging cafeteria doors, suddenly taller and walking with a confidence that reminded Amir of Loch. As they headed out to the truck, Loch looked over at Amir like she wanted to say something, but then changed her mind.

"Yes?" Amir said, smiling at her.

"I just wanted to say..." Loch paused so long Amir wondered if she was going to change her mind. It was the first time she'd ever seen her look nervous. "That it's not like I really think you're my girlfriend or anything."

"Well, that's a shame." Amir opened the truck door for her. She leaned in and brought Loch's face to hers, kissing her for longer than she should have in a high school parking lot and barely resisting the urge to do more than that. "Because that was my favorite part."

❖

Later, when they pulled up to Loch's house, Loch ran in to get her bag and swung it into the back of the truck before she climbed back into the cab.

"By the way," she said, looking through the back window. "What's all that stuff you have wrapped up in the back of your truck?"

"None of your business, ma'am." Amir reached over to put her hand on Loch's thigh.

"Don't make me get back there and get into it," Loch said with a smile that told Amir she was serious. "Because I will."

Amir started up the truck. "I'm taking you camping."

Loch just stared at her. "Are you serious?"

"Yep. You said you've never been."

She kissed Amir's cheek with an excited smile and sat back in her seat, sliding her hand underneath Amir's on the gearshift. "Do you know how long I've wanted to go camping?"

"Since you were a kid?"

She nodded. "I was supposed to go with Samia and Colleen twice, but both times, we got rained out. Then when I turned fifteen, I started working, so it just never happened."

"Well, I checked the weather, and there's no rain predicted till next week, so I think we're safe. And I reserved my favorite campsite, so all we have to do is drive in and set up."

❖

It was a short drive to Seawall Campground within Acadia National Park, and Amir followed the narrow camp road around until it came to the end and Amir parked, taking Loch's hand as they walked out to where the evergreens thinned and the land narrowed into the shape of an arrowhead. The farthest point of it pierced the clear blue sky, and sheer cliffs on both sides of it dropped into the sea below. Swirling waves crashed against the huge rocks at the base of the cliffs and launched cold white spray into the sky that hovered in the air, still and sparkling, an iridescent mist between the sea and the sun.

Loch walked slowly out to the point and stared down the two ragged cliff faces into the foaming sea below. She closed her eyes and breathed in the cold salt air, letting the water shake her like thunder as it crashed into the rock. Amir walked up behind Loch and wrapped her arms around her, pulling her close.

"This is so beautiful," Loch said, leaning back against Amir. "It's like you're standing at the end of the world, the last bit of earth before everything drops off into the ocean."

"And there's a full moon tonight," Amir said, her words soft against Loch's neck. "So, you'll still be able to see the waves spray up the sides of the cliffs even at midnight. It's gorgeous. It looks like liquid silver in the moonlight."

"I can't believe you brought me here. I totally didn't expect this." Loch turned around and slipped her hands underneath Amir's shirt, following the cuts of her abs with her fingers.

"God, Loch, you've got to stop," Amir said, closing her eyes and leaning into her. "If you start touching me like that, I'm not going to be able to stop."

"Maybe I don't want you to," Loch whispered, sliding her hands around to Amir's bare back and running her nails lightly up her sides.

"Jesus." Amir traced Loch's lip with the tip of her tongue, her hands warm against the sides of her face. "We've got to get the tent up before I take your clothes off right here and we get arrested."

Loch laughed at that and followed her back to the truck, where Amir handed her a green duffel bag. "This is the tent. If you want to, you can unpack this while I get the rest of the truck unloaded."

"Are you sure you don't want me to help you unload? There's all that wood and stuff."

"I think I can handle it." Amir winked at her and started stacking the wood by the firepit, but she kept an eye on Loch, who lined everything up in perfect piles on the ground. Rainfly, tent, footprint, and then the poles in three separate piles, with the poles and stakes across the top. Amir was unpacking the last of the equipment when she saw Loch holding the bag up and shaking it, looking inside it and feeling around in the corners.

Amir finally stood in the back of the truck and looked over at her, trying not to smile. "What's the problem over there, Battersby?"

"I have everything unpacked, but I can't find the instructions. I think I lost them somehow." Loch went over to the tent she'd carefully laid out and looked underneath it.

*Jesus*, Amir thought, watching her search carefully through the folded rainfly. *She's literally the cutest girl in the world.*

She hopped off the tailgate and took the bag that Loch was still peering into. "Don't worry, you didn't lose them. There are no instructions."

"But..." Loch shook the bag again, sudden worry wrinkling her forehead. "How do you know how it all goes together?"

Amir gave up trying not to smile. "I think between the two of us we'll be able to figure it out."

Loch looked doubtful but handed Amir the empty bag. "Okay, what happens first?"

Amir let Loch decide where she wanted the tent, and she chose the halfway point between the firepit and the cliffs, about thirty yards back from the edge of the cliffs. After the footprint was down, it only took about ten minutes to get the tent up and staked.

"I think we can skip the rainfly," Amir said, looking out at the cloudless horizon over the sea. "You can see the stars through the top of the tent if you don't have it up, and if we end up needing it, we can throw it up in under a minute."

Loch took off her shoes and climbed inside, lying back and looking up at the blue sky above her. "This is amazing. How have I been missing out on this all my life?"

"Stay right there," Amir said over her shoulder as she headed back to the truck. "I'm going to hand you some stuff."

She came back with two double camping pads and had Loch stack them on top of each other, then pulled a feather bed out of a canvas bag and shook it out.

"This goes on top," she said. "Then we'll put the sleeping bags over that."

After Loch had it all laid out, Amir handed her the first sleeping bag. "I didn't want you to feel like you didn't have your own space, so I brought two."

Loch looked at her for a minute and unzipped the bag, laying it out like a blanket. "That's so thoughtful, thank you." She looked up at Amir. "But I think tonight I'd rather end up in your space."

Amir smiled and handed her the last layer, a feather comforter, to lay over the top of everything, creating a lofted, cozy pile of soft layers.

"I'm positive my bed at home isn't anywhere near this nice," Loch said, looking up at Amir and smiling. "And something tells me you're actually a sleeping bag on the bare ground kind of girl if left to your own devices."

"Maybe." Amir crawled inside the tent and lay Loch softly underneath her on the bed. "But I know you're not used to camping, and the ground can get pretty cold. I didn't want you to be uncomfortable."

Loch looked thoughtful, then kissed her before she spoke. "I've never been with someone who takes care of me like you do. I guess it's always been the other way around."

Amir smiled at the memory of Loch that first morning outside the diner. "I think we've already established that you're hanging out with the wrong women."

Loch laughed, and Amir lay beside her, propped up on her elbow.

"This is none of my business, and you don't have to tell me, but what kind of girls do you date?"

"Mostly other models," Loch said, looking up at the sky. "I didn't realize it before, but I guess I've just been the more masculine person so far in my relationships."

"Being masculine doesn't mean you have to be in any certain role," Amir said gently. "There doesn't have to be roles at all. I think every couple is unique, you just have to see what develops between you, what your chemistry is."

"I guess I never thought about it that way." Loch looked up at Amir, thinking for a moment before she went on. "But I've definitely never dated anyone like you."

Amir smiled, her fingertips warm and light on Loch's neck. "So, you've never dated a butch?"

"No," Loch said. "Not even close."

Amir slid her hand under Loch's shirt and followed the lines of her body with her fingertips. "What do you think so far?"

"I think I've been hanging out with the wrong women."

❖

They spent the rest of the afternoon hiking down to the shore and back up. On the other side of the cliffs, the slope down to the water was much more gradual, and stairs had been cut into the steepest portions of the path. But even with those, Loch still had to stop and rest on the way back up the trail.

"Sorry," she said, accepting the water bottle Amir handed her as she sat on a step. "I don't know what's wrong with me. I usually have more stamina than this."

"There's no rush," Amir said. "If you never stop, you miss half the scenery anyway."

She watched Loch carefully as she spoke. She was paler than she had been before they'd started, and her hand shook when she lifted the bottle.

"What have you had to eat today?"

Loch looked up and shook her head. "I'm fine, I promise."

Amir raised her eyebrow and waited.

"It's not the same for me, Amir." Loch slowly peeled the label from the water bottle in her hand. "Models can't eat like normal people."

Amir shook her head and looked down at Loch's still trembling hands. "You don't eat enough, babe." She paused, holding her gaze. "But I know it's none of my business, and you can tell me to back off anytime."

Loch smiled and tangled her fingers into Amir's. "I kind of like you in my business."

Amir pulled her up and wrapped her arms around her. "Good, because I'm making you veggie chili dogs tonight."

Loch looked at her and narrowed her eyes. "Wait, does that even exist?"

Amir motioned for her to jump onto her back and slid her arms under Loch's legs as she started back up the trail.

"I'm going to pretend I didn't hear that."

Amir carried her the rest of the way to the campsite. When they finally got back to camp, the sun was just starting to go down, so Amir got what she needed out of the truck and lit the lanterns.

Loch lit the fire and got it going like a pro, and soon there were veggie dogs on top of the grate Amir placed over the fire, held at the right height by rocks on either side. The chili warmed in a cast iron pan beside them.

"When did you make the chili?"

"Last night," Amir said, stirring in raw onion and jalapeño. "I didn't have a clue what you'd like, but it's pretty hard not to like a chili dog."

"Maybe it's the fresh air, but I'm starving." Loch leaned over to kiss Amir's cheek.

The stars were dense, like drifts of pale ash across the black night sky, and the sea crashing into the cliffs thundered in the background like an invisible storm.

"Come here." Amir stood, brushing herself off, and held out her hand to Loch. She led them close to the cliff and leaned toward the edge. "If you stand here and close your eyes, you can feel the last of the spray hit your face."

Loch hesitantly closed her eyes and leaned closer to the edge, taking in a sharp breath when the icy mist touched her skin.

"I thought you were kidding," she said, looking back at Amir and turning back for more. "I can't believe you can feel it all the way up here."

Amir smiled. "I think the sea only sends it up when she notices someone watching."

When Loch finally got enough, she turned back to Amir, the silver mist shimmering across her face. The veggie dogs were ready when they got back to the fire, and Amir handed Loch a paper plate with a veggie dog in a bun, nearly buried in chili and topped with onion and cheddar.

Loch raised an eyebrow. "You know this is more than I eat in like three days, right?"

"What?" Amir leaned into her neck, the tip of her tongue moving silently to the edge of her ear. "You think I'm not going to work that off you later?"

Loch closed her eyes, memorizing the warmth of Amir's tongue as it moved around the edge of her ear to her mouth, drawing her lower lip slowly between her teeth, letting it go with a soft scrape.

"Amir," Loch whispered, her eyes still closed. "I swear I'm going to throw this amazing food off the cliff if you keep reminding me of what else I could be doing, so you might want to stop."

Amir smiled and leaned back, picking up her plate. "Eat, Battersby. Then I'll remind you all night."

The wind swept through the trees above the cliffs, the tops moving like paintbrushes across the night sky, leaving shimmering drifts of stars in their wake. A lighthouse foghorn sounded over the water, deep and resonant, the last faint remnants of sound colliding with the cliff face and falling into shards at the shoreline, fading like footsteps.

"So," Loch said, looking over and watching the firelight cast flames across the backlit amber of Amir's eyes. "Tell me something you've never told anyone else."

"Like what?"

"Anything." Loch licked sauce from the tip of her fingers. "Just something real."

Amir put her plate aside and shoved her hands in her pockets. "Okay. How about that I'm thirty, and I've never been in love."

"Whoa," Loch said, smiling, putting her plate down beside her. "That's way better than I thought I was going to get. Go on."

Amir looked at her plate with a raised eyebrow. Loch picked it back up and paused before she took another bite.

"Fine," she said. "But this had better be good."

"I think there's been a few different reasons," Amir said, answering the obvious question first. "But the biggest is that it's a small damn town, and I know too much about everyone."

"So, who do you date?"

Amir laughed, picking up her water bottle and taking a long drink before she answered. "No one appropriate. That might have something to do with it. Other than one serious girlfriend in high school that ended in disaster, I've tended to date casually, mostly outside of Innis Harbor. I've dated two women in town in the last couple of years, but they were wildly different. One was nineteen and the other was forty-six."

"This just keeps getting better and better." Loch kicked a log that had rolled to the side of the fire back onto the coals with her boot and rubbed her hands together in anticipation. "I want to know everything."

"No, you don't." Amir shook her head. "It's not that exciting."

"So, why didn't they work out?"

Amir just smiled, then went to the truck and brought back an armful of firewood. She stoked the fire before she sank one of the logs into the flames, watching them char the side of the cedar for a moment before she answered.

"Well, the nineteen-year-old was great, I still have a lot of respect for her, but she was just too young for it to go anywhere."

"And the older woman?"

"That was a little bit of a disaster." Amir looked up and ran her hand through her hair, then rubbed the back of her neck. "It was one of Anna's friends. Beautiful but crazy."

"Let me guess," Loch said, trying not smile. "She hired you to fix something for her."

"That's about right," Amir said. "She was newly divorced and wanted me to hang a porch swing for her."

"Recipe for disaster, obviously," Loch teased, stealing Amir's water and taking a sip before she handed it back. "What happened?"

"I'll give you the short version," Amir said. "We slept together twice, then she decided she was in love with me and told Anna, who's never let me forget it."

"Was Anna pissed?"

"Not at all. She said it was the best entertainment she'd had in ages. She still asks me about it all the time in front of my brother."

"Did he ever catch on?"

"Only because Anna flat out told him."

Amir laughed, shaking her head at the memory. "He told me I was an idiot, then wanted to know every detail the second Anna left the room. I think he may have been a little jealous actually, so that part was fun at least."

"What about the nineteen-year-old?"

"We slept together on and off for about a year, but I don't think either one of us really had romantic feelings for each other. The sex was good, but we didn't spend any time together outside of that."

"How did it end?"

"No drama, really. I introduced her to one of my friends, and they fell for each other right away. They're still together."

Loch put her plate down and sat closer, and Amir wrapped her hands around Loch's to warm them. "Are you cold?"

"Always."

Amir went to the truck and came back with a wool blanket that she wrapped around Loch's shoulders before she sat back down beside her and pulled her closer.

"So, you just happen to have a blanket in your truck the second I get cold?"

Amir leaned forward and dropped another log on the fire, wrapping her arms around Loch again when she leaned back against her.

"I figured we might need an extra one. I do know a few things about you by now," she said, dropping her voice to a warm whisper against Loch's ear.

"Tell me," Loch said, her hand warm against the inside of Amir's thigh.

"I know you make little complaining noises in your sleep if I get too far from you in bed." Amir ran her tongue across the soft skin just below Loch's ear. "I know it drives you crazy when I kiss your neck," she continued, pulling Loch's forehead to hers and looking into her eyes in the firelight. "And I know you're all I've been able to think about since the first night I met you."

Amir kissed her, pulling Loch into her body until she felt her fingers undo the first button of her flannel.

"Not so fast, Battersby," Amir said. "It's your turn to tell me something you've never told anyone else. Don't even think I'm going to let you off the hook with that one."

Loch unbuttoned Amir's shirt anyway and slid her hands under the T-shirt she found underneath. "Too bad, I forgot what I was going to say."

"If I take you to bed, will it help you remember?" Amir pulled Loch onto her lap, facing her, her hands wrapped low around Loch's hips as she kissed her, pulling her tighter against her body.

Loch nodded, closing her eyes as Amir's hands moved under her clothes to the bare skin of her waist. "If you keep doing that, I'll tell you anything you want to know."

"I'll hold you to that." Amir picked her up as she stood, then set her softly back on the ground. "I'm going to get the food put away. You go get warmed up in the tent. I'll be there in a minute."

Loch brushed her teeth at the water station that Amir had set up at the picnic table and watched as she took the trash out to the metal cans the campground provided at the edge of the road and put the food and the small cooler into the cab of her truck.

"Why did you put everything in there?"

Amir watched as the wind lifted the silver edges of Loch's hair, moving it gently across her face. She walked over and picked up her toothbrush.

"We do have a few black bears here," she said. "Not many of those in Manhattan?"

Loch laughed, trailing her fingers across Amir's back as she walked to the tent and disappeared inside.

After she had everything locked up for the night, Amir took her shoes off at the door of the tent and unzipped it, then reached up into the darkness and clicked on the lantern she'd suspended from the ceiling of the tent.

"Oh, that's much better," Loch said, slipping her lip balm back into the pocket of the folded jeans she hadn't been able to locate in the dark.

Amir watched as Loch climbed under the covers, wearing just a sheer white V-neck and boy shorts. Amir stripped down to her underwear, then slipped under the covers with her.

Loch's hand slid slowly across Amir's chest, fingertips brushing her nipples. Then she met Amir's gaze as she lifted her own shirt and dropped it beside the bed.

"God," Amir said, pausing, her gaze sweeping the length of Loch's body. "You're so beautiful."

She wrapped her arms around her, and Loch melted into Amir's strong chest, a perfect frame for the delicate contrast of her pale skin, the soft peaks of her breasts suddenly tense against Amir's fingers.

"Not getting out of it, by the way," Amir whispered against Loch's neck.

Loch looked up, distracted by Amir's touch. "Out of what?"

"Telling me what no one else knows about you."

Loch smiled, leaning back into the pillows, hands still soft against Amir's chest, sliding down to her abs and across her hips. "Wait, I didn't actually promise I would tell you anything." She buried her mouth in Amir's neck. "That question was just for you."

Amir's breath deepened as Loch kissed her neck. She wrapped her hands around Loch's hips, pulling them into hers. "I'm waiting."

Loch propped herself up on her side, visibly debating whether or not to accept the challenge. "What do you want to know?"

"Anything, just something you've never said out loud."

Loch turned her body into Amir's and whispered so softly against her shoulder that Amir had to ask to be sure she'd heard it correctly.

"Did you say you hate wearing a strap-on?"

When she nodded, Amir laughed, pulling Loch into her. "That was totally not what I was expecting."

Loch looked up at her, biting her lower lip. "I probably should have thought before I said that."

"No," Amir said, smiling at her. "That was perfect."

"But I'm not saying I wouldn't, I just..." Loch looked up at Amir, who touched her thumb to Loch's bottom lip.

"Loch," she said, replacing her thumb with the tip of her tongue. "If someone's strapped on, it's going to be me."

She slid Loch's underwear slowly down her legs and dropped them beside the bed. "I want to touch you more than anything," she said, holding Loch's gaze. "Just tell me I can."

"God, Amir," Loch said, closing her eyes. "Please."

Then she felt Amir's fingers soft as silk against her clit, stroking, then suddenly, deliciously, deep inside her.

Loch let out a deep slow breath, then buried her face in Amir's neck. "Don't…" She paused, then her voice dropped to a whisper. "Stop."

Amir stroked her slowly until she found the tense spot inside that begged her to stay, then she sank down between Loch's thighs. Amir's breath was warm and still against her clit, then her fingers were deep inside as she watched Loch's face.

Loch broke her gaze to arch her back, holding her breath. "God, Amir, please."

Amir circled her clit with her tongue, stroking her inside at the same time, lifting Loch's thigh over her shoulder. Loch's clit hardened against Amir's tongue as she pulled it slowly into her mouth, memorizing the feel of her, listening to every breath. She worked her until Loch's breath told her she was close, then slid her fingers gently out of her and reached up to brush her nipples with warm, slick fingertips. Loch's hips were restless, her clit straining against Amir's tongue. Amir slicked her tongue across it, slowly at first, then faster, feeling Loch's body tense suddenly and still underneath her.

"Amir," she said suddenly, her breath fighting the words. "Wait."

Amir moved up her body and took her in her arms. "What is it?" Her words were soft against her cheek. "Did I hurt you?"

"God, no…I'm just so close." Loch hesitated, then pressed her damp forehead to Amir's shoulder. "And I don't want this to be over."

Amir smiled as she pulled Loch tighter into her chest, her hands sliding up the length of her back. She let her go after a moment and lifted her chin, bringing Loch's gaze to hers.

"Baby," Amir whispered. "If you come for me, I promise I'll make you come again before you even catch your breath."

"Really?"

Amir nodded and bit Loch's lip gently before she moved back down her body to tease Loch's clit back into the heat of her mouth. She stroked it achingly slowly with her tongue, listening to Loch's breath quicken as she gave into it, hand tangled into Amir's hair. She held it there, the tips of her fingers whispering, her breath falling between them, one word hovering soft in the air.

"Amir…"

Loch's back arched to follow Amir's mouth, her body moving like flowing water, guided by the fingers inside her. Amir put Loch's thigh back on her shoulder, thrusting her shoulders against Loch's body in a steady rhythm, her fingers inside, fucking her in time with her breath.

"Oh, my God," Loch whispered, arching against Amir's tongue and lifting her arms over her head as Amir wrapped her arm around her back from underneath, pulling her harder into her mouth.

Time stopped as she came. Loch groaned, grinding into Amir, moved by the hand at the small of her back that pulled her hard into the slick heat of Amir's mouth. Amir held her as an orgasm visibly swept through her body, the heat between them flashing, intensifying, then flowing from Loch in a wet slick of lust.

Amir stayed inside her until her breath slowed, then moved back up her body, pulling Loch into her arms and smoothing the damp hair back from her forehead. She ran her fingertips up her back to her neck, circling the back of it with the warmth of her hand and holding her.

"Amir, that was…" Loch whispered against Amir's chest, her words open and soft. "That was so intense. I've never felt like that."

Amir kissed her forehead and felt Loch's breath soften and slow, then held her tighter and pulled the duvet up around her. She trailed a gentle finger across her cheek after a few minutes.

"Are you ready, baby?"

Loch stirred in her arms and buried her face deeper into Amir's chest, her breath already heavy with the rhythm of sleep. Amir smiled, reaching up to turn off the lantern. She held Loch in the darkness, staring up at the silver wash of stars above them. When she finally whispered the words, they hung in the air like the stars and refused to fade.

"I've never felt like this, either."

## Chapter Eight

When Loch unzipped the tent the next morning, Amir looked up at her from the fire, her hair wet from the shower. She'd worn a flannel shirt under her work jacket, but the morning chill still hung sharp in the air.

"Good morning." Amir laughed as Loch walked toward her with her hands over her face.

"Did I completely fall asleep on you last night?" Loch moved one finger aside and peered out at Amir.

"Yes." Amir poured Loch a cup of coffee from the blue enamel percolator on the fire grate and handed it to her with a little pot of cream. "And I can't think of a bigger compliment."

"Well," Loch said, taking the cup and kissing Amir before she sat on the log beside the fire. "If you think about it, it *was* all your fault."

"Absolutely. I take full responsibility." Amir sat beside her and pulled Loch into her, kissing her forehead. "So, do you remember that morning when you helped me with the pictures for the website?"

Loch nodded, holding her mug in both hands and scooting her feet closer to the fire.

"You said you had something to ask me that was guaranteed to be a pain in my ass, so you wanted to butter me up first."

"Now I'm embarrassed to tell you." Loch smiled at her. "And if you laugh, I'm getting right back into the tent and under the covers."

"Now I'm definitely going to laugh," Amir said. "I'm not sure that's the approach you want to go with considering getting you into bed is pretty much my goal anyway."

Loch laughed and snuggled closer to her. "Well, I have to show you. I can't just tell you."

"How about I take you to breakfast at the diner and then you can show me?"

"Deal," Loch said. "Although now you have to point me toward where you found a shower before I'm going anywhere."

❖

After Loch had showered and dressed, they drove into town and found a parking spot near the marina. The diner was busy, but Amir snagged a table by the window, sunlight warming the faded vinyl tablecloth between them. The waitress Loch had gotten to know from her morning coffee runs took their orders, then glanced at Amir as she gathered their menus and walked back to the counter.

"It was Cara, wasn't it?" Loch looked at Amir with a raised eyebrow, challenging her to admit it.

Amir smiled. "What about her?"

Loch leaned in and met her gaze. "The one who didn't need you to hang the porch swing?"

Amir shook her head and poured sugar into her coffee, smiling. "I'm not saying anything."

"Well," Loch said, glancing over at Cara ringing up a ticket for another customer. "I'm impressed. She's pretty young to pull that kind of thing off with no drama."

"I know," Amir said. "I've always thought the same thing." She realized suddenly what she'd said and tossed a ketchup packet at Loch. "I mean, in theory, of course."

The two plates of fresh blueberry pancakes and crispy bacon Amir had ordered over Loch's objections arrived blissfully quickly, and golden sunlight warmed the table as they ate. Amir carefully spread each of her pancakes with lashings of butter, then rolled each of them up like a little burrito and lined them up on her plate before she started eating.

Loch watched with one eyebrow raised, then picked up her coffee cup with a smile.

"I don't even know what to say about that, Farzaneh."

Amir looked up, pancake in hand. "Let's go with nothing. Although I'm sure Cara would love someone to laugh with about this. She's been teasing me since I met her about my pancake system."

Loch glanced up to the front of the diner where Cara was leaning against the counter, coffee cup in hand, not even trying to hide her amusement.

"It's just efficient," Amir said with a smile aimed at Cara and Loch. "I never have time in the morning to sit around with a plate of pancakes, so this just made sense. I can just take them with me. After a while, it just got to be a habit."

Loch shook her head, still smiling, and cut one of her pancakes in half, carefully separating it from the rest of the stack. She felt Amir staring at her and looked up, fork in hand.

"Not that I wouldn't love to dive face first into this entire plate, but I can't."

Amir started to say something, but Loch intercepted with a wink. "Eyes on your own plate, pancake freak."

After they'd eaten, they walked out into the bright sunshine, the glass doors closing silently behind them and taking the clatter and conversation of the diner with it. The sun glinted off the surface of the water, and the bright yellow ferry coming back from Bar Harbor was just pulling up to the dock, tourists dripping from every surface.

"Where to, Ms. Battersby?"

"My house," Loch said. "But just keep in mind you can totally say no."

"This is starting to sound like you're ordering a mafia hit or something."

"Well..." Loch bit her lower lip and looked up the hill toward her house. "You may consider doing that before it's over."

As they pulled up to the house and Amir cut the engine, Loch sat there for a moment, looking up at it. Amir watched her, waiting to see if she wanted to talk about whatever it was that was making that crinkle in her forehead. She'd either tell her, or it wasn't time. Either way, it was Loch's move.

"Remember when you found me on the dock that day and I'd been crying?"

Amir nodded, taking off her seat belt and turning toward Loch.

"Well, I'd just read a letter my aunt had left for me." She pulled the sleeves of her shirt down over her hands as she spoke. "She said I needed to clear out the house, that it was just stuff, and whether I wanted to keep it or sell it, I needed to get some fresh energy into the place."

"That makes sense." Amir picked up one of Loch's cold hands and warmed it between both of hers. "And now I can see why you didn't want to go home that night."

"Well, that and I just wanted to sleep with you."

Amir smiled and leaned over, bringing Loch's face to hers. "It was really hard not to touch you. But I'm glad you stayed." Amir kissed her, then sat back and ran her hand through her hair. "Ready?"

Loch nodded and got out of the car, and they headed to the house. When they got to the front steps, Loch took Amir's hand and led her around to the side, toward a detached garage with slate shingles and wide wooden doors. She pulled out her keys and squinted at the padlock, trying the same brass key several different ways before they slipped from her hand and clattered onto the stone path. Amir picked them up, opened the lock, then handed the keys back to Loch.

Loch stepped back and motioned for Amir to walk in first. Sunlight flooded in when she opened the doors, illuminating the dust hanging motionless in the air like fog. A restored 1956 Chevy 3100 truck filled almost every bit of the space, painted a brilliant yellow with a custom hardwood bed. Even in the low overhead light, the gleaming chrome fenders and white leather upholstery popped.

"Wow," Amir said, turning to Loch. "This was your aunt's truck?"

Loch nodded. "She rarely drove it. I think what she really loved was the process of restoring it. She came out here every few weeks and waxed it by hand even if it hadn't left the garage."

"This is gorgeous." Amir ran her hand over the smooth, curved lines of the truck bed. "And she left it to you?"

Loch shoved her hands into the pockets of her jeans and blew a lock of hair away from her face, which fluttered up and settled back down exactly where it had been. "Kind of."

Amir smiled and waited for her to go on. "Kind of?"

"It came with a caveat," Loch said. "Evidently, it's mine if I can learn to drive it."

"Ah, I get it." Amir opened the door and ran her fingertips over the chrome steering wheel and white leather bench seat. "Honestly, driving a stick shift is not as hard as it looks, even in an antique car. I mean, the no power steering always takes some getting used to, but you'll get used to it fast once you start taking it out."

"Yeah, that's kind of where you come in."

"Sure, I'll go with you." Amir shut the door, then looked back through the window at the ignition. "Do you have the keys?"

"I do," Loch said. "But they won't do me much good since I don't know how to drive."

"A stick shift?" Amir smiled. "Or at all?"

"I've never driven anything but a scooter," Loch said. "I'm from Manhattan. I take the subway everywhere."

"Well, you're in luck." Amir walked over and held out her hand. "Let's go. I know the perfect place to start."

Amir led Loch out of the garage, closing the doors and clicking the lock back into place.

"Wait, don't we need the truck?"

"Not at the moment," Amir said. "You should learn in a vehicle that's not quite so difficult to drive. Or expensive to fix."

"Wait," Loch said, hesitating as they walked back toward Amir's vehicle. "I can't learn in your truck. It's way too nice to let me wreck it."

Amir opened the door for Loch to get in, then wrapped her hand around the back of her neck gently and kissed her before she went around to the driver's side and got in. She looked over at Loch and winked as she put the truck into gear. "It's going to be pretty hard to wreck anything where I'm taking you."

Amir drove them about a mile out of town and onto a gravel road that wound down a hill into a green expanse of cut grass. Maple trees flanked them on two sides, and they were far enough from the road to see a car coming long before it reached them.

"Okay." Amir slowed to a stop in the middle of the field and put the truck into park. "This truck is an automatic, so it's great to learn on, but eventually, you'll need to master a stick shift."

Loch lowered her window and looked around. "Are you sure it's okay to be here? What if the owner drives by and sees us?"

"I think we're okay there." Amir smiled as she got out of the truck. "I am the owner."

"Shit," Loch said. "That was the last excuse I had."

Amir opened her door and wrapped Loch's legs around her waist, pressing her hips close into hers. Loch let out a slow breath as Amir kissed down her neck and back to her mouth, biting her bottom lip gently, thumbs grazing Loch's nipples as she let her go.

"I'll take care of you, baby," Amir said. "It's not as hard as you think it is."

Loch shook her head, sliding her hands under Amir's shirt and across her abs. "Well, if you value your truck at all, you may not want to distract me. I take no responsibility for my actions when your hands are on me."

Amir laughed and nodded toward the driver's seat. "Ready?"

Loch slid over into Amir's seat as Amir climbed into the passenger's seat, closing the door behind her. Loch was staring at the controls, her fingers white around the steering wheel. "Why is this so nerve wracking?"

"It's just unfamiliar. Everyone feels like that, I promise." Amir looked down at Loch's feet. "The most important thing to remember is that the gas pedal is on your right, the brake is the one right next to it."

Loch immediately put one foot on each, and Amir had to look out the window for a second to hide the smile on her face.

"You'll use just your right foot for both to avoid pressing them at the same time," Amir said. "But that was cute."

"Okay." Loch gripped the steering wheel and stared straight out the window like there was a cliff three feet beyond it. "What's next?"

"Next we're going to put it into gear," Amir said. "So, press your brake down and slide the gear shift down to the drive position."

Loch lowered her foot onto the brake and tried to shift, but it refused to budge.

"Press that button under your right thumb as you move it. That just keeps it from being knocked out of gear."

"Now the gas?"

"Take your foot off the brake first, and then the gas," Amir said. "But slowly. You just want to ease into it."

Loch pressed the gas pedal down, and the truck lurched forward.

"A little more lightly than that, babe." Amir reached over and snapped Loch's seat belt into place. "Just relax."

Loch bit her lip in concentration and pressed the pedal lightly with just the toe of her boot.

The truck moved slowly forward, but then she felt Amir's hand on her thigh.

"That was perfect," Amir said softly. "But you might want to open your eyes."

Loch opened her eyes slowly and loosened her grip on the steering wheel. "Look, I'm driving!"

"You are," Amir said. "Now give it a touch more gas. You don't want much speed. What you're really doing now is getting the feel of the pedals."

Amir took Loch through all the basics for the rest of the afternoon, and by the time they decided to head back to the campsite, Loch felt like an expert, or expert enough to drive slowly forward in an empty field, which was the same thing to her. On the way home, they stopped at the market in town, but just as they were about to go in, Amir's phone rang, and she looked at the screen.

"It's my mom," she said, looking up at Loch as she stepped out of the truck. "I may need to get this."

"Take your time," Loch said. "I need to get a few things anyway."

Amir watched Loch shut the door and walk toward the market before she picked up the phone.

"Hi, Ma."

It was a good two minutes before she got the chance to speak again.

"I know," Amir said finally, letting out a long, slow breath. "I've just been busy."

She looked toward the door of the market and watched as one of the shopkeepers stacked watermelons on the table beside it. He built a wobbly pyramid and stepped back to admire it as the last melon he'd placed tumbled to the sidewalk and burst open with a bright pink splash.

"Ma, I can't come to dinner tomorrow night, I've got to finish the plans for the greenhouse."

Amir closed her eyes and leaned her head back onto the headrest. She was wasting her time. Her mother always knew she was lying, and evidently, Hamid and Anna were already coming. Besides, the rising pitch of her mother's voice told her that another escape was unlikely.

"Okay," she said, watching Loch walk out of the market with a brown paper bag. "I'll be there at seven."

❖

Amir started a fire when they got back to the campsite, her mind spinning about dinner the next night. Loch had just walked to the restrooms, so she took the opportunity to text Hamid.

*Hey, Mom called me about dinner tomorrow night. I may bring Loch. What do you think?*

She stacked a few dried leaves under the kindling and watched as the smoke spun itself toward the sky. Her phone pinged after a few seconds.

*I think I'd better figure out where to buy tranquilizer darts on the fly.*

Amir looked up to see Loch coming back from the bathrooms. *Very funny.* She typed quickly. *Just make yourself useful and be sure he's had a drink or three before we get there.*

Loch reached the campsite and ran her fingers through Amir's hair as she knelt by the firepit.

"Now how did you know I wanted a fire?"

"Lucky guess."

"Hey, did I see a couple of skillets in the camping gear you have in the back of the truck?" Loch glanced back toward the equipment stacked neatly in the bed of the truck.

Amir nodded. "Do you need them?"

"I thought I might cook tonight if that's okay," Loch said. "I bought everything I need at the market on our way here."

"Hell, yes," Amir said. "You've already eaten the only meal I know how to make."

Loch set up a workstation on the water table and sliced onions into rings about a half inch thick while Amir secured the rainfly over the tent. Clouds had moved in sometime that afternoon, and it looked like it might rain overnight. Loch threw another log on the fire and lowered a grill over that, setting the cast iron skillet in the center to heat. Amir walked over and peered into the pan.

"So, what are you making?"

"I'm not telling," Loch said as she walked over to the fire. "That way, if it goes south, I can just call it something else entirely."

"Clever." Amir smiled, watching Loch drop a knob of butter into the sizzling pan and follow that with the whole onion slices placed carefully over the melted butter. She followed that with a generous pour of red wine vinegar and a scattered pinch of dark brown sugar.

"Actually, it's really simple. Just wild mushrooms, provolone cheese, baguette, and caramelized onions. Kind of like a vegetarian steak sandwich." She lifted one of the onion slices with a fork and peered underneath it. "Will you lift that grate up a bit so it doesn't get too hot?"

Amir placed it a notch higher and sat beside the fire. Loch followed and sat in front of her, leaning back into the warmth of

Amir's thighs. Dusk melted into navy night sky as the bats started stirring, swooping down from the trees and disappearing again over their heads. The fire crackled and popped tiny bits of ash into the cool evening air, and Amir wrapped her arms around Loch, resting her chin on the top of her head.

"So, my mom called while you were in the market," she said. "And it looks like I have to go to a family dinner tomorrow night." She leaned into Loch and kissed her cheek. "I was wondering whether you'd like to go with me."

Loch turned to look up at Amir. "I'd love to, but are you sure?"

Amir kissed her, her hand warm and soft against Loch's neck as she spoke. "Brace yourself," she said. "I have no idea how this will go over with my dad, although I know Mom will love you if we give her a minute."

Loch leaned forward and flipped the onions, which had turned a delicious caramelly brown on the bottom. She added more butter and scattered a pinch of salt, then sat back down. She was quiet for a moment and Amir waited, listening to her breathe. Loch's breath had always revealed more of her thoughts than the words she tried to wrap around them. When she finally spoke, she kept her gaze on the fire.

"Will they know we're together tomorrow?" she said. "Or should we leave that part out?"

Amir turned her to face her and held her face in her hands. "I said yes to dinner because I want them to meet my girlfriend."

Loch smiled as she stood and sat across Amir's thighs, hands sliding up her arms to circle her shoulders. "I think that might be the most romantic thing anyone's ever said to me."

After a few minutes, the onions had cooked to a perfect soft caramel brown with crispy edges, and Loch had taken them off the fire and scattered some wild mushrooms into the pan with a splash of white wine. As they warmed, a buttery sauce formed around them, and Loch layered them into two halves of a seared baguette lined with rich provolone cheese, then piled the onions on top of that with steak sauce and a sprinkle of fresh parsley. She handed Amir her plate with a handful of recycled paper napkins.

"Trust me," she said. "You'll need them."

"This is amazing." Amir picked hers up and breathed in the aroma of fresh bread, wine, and butter. "Where did you learn to cook like this?"

"I've never really learned anything specific, I've just spent a lot of time in other countries with my job. I love food, so I paid attention." She popped a seared mushroom into her mouth and closed her eyes as she ate it.

"So," Amir said. "Are you missing it yet?"

"What, modeling?" Loch looked up, her eyes thoughtful. Amir waited, shrugging off her flannel and draping it around Loch's shoulders.

"I loved the influence I was lucky enough to have, and I miss seeing my sister and my friends in the industry. But modeling?" She paused, gaze locked onto the fire. "No. Not at all."

Night fell as they ate, the air suddenly crisp and sharp at the edges. Electric blue sky faded slowly into a velvet purple sunset streaked at the edges with fiery copper. The last ribbon of sunlight slipped beyond the sea, and the darkness made the waves against the cliffs louder, as if they'd been waiting for their cue to take the stage.

"God," Amir said, giving Loch a look as she reluctantly slid most of her sandwich onto Amir's plate. "What's in this? It's amazing."

Loch laughed, glancing over at Amir, who was very focused on her plate. "It's just veggies. Nothing fancy."

"Well, now I'm going to beg you to make these not fancy veggies for me all the time because it's the best thing I've ever eaten."

"Actually, I learned a trick from Samia that makes all the difference, I think," Loch said. "Just as the onions finish cooking, you hold them in the flames for a few seconds to finish them, then make a sauce with some butter and the juices left in the pan to pour over the top."

"Well, you'll be lucky if I don't eat yours." Amir leaned over to kiss Loch and put a chunk of sandwich back on her plate. "But thank you for this. It's seriously the best meal I've had in ages."

As they were loading the last of the food and clean dishes into the truck, Loch grabbed Amir's arm and pointed toward the cliffs.

"I just saw a falling star!" She stared up at the smattering of stars dusted across the sky, dense and shimmering in the still night air. "I think I've forgotten how much I miss the stars. It's so bright in Manhattan you forget they even exist."

"You're in luck." Amir pulled a blanket from behind the seat and locked up the truck. "We have front row seats."

Amir took her hand, and they walked to the edge of the cliff and looked down at the waves, the sea sending silver mist up the face of the cliff to touch their faces like breath. Amir spread the blanket out a few inches from the edge and lay on her back, pulling Loch into her arms beside her. They looked up at the stars for a few minutes before Amir spoke.

"After I learned to drive my sophomore year in high school, I was almost never home. Mom didn't really worry about me. I guess she knew I could take care of myself."

"And she probably knew on some level she didn't have to worry too much about boys," Loch said.

"Good point." Amir pulled Loch closer into her chest. "Anyway, I watched the stars from a different cliff every night, just to see if they looked any different."

"And were they ever any different?"

"No," Amir said. "But I think that's why I liked it. It was a solid constant, something that was always the same, no matter what was going on at the time."

"I understand that." Loch slid her hand under the hem of Amir's flannel and held it warm against her skin. "I started really traveling for work when I was sixteen, and I felt like I was in a different bed every night. It was exciting in some respects, but it was also incredibly long hours, and sometimes, I just wanted to lock myself in a room for a week and sleep. You never relax when your life changes every day."

She let out a long, slow breath, something like dread settling back onto her chest as she thought about her real life.

"I just got used to it, I guess."

"Do you miss New York?" There was tension in Amir's voice, as if she already knew the answer she didn't want to hear.

Loch got up and climbed over Amir's body, dipping her mouth so close to her ear her lips touched her before the words. "I don't even remember New York."

Amir wrapped her hands around Loch's hips and held them against hers with one arm as she flipped Loch underneath her and lowered her body onto hers. Her mouth was suddenly everywhere as she unbuttoned Loch's shirt, then pulled her own over her head and tossed it aside.

Amir paused before she slid a thigh between Loch's and met her gaze, heavy with a desire that tightened its grip with every breath.

Amir leaned into her slowly, rhythmically, until she heard Loch's breath start to beg. She scraped Loch's nipples slowly with her teeth, pulling them hard into the warmth of her mouth when she felt Loch's hand at the back of her neck. Then, suddenly, Amir gave her what she wanted. Loch's hands tightened on Amir's back as she stroked her thigh hard and heavy against Loch. She let Loch set the pace until her breath caught and she started making the soft moans that Amir remembered from the previous night. She put one hand under Loch's head and bit her neck gently as she rocked her hips against Loch's. A rock from the edge of the cliff gave way and clattered down the cliff face to splash into the sea. It had been just inches beyond Loch's head. Amir slid her arms underneath her body and lifted her.

"Hang on, I need to move you down from the edge of the cliff."

"No." The word was quick and breathless, and Loch's gaze was locked on Amir's. "I want you to fuck me on the edge."

Amir paused, then her fingers found the button of Loch's jeans, her breath raw and deep against Loch's neck. Her fingertips brushed across the wet heat of her, then sank deep and strong inside. She slid the heel of her hand across Loch's clit and rocked against her, falling into an intense, steady rhythm until she felt Loch's walls tighten around her fingers. Her clit was tense against Amir's hand, nails digging into the backs of her arms, begging her for more. Amir paused, holding Loch's gaze just long enough to rip open her own jeans, then lowered herself back down, her own clit slick and tight against the same hand she was using to fuck Loch. Neither noticed the warm rain that had started to fall fast, sliding from Amir's body to Loch's.

Loch's hips followed every thrust Amir gave her, her breath shallow and fast. Amir moaned and sank deeper into her, bringing them both closer with every stroke. They moved together, silent and strong, until Loch raised her hands above her head and grasped the raw edge of the cliff behind it, feeling the sharp earth crumble and give way under her fingers. Loch arched her back, grinding her hips hard against Amir's hand until she forgot how to breathe and shuddered to a blindingly intense orgasm.

Amir's voice was a growl against her neck as she rocked Loch between the edge of the cliff and her body, crying out suddenly as she came. The sound echoed over the water, fading into the crashing waves before Amir finally pulled away with a soft bite and collapsed beside her.

Loch sat up and looked toward the tent, looking suddenly worried as Amir pulled her back on top of her and smiled.

"Don't worry," Amir said. "I checked the weather and put up the rainfly before you woke up this morning."

Loch glanced over her shoulder. "How did you even think of that this morning? The weather was beautiful."

Amir smiled and stood, offering her hand to Loch. "Not my first camping trip, baby."

They raced back to the tent, and Loch went on to the bathrooms, splashing through the puddles that were forming at the sides of the trail. Amir brushed her teeth and dove into the front vestibule of the tent, taking off her clothes and boots and leaving them outside the main room. Loch did the same a few minutes later, dropping her clothes in a soaked pile by Amir's and climbing naked into bed beside her.

Amir rolled over on top of her, pressing the warm length of her body against Loch, trying to stop her shivering. "I shouldn't have let you stay outside in the rain."

"There's no way I would've let you stop."

Loch ran her hands down Amir's shoulders and back to her ass. She looked up at her and whispered, pressing her hips into Amir's, "I see you didn't take everything off."

Amir ran the tip of her tongue down the side of Loch's neck. "Not everything," she whispered.

Loch brushed the buckles of the harness with her fingertips. Amir bit her shoulder lightly and moved to her nipples, her tongue hot against the chill of Loch's skin. The warmth of Amir's breath was intense as she pulled it into her mouth, her hand strong under Loch's back, holding her body hard against her own.

"Amir..." Loch said, her eyes shut tight. "Jesus."

Amir reached back and pulled her knee up on one side, her fingertips trailing softly down the inside of Loch's thigh. She slid down her body, slicking her tongue across Loch's clit, then back again when she felt Loch hold her breath. Amir looked up, then held Loch's gaze as she settled between her thighs and waited for Loch to whisper *please* twice before she slid slowly inside her. Amir waited, eyes closed and breath still, fighting the urge to come as she felt Loch tighten around her. Loch arched, hands sliding to Amir's hips, pulling her deeper inside.

Amir groaned, raw and urgent, her mouth hot against Loch's neck. Still deep inside her, she angled her hips so Loch's clit slid hard against the front of the leather harness and pulled her hands above her head, keeping them there with one of hers. Amir felt Loch's legs wrap around her waist and her body move with hers as she rocked against her. She tightened her hands against Loch's as she bit the soft skin at the base of her neck. Loch shifted, and Amir held her eyes as she tightened her grip on her wrists to keep her arms above her head.

"Baby," Amir said. "I'll always stop the second you tell me to. But until then, I'm going to take you like you're mine."

Amir pressed her wrists harder against the bed when Loch shifted underneath her, and Loch smiled, holding her gaze.

"I am yours." Loch bit her lip and looked at Amir's mouth as she spoke. "I need you to fuck me like you know that."

Amir closed her eyes as she slid hard and deep inside Loch,

letting her wrists go and holding her against the bed with her hand just below the base of her neck. She felt herself fall, felt her orgasm crash over her like a seventh wave, Loch's words shimmering in her mind as her climax shook the breath from her lungs.

She touched her forehead to Loch's for a moment, then flipped her over on top and wrapped her hands around her hips. Loch's hair fell wild across her face as she looked down with soft eyes, slicking her tongue across her lower lip. Amir lifted her and slid deep inside, using her thumb to stroke her swollen clit as she started to move Loch's hips back and forth.

"Lean back, baby," Amir said. "Hands behind you on my thighs."

A slow flush moved across the damp skin of Loch's breasts as she leaned back, her hands tight around Amir's thighs as she pulled one of her knees up to let her rock her hips harder against the harness. Loch's eyes closed as Amir stroked her clit, steady and constant, her other hand strong at the base of her back, pulling Loch harder against her body.

It was only a few seconds before Loch started to tremble, her rhythm faltering as she started to come. Amir took over and thrust deeper into her as Loch's orgasm moved through her body, her head thrown back as she rode her, thighs tight against Amir's hips, muscles taut and straining.

After the last waves had faded, Amir pulled Loch down into her arms, kissing every inch of her as she slowly settled onto her body. Loch's breath relaxed into sleep after a few moments, and Amir held her close while she listened to the waves break and shatter against the rocks below. Then a weight the size of the cliffs settled onto her chest as she closed her eyes against it.

## Chapter Nine

Loch rolled her eyes as she sifted through the closet for her navy cashmere crewneck, balancing the phone between her cheek and shoulder. Amir was picking her up for dinner with her parents in ten minutes, and all she'd managed to put on was a pair of white jeans.

"Harvey," she said, struggling to keep her voice even. "You signed me at fifteen, and I've been working every day since. I need some time."

"Loch, you can't just take a year off in this business, you know that." Loch listened to him take a slow breath and choose his words. "If you put your career on a shelf, it'll stay there. I've seen it happen."

"I know it's a risk." Loch pulled the missing navy sweater out from the bottom of a stack that threatened to tumble without it. "But I can't keep doing this."

"I can get you out of what you have booked at this point, but let's give it some time and revisit this, okay?" Harvey paused. "You've never been more in demand than you are right now, and at this point, you have the freedom to take your career in a whole different direction if you want to. You don't want to lose that."

Loch pulled the sweater over her head and rubbed her temples slowly before she answered. "Okay."

"Just get some rest, and I'll call you in a few weeks."

The phone clicked off just as Amir knocked on the front door. Loch ran a hand through her hair, took a last look in the mirror, and slipped into the shoes she was carrying as she opened the door. Amir stepped in and immediately picked her up, wrapping Loch's legs around her waist. She held her against the door as she ran her tongue slowly down the side of her neck, pulling away with a soft bite on her shoulder.

"Can't we just skip this and stay in bed?"

Loch laughed as Amir put her down and glanced back to the bedroom for emphasis. Loch just handed her a dish from the side table as she grabbed her keys and jacket, pulling the door shut behind them.

"What's this?"

"It's saffron and rosewater cookies," Loch said. "I made them for your mother."

Amir looked at the beautiful antique dish with the glass top. The cookies were a perfect warm pink, and rose petals crusted with sugar had been scattered on the top. She leaned in and kissed Loch's cheek as she spoke. "How in the world did you know how to make these?"

"I didn't," she said. "When you dropped me off this morning, I did some research, then took the recipe to that restaurant in Bar Harbor and asked the ladies there what I needed. One of them gave me a little glass jar of homemade rosewater to use. But when I tried to pay, they wouldn't let me."

"I'm sure they recognized you," Amir said, taking her hand as they started toward her truck. "You're kind of hard to forget."

"I don't know." Loch bit her lip as she thought back to the day Amir had taken her to the restaurant. "I'm not sure I even saw them there that day."

"Trust me," Amir said, staring straight ahead as she started the truck, "they saw you."

❖

When they arrived at the house, Amir took Loch's hand as they opened the front door. The warm scent of red curry, onion, and plum chutney enveloped them as they stepped into the entryway, and Amir took Loch's coat to hang on the wall.

The home was immaculate, decorated with antiques and scattered collections of tiny glass bottles, intricately decorated with gold etchings. Pictures of Amir and Hamid crowded every available surface, and an old organ in the corner of the living room held a newer collection of photos of Hameen and Yasmin. Beautiful Afghan rugs lined the hardwood floors, including a small but beautifully patterned one set apart directly under a window.

"This one is so interesting," Loch said, walking over to it to look closer. "The design reminds me of something. Why is it over here by itself?"

"Muslims pray facing east, and this is a prayer rug," Amir said, crouching down to trace the patterns with her finger. "The design shows you how to position your body for prayer. These squares here are where your knees should be, then your hands are here," Amir said, pointing. "And the ornate part at the top indicates where your head would be during prayer."

"It's beautiful," Loch said. "I love it."

Hamid rounded the corner from the kitchen suddenly and handed Amir a beer. "It's about time. I was beginning to think you just kept driving."

Amir looked over Hamid's shoulder and dropped her voice. "Don't think I didn't consider it." Hamid stepped past Amir to Loch, kissing both her cheeks in greeting. "I'm so glad you came. Can I get you something to drink?"

"No, I'm fine at the moment." She smiled as she said it and held out the dish of cookies. "But where should I put these?"

Just then, a short, plump woman in a traditional Muslim headscarf came around the corner, wiping her hands on her apron and smiling before she stopped dead in her tracks.

"Mom," Amir said, taking Loch's hand and stepping forward. "There's someone I'd like you to meet."

Amir's mother nodded, then disappeared back around the corner, mumbling under her breath about something in the oven.

Anna appeared from the hall and took the dish of cookies from Loch. "Brace yourself, girl." She squeezed Loch's shoulder and headed toward the kitchen with the cookies. "This could be a rough ride."

Amir pulled her close and touched her forehead to Loch's. "I'm so sorry. We don't have to stay."

Loch shook her head and smiled. "Are you kidding? I'm used to being stared at. That's nothing."

Hamid laughed. "You're tougher than you look," he said with a wink. "But that said, I'm still getting you a beer."

Suddenly, Yasmin was tugging on the back of Loch's sweater.

"She wants to show you her dollhouse," Hamid said. "It's in the living room. I think she loves it more than me." He thought for a moment, glancing down at Yasmin and pausing for dramatic effect. "That might be because she *told* me she does."

Yasmin nodded in agreement and took Loch's hand, pulling her over to her dollhouse set up in the back of the living room.

"Jesus Christ, man." Amir rubbed the back of her neck with her hand when she was sure they were out of earshot and looked toward the kitchen. "We're barely past the front door. What was that all about?"

"They've both been acting weird since we got here. Dad's been upstairs on the phone most of the time." Hamid glanced up at the staircase. "Something's up with him."

"Great." Amir followed him down the hall to the kitchen. "That's all I need tonight."

The kitchen was empty when they turned the corner, and a pan of basmati rice was starting to smoke on the back burner. Amir pulled it off the burner and looked around.

"Where did Mom go?"

Hamid looked toward the stairs. "One guess."

She slumped against the counter and closed her eyes, taking a breath and letting it out slowly.

"Look," Hamid said, opening the fridge and perusing the contents, "Loch's a great girl, they're just going to have to get over it."

"I don't remember you bringing Anna home." Amir took a long swig of her beer. "What was that like?"

"It was okay, but only because they didn't know she was pregnant." He looked over at her and grinned. "Which I'm assuming isn't the case with Loch."

Amir half laughed, half choked on her beer as her mother walked back into the kitchen. She glanced at both of them and turned on both the taps full blast, turning away from them and reaching for the rice pan.

"Mom, I'm sorry," Amir said after a moment, her hand warm against her mother's arm. "I should have told you I was bringing someone."

Her mother busied herself with scraping the burned rice into the garbage disposal and said nothing.

"But," Amir said, looking over at Hamid, who nodded in encouragement, "please try to be nice. I really like this girl."

Their mother stopped suddenly and stared at them, the pan of scorched rice still in her hand. "What is it with you two and the white girls?"

"*Mom!*"

Amir and Hamid said it together, followed by Hamid peering around the corner to make sure Anna was out of earshot.

"What? Is it wrong that I want at least one of my children to have a traditional Muslim family?"

"Mom, seriously, I can't believe you just said that. What's wrong with you?" Hamid leaned over and plucked an olive off the top of one of the dishes. "You know this family has never been 'traditional Muslim' or whatever that means. I can't remember the last time we went to the mosque. And didn't that dream fly out the window anyway when super butch here came home with that Mohawk in eighth grade?"

"Look at you using the new word we taught you." Amir gave his arm a playful shove. "Although if you ever refer to me as 'super butch' again, I'll smack you."

Hamid rolled his eyes and put his arm around his mom, pulling her into a reluctant hug. "Besides, Anna adores you, and I happen to know you feel the same about her." The smile she didn't manage to hide made it clear he was right. "And you don't know her yet, but that girl out there is one of the nicest people I've met in a long time."

Mrs. Farzaneh looked at Amir, then back at Hamid. "It's just…" She paused, searching for the right words.

Amir and Hamid tipped their heads in the same direction, waiting.

"Well," she said finally. "You have to admit she's unusually tall."

A smile swept slowly across Amir's face. "Seriously, Mom?"

She turned to look at Hamid, who was already laughing, and then even their mother was giggling so hard that she finally wiped a tear from her cheek and glanced toward the door.

"Shh," she said. "They'll hear us."

"So, that's really all you've got?" Hamid said, not even trying to keep a straight face. "That she's too tall?"

Their mother swatted at them with a kitchen towel and pointed toward the living room, shaking her head and smiling as she poured new rice into the pan to simmer.

They walked back into the living room just as Mr. Farzaneh was coming down the stairs, his gaze coldly fixed on Loch.

"Here we go," Hamid whispered, squeezing Amir's elbow.

"Dad," Amir said, clearing her throat and taking Loch's hand, "I'd like you to meet my girlfriend, Loch Battersby."

Her father stopped at the base of the stairs. The grandfather clock behind him ticked, the seconds stretching heavy and silent across the room. He finally opened his mouth to speak just as the doorbell rang at a ridiculous volume, and Loch let out a soft breath as he left the room to answer it.

"Well," Hamid said, still staring in the direction of his father. "This takes awkward to a whole new level."

Amir looked over at him and drank the last of her beer. "At least he knows. That was the hard part. It can't get any worse now."

Just then, Amir's father rounded the corner and walked back into the living room accompanied by a nervous-looking young man carrying flowers. His hair was slicked back in a shiny black wave against his head, and he scraped one damp palm against his pants leg as Mr. Farzaneh took his coat and went to hang it in the hall closet.

Hamid looked at Amir. "Apparently, it can."

As her father walked back into the room, Amir leaned closer to Hamid and whispered words so taut they shot across the room. "Hamid, *please* tell me this isn't what it looks like."

"No can do, sis." He looked the visitor up and down. "This is exactly what it looks like."

"Amira," her father said as he gestured toward the nervous man standing beside him. "This is Zayan Azzi, and he'll be joining us for dinner this evening." He looked briefly at Loch, then fixed his gaze back on his daughter. "I invited him here to meet you."

The man stepped forward and awkwardly offered the flowers to Amir. She took them but kept her gaze locked on her father.

Anna excused herself to check on the children, both of whom were playing with the dollhouse across the room, and gestured for Loch to follow.

Outside, Anna led Loch to the end of the front porch, where she tugged two chairs together and set her beer on the porch railing in front of them. They sat silent for a minute until Loch finally spoke, shock still frozen on her face.

"What the *hell* was that?"

"That," Anna said, "was watching a car skid into a brick wall in slow motion. Or as Mr. Farzaneh likes to refer to it, matchmaking."

"You're kidding."

"Unfortunately not." She shook her head and glanced back at the door. "I've heard him mention it a few times in the past, but he knows Amir is gay. It never occurred to me he'd actually do it."

"Why now?"

"My guess is he heard Amir met someone. It's a pretty small town, and when you're part of the Muslim community between here and Bar Harbor, it gets smaller by the minute."

"Do you think Amir is okay?" Loch glanced back toward the door. "Maybe I should go back in there."

"God no," Anna said, closing her eyes and rubbing her forehead with her fingertips. "She's more pissed off than I've ever seen her, so if you go back in there and he says something disrespectful to you, it may tip her over the edge."

"So, what was he expecting?" Loch leaned back in her chair and ran her hand through her hair. "That his obviously gay daughter would suddenly do a one-eighty and marry a dude?"

"In a word, yes." Anna looked at Loch and paused before she went on. "I'm not saying arranged marriage never works. The Farzanehs were married the day after they met, and they've always been happy. But obviously, it's not the right choice for Amir."

Anna tapped her fingertips on the armrest of the chair, glancing at the door as if she was afraid of who might come out next.

"He and Amir were so close before she came out. After that, they were still cordial, but it changed everything between them."

"What did he say about it?"

"That's the thing," Anna said. "He never said a word. He just pretended she never said it. It was like he only loved her if that part of her didn't exist."

"Wow," Loch said, nervously peeling the label from her bottle. "That must have been awful."

"It was. She wouldn't even talk to Hamid about it, and they've always been close."

Hamid stepped out onto the porch and let the screen door slam shut behind him, which made Loch and Anna jump. He looked straight ahead, the muscles in his jaw visibly tense.

"What's going on in there?" Anna asked, her voice just above a whisper.

Hamid just shook his head. After a moment, he looked over at them, his voice low and taut. "Loch, I'm sorry. This is my fault. He knew you were coming over because I told him yesterday. I thought giving him a heads-up might make things easier."

"Did your mom know this was going to happen?" Anna's words were still a whisper.

"No." Hamid shook his head. "I asked her before I came out here. She had no idea."

"Then this must be so hard for her." Loch looked again at the door. "This is not even close to your fault, Hamid. But how is Amir?"

Hamid looked over to Loch, his face softening for the first time. "She's pissed, but she's dealing with it."

"Guys, don't worry about it. I was half expecting this anyway." Loch pushed away the lock of silver hair the breeze had brushed across her eyes. "Of course he doesn't like me. Amir was so nervous on the way over here, I figured it wasn't going to be easy."

Anna dropped her voice to a whisper and glanced over at Loch. "What does he know about her?"

"You mean does he know she's a model?"

Anna nodded.

"Nope," Hamid said. "I thought I'd save that one for later in case we got bored."

Loch laughed as Mrs. Farzaneh opened the door, bringing a warm waft of jeweled rice with her.

"Dinner is on the table," she said, glancing down the hall behind her before she spoke. "And, Hamid, please try to be patient with your father."

"You're kidding me," Hamid said, looking past her into the house. "That guy is staying for dinner?"

She shot him a look as she disappeared back into the house.

As they followed her into the dining room, Amir motioned for Loch to sit in the chair next to her and leaned close. "Are you okay?" she whispered.

"I was just about to ask you the same thing." Loch glanced across the table at the young man deep in conversation with Amir's father. "But it takes a lot more than this to rattle me, I promise."

Amir smiled as she squeezed Loch's hand under the table and took the dish her mother handed her, passing it to Loch when she'd finished.

"So, Zayan," Mrs. Farzaneh said, finally breaking the silence when it was clear no one else was going to do it. "What is it that you do?"

"I'm an accountant. I work at my father's firm in Bar Harbor."

Silence settled back into place, and the only sound in the room was the clink of cutlery against the plates, until Hameen held his fork in the air and waved it.

• 121 •

"Hameen," Anna whispered, taking the fork from his hand and placing it back on his plate. "Please remember the manners we talked about this morning."

He looked around at the other adults. "They aren't doing manners." He raised his eyebrows, as if his point was obvious. "They're not even saying nothing."

Zayan choked on the water he'd been drinking and put the glass down, the beginnings of a smile forming against his will.

"Little man has a point," Hamid said, glancing at his father.

Mrs. Farzaneh looked at Loch, clearly determined to start a conversation. Any conversation. "I'm sorry, I had to run back into the kitchen and didn't catch your name when we met before dinner."

"My name is Loch," she said, meeting her gaze and smiling. "And I'm sure it's hard to do anything else when you're cooking a meal like this."

"Locks like on a door?" Hameen looked up from his plate, holding a piece of bread aloft. "My aunt Amira does locks."

This time, it was Anna trying to hold back a smile. Hamid didn't even bother, clearly amused by the direction of the conversation.

"It means 'Lake' in Scottish, right?" Zayan looked over at Loch, who smiled back and nodded.

"You look so familiar to me." Mrs. Farzaneh took in Loch's face, studying her eyes. "Is your family from Innis Harbor?"

"No, I'm from Manhattan, but my aunt lived here. She passed away recently, so I came to take care of things for her."

She looked into Loch's eyes as she put down her napkin, then spoke as if she already knew the answer. "And what was your aunt's name?"

"Samia Battersby. She lived in the Cape Cod just up from the docks."

Mrs. Farzaneh sat back in her chair and looked pointedly at Amir's father, who just shook his head, his gaze falling to the table and staying there.

Amir looked at one of her parents and then the other. "What?"

Her mother cleared her throat, still looking at her husband. "Do you remember that wreck I was in when you were ten?"

Hamid and Amir nodded.

"Yeah, you almost died," Amir said. "The car in front of you hit black ice, and a bunch of cars plowed into yours from the back."

She nodded. "By the time I came to, my car was on fire. I couldn't see anything but black smoke."

"And you were trapped somehow, right?" Hamid said.

She nodded again, closing her eyes tight against the memory. "The seat belt latch was buried under the passenger dashboard, and I couldn't get out of it."

"Wait," Hamid said. "Didn't one of the other drivers pull you out or something?"

"No," she said, holding her husband's gaze. "They wouldn't come near the car because it was on fire. I was just trapped there, watching them back farther and farther away."

"I never knew that," Amir said, looking from one to the other, her voice soft. "I remember you recovering after the wreck, but you never told us what really happened."

"What happened," she said, turning to Loch, "is that I was losing consciousness when your aunt threw the door open, cut me out of the seat belt with her knife, and carried me across the road about five seconds before the fire hit the gas tank."

Hamid set his glass slowly onto the table, which was suddenly the only sound in the room. "Did you stay in touch after that?"

Mrs. Farzaneh caught a tear on her cheek and wiped it away before she answered. "We were friends until the day she died."

❖

After the dishes were done and Amir had helped clean up, they said their goodbyes as Mr. Farzaneh disappeared upstairs.

Hamid watched and shook his head, his jaw tense with unspoken words.

Mrs. Farzaneh pulled Loch into a warm hug as she said goodbye. "I forgot to thank you for the cookies, dear, they're beautiful. Where did you get them?"

Loch hesitated, but Amir stepped in. "She went to the restaurant in Bar Harbor to get the ingredients from your sisters, but she made them herself."

She looked at Loch with soft eyes and squeezed her hand. "You're so much like Samia." She looked up the staircase. "And you're welcome in our home anytime."

As they walked to the truck, Loch took Amir's hand. "I can't drive just yet, but I have somewhere I want to take you."

"Sure," Amir said, her voice tense. "Anywhere but here."

Loch stopped in her tracks, then smacked Amir lightly on the arm. "Well, great. I was going to suggest we go back into the house for a game of Trivial Pursuit." She hesitated again. "So, that's totally out of the question?"

Amir laughed as she opened the passenger's side door for Loch, then walked around the truck and got in. "All right, boss, where are we going?"

"That," Loch said, as Amir started up the truck with a jolt and headed down the driveway, "is up to me, so you just pipe down over there and head for the water. I'll tell you when you need to know."

Amir smiled and looked out the window. She was quiet as she drove out of town and onto the winding seaside roads leading to Acadia National Park. Loch finally glanced over and picked the question out of the air, turning it over a couple of times before she asked it.

"Do you want to talk about it?"

"God, no."

Amir's gaze was on the road, and she didn't look over as she answered, just drove the wide curve of road around the edge of the sea as night fell in sheer navy sheets around them. Amir hit the lights and placed her hand on Loch's thigh as she lowered her window and let the wind rush past her face, drying the tears Loch had already seen. After a few minutes, Loch had her pull off onto a dark side road and up to the edge of a remote sixty-foot cliff. The granite drop-off was raw, with a jagged edge that looked as if it had been torn off centuries before and tossed into the sea. The tires rolled slowly to a stop a few feet from the edge, crushing the gravel beneath them.

"I'm impressed," Amir said, her gaze tracking a hawk it was

almost too dark to see as it glided past the drop-off toward the rising moon. "Most people don't even know where this is."

"You keep forgetting I'm not a tourist."

Amir reached out in the darkness and slowly traced Loch's lower lip with her thumb. Loch touched it with her tongue, drawing it into the warmth of her mouth.

"Fuck, baby." Amir leaned back against the headrest, her eyes closed. It was forever before she opened them and shifted the truck silently into park.

Loch wanted to ask her a thousand things, pull her into her arms, tell her how sorry she was about what happened, how much it didn't matter. But it did matter, so there was nothing to say.

Amir got out of the truck, walked around front, and opened Loch's door. She pulled Loch's body against her hips in one smooth motion, her words low and hot against Loch's neck.

"Kill the lights."

Amir wrapped Loch's legs around her waist, hands strong against her back, and kicked the door shut with her foot as she carried her to the front of the truck. Loch sat on the hood and leaned back until she felt the cold metal against her back and looked up at the sky dusted with stars so close they left a sheer haze of light across her body. The air was soft, as warm as bare skin, and the wind shifted the treetops gently across the night sky.

Amir slid Loch's jeans off and tossed them on the hood, then ran her tongue up the inside of Loch's thigh, lifting it to rest on her shoulder. She held Loch's gaze as she laid her palm against the center of her chest, slow and strong, holding her between the truck and the stars. Loch felt the heat of Amir's mouth slide across her clit and arched her back as Amir slid her fingers inside. Amir flicked her tongue against it, then pulled it lightly into her mouth, swirling around it with just enough pressure to make Loch arch and tangle her fingers into Amir's hair. Loch's thigh tensed against her shoulder as Amir slicked her tongue around her clit until it was taut and aching and Loch was whispering for her to let her come.

"Amir," she said, barely moving but breathless. "More."

Amir slid a third finger inside and fucked her strong and slow, stroking her clit with her tongue until she felt Loch's thigh start to tremble against her face. She pulled Loch down the hood of the truck until she had both of Loch's thighs over her shoulders and rocked back and forth against her hips, her fingers deep inside. She kept her tongue on Loch's clit, reaching up to run her palm across her nipples or biting her thigh hard into her mouth when she got too close, until Loch was begging her for it, breathless and wanting.

"Baby," Loch said, back arched, every muscle in her body tensed against the cold steel of the truck hood. "Make me come for you."

That was all Amir needed to hear. She drew Loch's clit into her mouth and rocked into her, holding her strong at the small of her back as she came. She cried out into the darkness, the sound echoing off the undulating sea below, but Amir didn't stop fucking her, just slowed until she felt Loch's body start to move with her again and she heard her cry out again a few seconds later, the sound repeating as it bounced off the cliff faces below, finally sinking into the dark seawater.

Loch sat up when her breath slowed and pulled Amir to her, kissing away the tears she found on her cheeks. Loch held her as she cried, then tighter as she listened to Amir's body whisper what she wasn't willing to hear herself say.

They drove home that night, the silence dense and intimate, with the moonroof open to bring the stars closer. Loch never asked, just held her hand over Amir's heart as she fell asleep.

## Chapter Ten

The next few days sped by in a blur. The women's shelter came in and retrieved Samia's furniture, quickly and sensitively, but Loch decided five minutes into the process that she'd be better off down at the café reading what was left of the newspaper.

When she returned a few hours later, the house was empty, silence hanging in the air with the dust as if looking for a place to settle. Loch walked into the kitchen, looking around with fresh eyes. The house was suddenly expansive, with wide beams of sunlight falling in from the tall windows like a watercolor wash of pale gold, highlighting the faded spaces where photos and paintings had been on the walls for decades. She traced a wide square of faded wallpaper with her fingertip where a picture of Samia and her father had always hung. It had been taken at the diner in town sometime in the fifties, and it was Samia's favorite. Loch had packed it up carefully before the shelter came for the furniture and put it in the attic with the others she'd saved for Skye and their mother.

She ran a hand through her hair and turned where she stood, feeling the burn of tears behind her eyelids. Memories swirled around her as if she'd somehow sunk beneath the cold surface of the ocean, and she held her breath as they played out against the backdrop of the murky water around her. Samia walking into the kitchen through a path of white sunlight from the skylight in her studio with a paintbrush tangled into the center of a bun on top of her head. Her hair changed over the years from a silver shock of wild curls to a thick white drift, but it was always wound around a random paintbrush piercing the center. Loch had watched her pick up a paintbrush more than once that was still dripping paint and wedge it into her hair, her eyes intense and focused on the canvas in front of her. Loch's favorite was blue. Somehow, the blue tints never really washed out, and Samia was left with swirls of pale azure tint in her hair, like wispy white clouds swirled with blue summer sky.

Loch shook her head, but the memories seemed to press in around her, stealing the air. Somehow, the empty house was harder to take than when it had been full of Samia's things. She could still look around then and see her aunt all around her, but now, Samia was gone, and it seemed the house had exhaled, then never took another breath. It was time to make it her own, whether she decided to keep it or sell it, and she felt like a traitor. She turned in slow circles, trying to imagine the walls a different color, with furniture that reflected her more urban style, but everything was too different already. She should have prepared better or known by now what she wanted to do. She closed her eyes and fought the urge to slide down the wall and do nothing.

A hard knock at the door jerked her back to reality. She considered not answering it, but by the time the thought crossed her mind, whoever it was had found the doorbell. She pulled on her hoodie and shoved her hands in her pockets, pausing before she opened the door, hoping whoever it was would just give up. No such luck.

She opened the door to find a burly man in white overalls, holding a toolbox and a paint-splattered bucket of brushes.

"Good morning, ma'am," he said in a thick Southern accent. "Where do you want us?"

Loch paused. "I think you might have the wrong house. Are you sure you're looking for 333 White Street?"

He nodded, then looked over his shoulder as two more trucks pulled up and more guys piled out, reaching into the truck beds for ladders and paint cans. The logo on the truck doors caught her eye, just as yet another pulled up to the curb and parked.

*Lock Up Your Daughters.*

"Ma'am?" The guy in the white overalls still standing on her porch pulled off his cap and looked at his watch, which was also splattered with paint. "If you just want to tell us where to set up, we can get started."

"I'm sorry," Loch said, smiling as she saw Amir get out of the truck and start toward the house. "Please, come in."

He gestured to the rest of the crew and stepped past Loch, leaving her on the porch as Amir climbed the steps and pulled Loch into her arms.

"I'm sorry, babe," she said, whispering into her hair as she held her close. "I meant to be here to explain before my guys took over your house, but her plane was late."

"Explain what?" Loch pulled back just enough to see Amir's face. "What *is* all this?"

Then something caught her eye over Amir's shoulder, and Loch peered down at the truck as the passenger door opened, the glare of the sun glinting off the window in a blinding arc as someone stepped out.

Loch took a breath, then took off running, throwing her arms around her sister before she'd even had a chance to drop her bags. "Skye!" Loch said, breathless, her cheeks wet with sudden tears, letting her go only to hug her again. "Where the hell did you come from?"

"Your girlfriend thought you might need some help picking out paint colors, so I told my coach I had mono." Skye winked at Amir as she walked up behind Loch. "And not that I really care, but I think he bought it."

Amir smiled and squeezed Loch's hand. "I knew the shelter was coming today to help clear out, and I thought you might need some company."

"How did you even know how to contact her?"

Amir smiled, picking up Skye's bags and dropping them into the back of her truck. "It took me three seconds to find her on Facebook. She did the rest."

"Well, that's complete BS." Skye gave Amir's shoulder a

playful punch. "She set everything up. All I did was get my ass on the plane this morning."

"All right, girls." Amir smiled as she held out the keys to her truck. "Which one of you wants to drive?"

Loch and Skye looked at each other and laughed as they watched the reality of the situation dawn on Amir.

"Seriously?" she said. "Skye, you can't drive, either?" She dropped her keys back into her pocket and nodded down the hill toward town. "Okay, New Yorkers," she said, smiling. "Walter is waiting for you at the hardware store. He's the owner. Get down there and bring me back some paint chips in whatever colors you decide on for the house. I gave him a layout of the house this morning, so all you have to do is pick your colors and tell us where they go."

"So, that's what this is?" Loch looked back into the house where ladders were quickly going up and strips of tape were being laid down. "You sent your crew to paint my house for me?"

"Yep," Amir said. "I know how overwhelming it can feel to have to do something like this. I didn't want you to feel like you had to do it alone."

Loch caught a tear on her cheek with the heel of her hand and leaned into Amir.

"God," Skye said, looking Amir up and down. "Please tell me you have a single brother."

"Just missed him, I'm afraid," Amir said. "He's all kinds of married."

"Just my luck." Skye slipped on her sunglasses and looked toward town. "Let's get going so I can pick out all my favorite colors for the house." She paused, looking back at Loch over her shoulder and sliding the sunglasses down her nose. "I mean *your* favorites."

Amir pulled Loch into a quick hug. "We'll sand and prime while you're gone, so take your time. Just let him know what colors, and I'll get with Walter later as far as how much paint we need."

❖

After Loch and Skye had spent the better part of the afternoon comparing dozens of colors with names like Tart Hibiscus and Wild Bluebell, they finally narrowed it down to their favorites and brought samples back to the house to tape onto the walls. Loch also brought back a box of handmade sandwiches from the market and a case of beer for the crew, which seemed to make her some sort of instant rock star. They all settled onto the back deck and soaked up the sun while Loch and Skye walked around the house and tried to decide which colors went where. Amir taped the color samples up on each wall as they decided.

"By the way," Skye peeked through the empty rooms, "where are we sleeping tonight? They already have tape and drop cloths all over the room you're staying in."

"You're both staying at my house," Amir said, ripping the painter's tape off the roll with her teeth. "Well, kind of, anyway. My family has a short-term rental at the lake that's empty at the moment. It will keep you out of the fumes while we get everything painted."

The doorbell sounded again, and Skye went to answer it. She was back a few seconds later. "It's the police." She glanced back toward the open door and lowered her voice. "And they want to speak to Amir."

Loch took a paint color strip out of her mouth and looked at Amir. "How did they even know to look for you here?"

"It's a small damn town." Amir wiped a white haze of primer off her hands with a rag. "I'm sure it's nothing. I'll be right back."

Loch and Skye peered around the corner and watched her step out onto the porch and shut the door behind her.

Skye looked at Loch. "What the hell was that about? There's like three of them out there."

"I have absolutely no idea." Loch returned the tape roll to the top of the ladder. "But I guess we'll find out."

It was a few minutes before Amir returned, but when she did, it was clear that whatever the police wanted to talk to her about, it was not nothing.

"I need to go down to the station for a few minutes." Amir

pulled on her sweatshirt and ran a hand through her hair. "I spoke to Chris, my foreman, and he's going to drive you out to the house when you let him know you're ready. I'll call you when I'm done."

Loch watched a vein in Amir's neck tense as she spoke and saw that the hand that wasn't holding her keys was clenched into a fist.

"What is all this about?" Loch kept her voice steady and light, but she felt knocked a bit off her feet, as if a wave had suddenly hit her from behind.

"I'll tell you what I know tonight. I'll bring dinner out to the house after I'm done."

"Don't worry about it," Skye said as she looked at her watch. "I'm making dinner tonight. Just bring yourself when you're done, and we'll put a beer in your hand before you even make it through the door."

Amir looked at her with a sudden flash of gratitude and whispered to Loch as she leaned in to kiss her. "Don't worry, baby. I'll explain everything tonight."

And then she was gone. The house felt suddenly emptier, cold, as if all the promise had been sucked out of it. Chris, the burly redhead who Loch had met at the door, popped his head in an hour later and asked if they'd decided on colors, so they handed him the three-page list of directions they'd just finished, which didn't seem to faze him in the least. Loch packed an overnight bag and gave it to Chris. He promised to lock up the house when the crew was done for the day, then offered to take them out to the lake house if they were ready. He had a deep Southern accent, a red beard that made him look like he should be wearing a kilt, and a gun rack in his truck that was bigger than Skye.

"Are all those guns yours?" Skye asked as he took out the guns and carefully stacked them in a stainless steel box bolted to the back of the truck so there was room for her to sit.

"Nope," he said, clamping the locks shut with the heel of his hand. "This is my wife's pickup. I have the big ones in my truck at home."

Chris got Skye settled and opened the passenger door for Loch.

Skye leaned up to Loch's seat with a raised eyebrow. "I think

I might have forgotten what a gentleman is after all these years in the city."

Chris made a stop at the market in town for Skye to get what she needed for dinner, and as they climbed back in with their grocery bags, Skye handed him an enormous strip of the homemade beef jerky the market kept by the register in the summer. He winked at her, folded the length of it easily into his mouth, and fired up the truck.

A few minutes later, they pulled up to the house Amir had loaned them, and Chris carried in their bags before he handed them the key.

"If y'all have any trouble with anything, just give me a call." He leaned into the door and looked toward the kitchen. "Walter at the hardware store has my number, but I manage some of the Farzaneh properties, so I think it may even be on the fridge in there if you need it."

As his truck roared to life again and disappeared down the road, Skye grabbed the beer out of the grocery bag on the way to the deck. The house was a chalet-style cabin built on a rocky cliff with a wide redwood deck that extended out over the water, making it look like it was hovering above the sea. They sank down into the green cedar lounge chairs and popped the top off the bottles with the house key Chris had given them, listening to the waves break below the deck.

"So, tell me."

Skye looked at Loch as the wind picked up the edges of her hair and brushed them against her face.

"Tell you what?"

"Tell me what's going through your head." Skye shifted in her chair to face Loch. "I know when you're worried about something."

"I don't know." Loch unzipped her hoodie and leaned back in the chair to let the sun fall across her face. "I know it's probably nothing, but I just don't…" Her voice trailed off, and she stared over the deck railing.

"You just don't have a good feeling about this?"

"Yeah," Loch said. "I don't."

"Want to talk about it?"

Loch threw the bottle cap beyond the railing into the white caps below. "Hell no. I want to pretend it's not happening."

"Well, I bet I can take your mind off it." Skye leaned back in her chair and balled up her jacket behind her neck, her eyes melting closed under the warmth of the sunshine. "I've been fucking a girl on my swim team."

Loch sat straight up in her chair and shaded her eyes. "Holy shit! How the hell did that happen?"

Skye looked over at her and smiled. "Well, if you need me to go over the ins and outs of lesbian sex, I guess I have a few minutes."

"You know what I mean!" Loch tossed her sunglasses at her. "Who is she?"

"She's been on my swim team at Columbia for about a year. I'd noticed her, but we're in completely different friend circles, so we never talked."

"What is she like?"

"Honestly, that foreman reminds me of her."

"So, she has a red beard?" Loch paused, nodding before she continued. "That's kind of what I was picturing."

Skye laughed, tipping her beer up and finishing the last half without taking a breath. "Very funny."

She paused, choosing her words carefully, as if they were unfamiliar.

"It's hard to describe. She's just got something about her. She's black, with these sexy as hell shaved lines in her hair on the sides. She walks like a guy, with broad shoulders and a banging body, doesn't talk much but sounds like an Alabama senator when she does. She's just…hot."

Loch grabbed her sunglasses and lay back down on the chair. "Jesus. I can't believe you didn't lead with this little tidbit like the second you got here." She paused. "Wait, what happened to the cold oatmeal dude?"

"I had to cut him loose. I think I was a little too much for him."

"Really?" Loch sifted her hand through her hair. "Or was it that he wasn't enough for you?"

"I'm starting to think the latter may be true."

"So," Loch said, sliding her sunglasses back on and leaning back in her chair. "How did this happen anyway?"

"We had a swim meet in Atlanta a few weeks ago, and our flights got messed up, so everyone was stuck there for an extra day. They got us a hotel, but I guess she's from Georgia, so when I walked out of the meet, she was starting up a black Jeep in the parking lot. We've been swimming on the same team for a year, and she's never said a single word to me, but suddenly, she just leans out the window and says, 'Get in, I'm gonna take you somewhere.'"

"And you got in?"

"Of course." Skye peered over her sunglasses. "Why would I *not* get in some random chick's Jeep and take off? Where's your sense of adventure?"

Loch laughed and raised an eyebrow, waiting for her to go on.

"So, I just got in, and she turned up the music…"

"What was it?"

"Oh, my God, it was *country*. Jason Aldean."

"Well, don't tell anybody. We'll never be able to live in Manhattan again."

"Fuck no, I'm not telling anybody!" Skye reached for another beer from the six-pack between them and cracked it open. "Anyway, she drives us out of Atlanta and into some backwoods Georgia town, and I swear, I felt like I was in a country music video. At some point, we got off the real roads and turned down this red dirt road, and we ended up at this gorgeous lake. I guess her friends heard she was going to be in town and just packed up and headed out there to camp for the night."

"What the hell were you thinking?" Loch stretched her arms out in the sun, then pulled her shirt over her head and dropped it on the deck. She settled back onto the lounge chair, face turned toward the sun. "I would never just let some random person drive me out into the boondocks."

"Of course you wouldn't, that's why my life is so much more interesting than yours."

"Fair enough." Loch shook her head, smiling. "Then what happened? Do you even know her name at this point?"

"Of course," Skye said, peeling the label off her bottle. "I remembered it from the swim roster. Her name is Hayden. Anyway, we got out there, and there was a big bonfire and tons of trucks with the tailgates down, more coolers than I've ever seen in my life, and all her friends treated me like they'd known me forever. I actually had a kick-ass time."

"So...what was it like to kiss a girl?"

"Oh, my God." Skye paused, turning toward Loch and sliding her sunglasses down her nose. "It was so hot. She offered more than once to take me back to my hotel, but I wanted to stay, so she pulled some sleeping bags out of her truck, and we slept down on the dock under the stars."

"And...?"

"And since then, we've spent every night together." Skye smiled at Loch, shading her eyes with her hand. "Which reminds me, I've got to find an apartment and get the hell out of Mom's house before she asks me one more time if I'm on birth control."

Loch clinked her beer bottle to Skye's and laid back. "Well, welcome to the club, little sis." She looked over at Skye and opened one eye against the piercing sunlight between them. "But just for the record, I've known for years."

"Seriously?" Skye took her shirt off and tossed it in Loch's direction. "And you didn't think to mention to me that I might want to try dating girls?"

"Nah." Loch tossed the shirt onto the deck with hers. "I knew you'd figure it out."

They lay back in the chairs for a few minutes and soaked up the sunshine. In Manhattan, summer days were intensely hot, as if the heat bounced off all the concrete and intensified, hovering in an impenetrable layer over the city. But the breeze swept up from the sea in Innis Harbor stirred coolness into the bright summer days and made the nights more crisp than sultry.

Just as the light was starting to drop back behind the cliffs, they heard a car drive up and shift painfully through several gears before settling on park. Loch pulled her shirt on and tossed Skye hers just as they heard a knock at the door. They walked from the deck back into the house as Loch shot Skye a look.

"Who even knows we're here?" she whispered. "It's not Chris or Amir, they can actually drive."

Skye just shrugged and opened the door to a slender, impeccably dressed man with a pile of designer luggage at his feet and a Fendi bag on his shoulder.

"Graham, you came!" Skye shrieked, wrapping her arms around his neck before he even stepped inside. "I thought you had to do makeup for that runway show in L.A."

"I'm sick to *death* of those shows, honey. After I got your text about coming out here, I gave the LA show to my assistant, and this town is the size of my suitcase, so it didn't take long to find you."

He dragged his suitcases over the doorstep as if they were stuffed with concrete.

"It's worth it to see my favorite supermodel." He paused, giving Loch a wink as he dropped his Fendi bag on the couch. "And Loch, of course."

He pulled Loch into a warm hug, then kissed both her cheeks. "God, girl, you look amazing! Vacation does a body good." His gaze swept her body, then settled on her face with a concerned grimace. "But those brows are out of control. Thank God I got here when I did."

"Don't even tease me, Graham," Loch said, rolling her eyes. "I'm getting fat. I'm going to eat myself right out of the shows I'm scheduled for."

"Oh, Lord, you've gained two pounds and are all the way back up to the triple digits?" Graham fanned himself dramatically and shook his head. "Fuck them, they're lucky to get you at all, and they know it."

He looked around at the house and peered out onto the deck. "Skye said she was headed up here to see you, so I thought I'd come check for myself that you didn't drop off the face of the earth. Everyone everywhere is talking about it. They all think you've been abducted by aliens." His voice softened then, and he squeezed her hand. "I'm so sorry about your aunt. I know you were the closest one to her."

Loch, Skye, and Graham eventually settled into the sofas with drinks in hand, catching up on gossip and leisurely downing bottles of Graham's favorite French rosé that he'd smuggled back in his luggage from his last shoot in Paris. Graham was known as the best makeup artist in the business. Loch had worked with him on various shows and shoots for years, and they had clicked immediately and remained close over the years. He'd met Skye several times backstage when she was there with her.

"So…let's see it." Loch smiled at Graham and peered at his left hand.

"What? This little thing?" Graham held out his hand and showed Loch a white gold band covered in what looked like Broadway lights. "He did well, didn't he? I told him I'd better need Ray-Bans to look at it, and he went all out."

Graham had recently gotten engaged to his longtime boyfriend, a movie producer, and the wedding was scheduled for the following May.

"Now the only problem is learning how to dance to his music for the wedding. I love him, but I cannot believe there's going to be country music at *my* wedding, for fuck's sake." Graham balanced his wine glass on two fingers. "Needless to say, I saved on a videographer. The last thing I need is a record of his crazy Texas family two-stepping around our Manhattan posse."

"Graham," Skye said, nudging him with her foot. "That's exactly why you need to hire a video guy for every corner, so you can catch that from every angle!"

Loch laughed and got up to start the grill on the deck. They'd bought steak for dinner at the market, with a huge portobello mushroom for Loch, and after all the wine, she'd actually started to consider eating. She turned to look at Graham over her shoulder on her way out.

"Is the wedding cake going to be shaped like a cowboy hat?"

"Hilarious, Battersby," he said, pelting her with one of the throw pillows from the couch. "You'd better not know something I don't know!"

Loch looked the grill over once she got outside, but it was a gas grill, seemingly with no power switch, which was confirmed five minutes later when they'd all inspected it and come up with the same conclusion. Darkness fell over the glossy surface of the sea as they stood on the deck, until only the whitecaps were visible. Pelicans glided across the water looking for easy evening prey, and the scent of cold pine drifted in from the evergreens dotted around the cabin. Graham was keeping everyone laughing, but it was all Loch could do not to panic about what was happening with Amir. The worst part was not knowing the whole story, and Loch was trying not to wonder if she might have missed some chapters.

"Okay," Skye said, winding her glossy blond hair into a knot at the nape of her neck. "How is it possible that three grown-ass adults can't figure out how to light a single grill?"

"Look at me, honey," Graham said with a dramatic sniff, adjusting the wildly expensive watch on his wrist for emphasis. "Do I look like I'm firing up a grill in the backyard every weekend?"

"Wait a minute." Skye headed back into the house and pulled her phone out of the back pocket of her jeans. "I have an idea."

Loch leaned against the railing, scanning her phone again for a message from Amir. What could possibly be taking so long? It had been five hours since she'd gone to the police station, and Loch's uneasiness was increasing by the moment.

❖

Skye convinced Chris to come back to the cabin and look at the grill for them, then invited him to stay for dinner. Afterward, when Graham said he wanted to surprise his new husband by learning to dance to country music at the reception, Chris started a Gary Allan song on his phone and laid it on the table. He stood and offered his hand to Graham, who assumed he was kidding until Chris asked him whether he wanted to learn to lead or follow. Surprisingly, Chris turned out to be a great teacher, and by the end of the night, Graham had learned the steps to a few of the more popular country dances. Of course Skye posted the funniest moments on Instagram Stories before Graham had a chance to stop her, then begged Chris to teach her how to line dance.

After Chris went home at the end of the evening, all three collapsed on the couch, and Loch checked her phone again, trying to push down the rising feeling of dread getting worse with every passing minute. She poured the last of the rosé into her glass, then looked up when she noticed the room had suddenly fallen silent. Graham and Skye were looking at his phone, and Loch watched Skye's face pale before she covered her mouth with one hand and slowly handed her the phone with the other.

It was a post on a celebrity gossip blog, well known in the entertainment industry. Loch read the headline and felt sick, sinking back into her chair as she read it again and noticed that the link for the article had already been retweeted and shared more than two hundred thousand times. At the top of the article was a picture of Loch and Amir, eating lunch by the window in the diner, followed by the headline.

> *Loch Battersby has finally reappeared, and it looks like the modeling world's feminist darling has shacked up with a convicted rapist in Maine. Not such a role model now, are we, my dear?*

Loch's phone buzzed as she stared at the picture of her and Amir. It was her agent.

## Chapter Eleven

"Amir Farzaneh?"

Amir looked up at the two detectives entering the room with a tape recorder and nodded in their direction. A single lightbulb buzzed overhead where Amir sat at a small brown table, the only furniture in the room. The fake wood trim had curled back from one of the ends, leaving the dirty plywood edge worn smooth by countless nervous hands. They'd put her in the room three hours earlier, and she hadn't seen anyone since.

The detectives wore dress pants with long-sleeve button-ups, and each carried a Glock in a holster and a ridiculously shiny badge attached to his belt. The heavier one with combed-over gray hair spoke first.

"Ms. Farzaneh, this is Detective Carson, and I'm Detective Barton with the Bar Harbor sex crimes division."

The words hit Amir in the stomach so hard she had to concentrate to keep from doubling over.

"Someone needs to tell me what's going on here." She slid her hands under the table. "Am I under arrest?"

"No, not yet, but we need to ask you some questions first."

"First?" Amir shook her head to clear it. "What the hell do you think I did?"

The words came out of her mouth, but they were a waste of breath. She knew the answer. She'd been here before.

❖

"Who the fuck is that?" Graham slid closer to Loch on the couch and peered at the picture, partially hidden by the glare of the diner window. "Do you have any clue what they're talking about?"

Loch wanted to answer him but couldn't. She concentrated on the feeling of her heartbeat in her neck, uneven and silent. It was the only sound in the room.

"That's Amir, isn't it?" Skye leaned closer and put her hand on Loch's knee until Loch looked up and nodded. "Do you know what he's talking about? Did she tell you anything about this?"

Loch locked gazes with Skye, and a tear rolled down her cheek and fell onto the phone screen before she gathered enough words to speak. "I have no idea. I don't know anything."

"This could be nothing still, remember that," Skye said, squeezing her hand. "We don't even know the story yet."

"It wouldn't be the first time some dickhead has made up a story to sell to the press."

Graham's words were kind, but Loch looked up just in time to see the look he shot in Skye's direction.

❖

Amir waited while the detectives shuffled papers and took their time before they got to the point. "Do you know why we brought you in to answer a few questions today?"

"No, I don't." Amir struggled to keep her voice even. "I thought we covered that already."

"Really?" This was from the second detective, Carson, who from the look of him, would rather be in the gym. "Because I think you do."

"Then why don't you just save us both some time and tell me?"

Amir knew as it came out of her mouth that she was tanking her chances of getting out of the room before her hair turned gray, but she was tired, covered in paint, and a friendly game of déjà vu just wasn't what she was in the mood for.

Detective Barton tapped his pen on the table. Amir wondered after a few seconds if he was even going to speak. "There's been an allegation of sexual assault made against you in Innis Harbor." Carson leaned in, locking his gaze with Amir's. "Again."

"Who said I assaulted them?"

"Well," Barton said with a glance at his partner. "Let's start with the most important factor. The alleged victim is fifteen, so she's underage."

"Way underage." Carson cleared his throat. "Again."

Fuck. It was happening again. This would push the life she'd built since the last time over the edge of a two-hundred-foot cliff. Amir sat back in her seat and rubbed her forehead with the heel of her hand.

"This is bullshit," she said. "I can't do this again."

"Here's a news flash, sunshine," Carson leaned forward on his elbows and spat the words across the table. "We're all sitting here because you can't seem to learn to keep it in your pants or whatever your kind wants to call it. There's a shit ton of other things I'd rather be doing today, too, so let's stop wasting each other's time."

"Look." Barton leaned back in his chair, his belly testing the limits of the cheap, translucent buttons threatening to pop off and ricochet around the room like bullets. "I'm gonna be straight with you about this. This girl is alleging that you came into her bedroom at her parents' home in Innis Harbor, stripped her naked, and forced yourself on her."

"Oh, my God." Amir closed her eyes to stop the room from spinning and leaned back in her chair. When she felt tears burning behind her eyelids, she counted the tiles on the ceiling until she could talk. "I've never, *never* forced any woman to do anything sexual. And if you're talking about Charlotte Clancy, she came on to me."

Carson slapped his hand on the table hard enough to make his notebook shudder.

"Well, you should have told us that! That makes it *completely* okay to have sex with an underage girl." He narrowed his eyes and locked them onto Amir. "Look, I don't care whether she gave you an engraved invitation and handed you her clothes on a silver fuckin' platter, she's a *child*."

"I can't do anything but tell you the truth." Amir leaned forward in her chair. "I didn't do this. It's her word against mine, but I would never do that to anyone, especially a child."

"That's touching." Carson held his hand to his heart and dabbed at his eyes with his sleeve. "That really gets me right here." He tapped his heart and glanced at his partner, who shot him back a look. Then he opened his bag and pulled out an iPad. "But maybe we should just watch the tape."

❖

Loch woke to the sun streaming into her window and Skye standing by her bed, dangling a hoodie over her face.

"Wake up, sleepy butt."

Skye dropped the hoodie onto Loch's head and sat beside her, handing her a cup of steaming black coffee she'd put on the nightstand.

"What time is it?"

"Time for you to get your ass out of bed." Skye stood and opened the curtains wider, filling the room with light. "Graham is at the door waiting. He only eats diner food when he gets out of the city, so he's been talking about bacon since he woke me up at six this morning."

"Oh, Lord. I forgot about that." Loch traded her undershirt and boxers for a pair of faded skinny jeans and the Columbia swim team hoodie that Skye had dropped on her. "He counts every freaking calorie when he's working, but God help anyone who gets between him and a patty melt outside of Manhattan."

She pulled on her boots and looked up at Skye, who was winding a hair tie around a slick of blond hair falling through her fingers. "What am I going to do if this is true?"

Skye pulled on one of Loch's hats and pulled her ponytail through the back of it. "Do you love her?"

Loch nodded, biting her lip and jerking on her laces harder than necessary. "I can feel myself falling in love with her, so that makes this even worse. How could I not have seen this about her?"

"Listen." Skye sat on the bed beside her and pulled a tissue out of the box on the nightstand. "I'm not going to sugarcoat this for you. It could turn out that she's not who you thought she was, but we don't know that yet. And if you feel this strongly for her, you owe it to both of you to find out what's really happening."

Loch and Skye looked at the door when they heard the clomp of boots hitting hardwood. Graham peered around the corner and tapped his watch.

"Um…I know models don't eat, but I'm planning on eating a stack of pancakes the size of my head this morning." He raised one perfectly shaped brow. "So, let's go."

❖

The diner was busy as they pushed open the smudged glass door, but only two old ladies in the corner even bothered to look up when they came in.

"I can see why you like it here, my little hermit." Graham took off his sunglasses and settled into the booth farthest from the windows. "It appears no one gives a shit who you are."

"Yes, thank God, not a camera in sight."

"It is kind of refreshing," Skye said, sliding her silverware out of the little white paper bag next to her coffee cup. "I can't say I love being constantly referred to as the 'fat twin.'"

Graham lowered his menu long enough to give her a look. "Please tell me you don't actually let that bother you."

Skye flashed him a wide smile and winked. "Hell no. I'm fabulous. And all this muscle means I can kick anyone's ass in the pool."

They were all studying the menu as Cara came over to take their order, pen in hand. She glanced at Loch as if to ask if she'd heard, and Loch nodded.

"Well," Cara said. "I guess you know what's happening."

"Pancakes," Graham said. "Pancakes are happening. Then we can figure this steaming pile of shit out."

Cara laughed and got out her order pad, raising an eyebrow at

Graham's lengthy order. Finally, Loch and Skye told her what they wanted, and Cara took it to the window, returning in a few minutes with the coffeepot. She filled everyone's cup and one for herself, then slid into the booth beside Loch, who introduced her to Graham and Skye.

"So, here's the latest." She softly bumped Loch's shoulder with her own. "Hamid was just in here on his way to see if he can bail her out of jail, so she should have access to her phone at some point today and be able to call you."

"What did they charge her with?" Graham poured the fifth packet of sugar into his cup and looked up at Cara.

"Aggravated sexual assault of a child."

"I can't believe this." Loch pushed her coffee cup away. "What even happened?"

"That's a good question. Even Hamid didn't know. All we know is that Amir did a one-day job on the Clancys' deck a few days ago, and now Charlotte is saying she assaulted her."

"Who the hell is Charlotte?" Skye looked around and lowered her voice. "Do you know her?"

"Yeah, and she's a piece of work. She goes to some fancy boarding school in Boston. I think she's just back for the summer."

"How is Hamid?" Loch said, then remembered to explain to Skye and Graham who she was talking about. "Hamid is Amir's older brother. He's a great guy."

"He *is* a great guy," Cara said. "But he's pissed as hell. He just wants to make this all go away and he can't."

"So," Skye said, glancing over at Loch. "I hate to ask this, but I read in the media yesterday that Amir has a previous conviction for rape. Is that true?"

"Wait a minute," Cara said, lowering her voice. "No one even knows about Amir's arrest yet, where the hell did you read that?"

"In a celebrity blog out of New York. It's been shared over two hundred thousand times at this point. It's everywhere by now."

Cara got up quickly when she heard the cook slam his hand on the bell and start to load up the plates in a precarious stack at the window.

"Wow," Graham said. "She really doesn't have a clue who you are, does she?"

"It's a small town. No one really follows celebrity news like they do in the city," Loch said quietly. "And that's my favorite part of it."

Cara came back and handed out the plates, making sure everyone had what they needed before she sat back down.

"I had no idea anyone even knew about that beyond her family," she said. "Why the hell does someone in New York City care what's happening in Innis Harbor?"

Graham held up his iPhone with one hand and poured a lake of syrup across his plate with the other. Cara took it and scrolled through the images, one by one, until she finally looked up at Loch. "Holy shit, is that you and Taylor Swift?" She looked closer at the picture of Loch and Taylor from an awards show the previous year. "You're an actress?"

"No," Loch said, pushing her plate away. "I'm a model."

"Okay." Cara handed the phone back to Graham. "Now this is starting to make sense."

All three of them looked up at her, even Graham, although he did continue to stuff his face with pancakes as he listened.

"The other day, this guy came in with the biggest camera I've ever seen and asked about Loch."

"What did you say?" Skye asked, stealing a piece of bacon off the edge of Graham's plate since she'd already eaten her own.

"I said you came by for coffee every once in a while, so he waited here all damn day. He asked where you lived, and I told him to fuck off." She flashed an angelic smile. "Nicely, of course."

"That's how they got that pic of you and Amir in the diner window." Skye met Loch's gaze and pushed her plate back toward her with a pointed look.

"I'm sorry, girl," Cara said. "I shouldn't have said anything."

Loch shook her head. "It's not your fault, you didn't know. They always find me anyway."

The door opened, and Amir's foreman Chris walked in wearing paint-splattered clothes, heading for their table when he saw Cara.

"Hey," he said. "Have you seen Amir? There was a group of guys up at Loch's house with cameras just now, and Amir hasn't shown up yet. I've worked for her for the last nine years, and she's never even been late."

"Holy shit, are you talking about Loch's aunt's house?" Graham said. "What did you tell them?"

Chris looked confused. "What, the dumbasses with the cameras?"

Cara laughed. "Yeah, them."

"Well, the house is empty because we're repainting, so I opened the front door and asked them if it looked like anyone lived there, then told them to get the fuck off the property."

Graham put down his bacon and stared at Chris. "I know you're straight, but, Christ, that's sexy."

Skye shot him a look.

"No offense, of course," Graham added, trying his best not to smile.

"None taken." Chris winked in his direction. "Best compliment I've gotten in a while, actually."

"Do you think they believed you?" Loch asked.

"Yeah, the place looks deserted, and there's no visible furniture or cars parked outside, only the work trucks, so they left." Chris looked at Loch and Cara, but no one spoke. "Can anyone tell me what the hell is going on?"

Cara reached over and dragged a chair from one of the tables. "Have a seat. This may take a while."

❖

Amir watched the black and white video start playing and leaned in to read the date on what looked like security footage.

"Is this the day I was there to fix the step on his back patio?"

"So, you're admitting to being in the Clancy home on June first?"

"Yeah, of course," Amir said. "Mr. Clancy is a real estate agent, so he and my dad have worked together on a few houses they've bought and flipped over the years. Our families know each other. He asked me to come fix a broken step on his back patio." She looked closer at the images on the screen. "Is this footage from their home security system?"

They didn't answer, so Amir kept her gaze on the screen and watched herself come into the house and start setting up for the job. She'd brought in her tools from the truck, taken a look at the back step, then stopped to read a note left for her on the kitchen counter.

"What were you doing right there?" Barton asked, popping the top on a Dr Pepper someone had just handed him through the door. Foam bubbled up and threatened to spill over the edge of the can, and Carson shot him a look, finger poised over the pause button.

"You ready now, Detective?"

Barton nodded, and they watched Amir turn the note over and read it again, then start up the stairs.

"What did the note say?"

"It asked me to take a look at the bathroom faucet in his daughter's room."

He looked back at the tape and pointed to Amir on the stairs. "Then why didn't you go up there with any tools?"

"Because I hadn't even seen what the problem was." Amir tried to ignore the feeling of being swallowed by slow-moving quicksand. "I didn't know what I'd need."

She shook her head as she watched herself walk down the hall and enter Charlotte's bedroom. Detective Barton stopped the tape. "Do you want to tell us what happened after you went in, or should I just press play?"

"Nothing happened," Amir said. "Before I even got to the bathroom, Charlotte came out of the bathroom in a towel, so I apologized and started to leave."

"Funny," Carson said, turning his pen through his fingers. "Because this footage shows that you definitely didn't come right back out. In fact, you didn't come back out that door for twelve minutes and seven seconds."

"She said to just go ahead since I was there, so I went in to take a quick look while she was in her walk-in closet." Amir rubbed her temples slowly, listening to the noise in the hall outside. "In hindsight, I should have just left."

"Well, that's the understatement of the year because Charlotte says you locked the door and assaulted her on the bed."

"You gotta be kidding me! What she did was come into the bathroom, drop her towel, and ask if I wanted to touch her. I said no, but she was between me and the damn door. I couldn't leave."

"What else happened?" Barton asked with a glance at Carson.

"She tried to kiss me, but I kept telling her no. I eventually got past her and left."

Carson pulled a folder from the stack in front of him and pulled out a glossy photo the size of a sheet of paper. "Then how the hell did *this* happen to Charlotte?"

❖

Loch pushed through the glass double doors of the Bar Harbor police station and saw Hamid sitting in one of the white plastic chairs that lined the waiting area, staring into the silent TV in the corner. She sank down in one of the chairs next to him, and he pulled her into a hug.

"How are you holding up? I know this has to be stressful for you." He looked like he'd been there all night.

"I'm okay, but I'm sure it's worse for you. Any news?"

"She was arraigned early this morning, and I'm just waiting to be able to post bail for her. It's taking forever."

"I need to ask you something." Loch felt suddenly as if she was about to cry and pulled at a thread on the cuff of her hoodie until she could go on. "Does Amir have a previous conviction for rape?"

Hamid sighed and sank back in his chair, rubbing the deep lines in his forehead with the heel of his hand.

"She does. And she should have told you." He looked over at her and saw the tears welling in her eyes. "I'm sorry, Loch."

Loch shook her head, staring at the half-full coffeemaker in the corner until she felt steady enough to speak. "What were the circumstances?"

"She should really tell you herself," Hamid said. "But it was a long time ago."

"This is so surreal," Loch said, her world fading into black and white around her. She watched the last shards of colors shatter at her feet before she heard herself speak again. "I just can't believe this is happening."

She put her sunglasses on and walked back out the doors, fading slowly into the glare of the sun.

❖

It was two weeks before Amir stopped leaving messages on Loch's phone. Four weeks before her mother spoke to her again. And six weeks before Amir felt the stares of everyone in town start to wane. Most of her crew had never come back to work. Chris was the only one who stayed on, which allowed her to complete the projects she had contracts for, but calls for additional jobs had slowed to less than half her usual number of projects. The trial was set to start in another week, so she'd told herself maybe that was better anyway. She'd tried to bring it up one day as she and Chris were setting up for a painting job, but Chris had cut her off before she got her sentence out.

"Look, boss, I don't care what everyone in town is flapping their gums about. I don't believe that shit for a second. You and I have been working together for nine years, and I ain't stopping now."

"But I just wanted to explain—"

Chris tossed her a paintbrush and pulled his cap down over his head. "Nothing to explain."

He flashed her a smile and switched the radio to country music. "Now shut up and paint."

❖

Amir was starting her last job before the trial, and as she got out of her truck, the midsummer sun shimmered off the water just past the docks, and tourists lined the sidewalks. Her truck door slammed shut, and for the hundredth time, she wished she could stop into the café for coffee. She'd tried once, weeks earlier, but as she'd walked in, the conversations at the tables had suddenly stilled, and she waited at the counter for her coffee in near silence, trying not to notice the icy stares following her as she left.

The bell on the door clanged as she pushed it open now, and thankfully, most people didn't look up. Either the crowd was mostly tourists or things had finally started to die down, but it was a welcome change.

"Hey there, stranger." Cara turned over a coffee cup and started pouring. "I was wondering when I was going to see you again."

"Well, you're the only one." Amir took another glance around before she reached for the sugar and poured it into her coffee.

"Hey," Cara said, pulling the cream out of the fridge and pushing it over to Amir. "I don't want to bring up a sensitive subject, but have you heard from Loch?"

"No. I've tried for weeks, but she won't answer." Amir picked up her cup and blew on the surface to cool it. "Not that I blame her."

"Listen." Cara touched her hand to get Amir to look up at her. "You'll have a chance to lay it all out there at the trial. People around here think they know everything, but they don't."

"One of Hamid's college buddies is a defense attorney in Boston, so he took my case. I'm sure he's great at what he does, I just don't have much to defend myself with." She ran her hand through her hair and rubbed her thumb over the back of her neck, trying to quell the near-constant headache she'd carried around since this all started. "It's her word against mine."

"Is that picture admissible at trial?"

Cara had stopped by Amir's house shortly after she'd gotten out of jail, and Amir told her about the picture of Charlotte the detectives had shown her when she was being questioned. She'd had bruises around her arms and at the base of her neck and a bloody scrape over one eye. It was painful to look at, and Amir still saw it every time she closed her eyes.

"I don't know. He's trying to keep it from being included in evidence, but we don't know yet."

"She comes in here all the time with her friend Amy," Cara said. "I think they used to cheer together before her parents shipped her off to that fancy boarding school. They just sit there and gossip like there's nothing wrong."

"Cara." Amir raised an eyebrow and smiled. "You know you can't punch them, right?"

"Yes, I can," Cara said, wiping down the counter before she paused, turning back to Amir. "Although I've given it some thought, and I feel it's more appropriate to just knock their stupid heads together."

"I appreciate it," Amir said, trying not to smile. She wasn't entirely sure Cara was kidding, and it was safer not to encourage her. "But let's not both get arrested over this, okay?" Cara looked at Amir and winked. "No promises."

❖

Loch waited in the plush lobby area of her modeling agency, waiting to be called for her appointment with her agent. She'd taken a few weeks off after she'd gotten back to Manhattan but knew the best thing for her was to get back to work. Anything to keep Amir from flashing through her mind every waking minute.

"Loch Battersby?"

The receptionist scanned the room, and Loch stood, slipping her bag over her shoulder and following her down the hall to Harvey Goldberg's office. Harvey was the best in the business, and they'd worked together for the bulk of Loch's modeling career. He seemed thrilled when she'd called and told him she was ready to come back to work, and he'd started booking shows for her before she'd even decided what date she wanted to start again.

The receptionist knocked lightly on his door and opened it, gesturing for Loch to step in. Loch sank down into the chair across from his desk and put her bag on the floor.

"Hey, Harvey," she said. "Thanks for fitting me in today, I know it's short notice."

Harvey's gaze was locked on her body, and he looked her up and down twice before he shuffled the papers on his desk and looked her in the eyes. "Stand up."

"What?" Loch said. "Why?"

"Just stand up. And take off your jacket."

Loch did as he said, staring at the wall while he scanned her body. It had taken a second to realize, but now the realization of what was happening settled in her stomach like an anchor. He told her she could turn back around, then buzzed his receptionist.

"Christine, can you come in here for a moment?"

Loch set her jaw, avoiding his gaze in the tense silence that followed until Christine knocked lightly on the door and stepped inside the office. She was tiny, with her hair pulled back in a slick bun and cheekbones that made her look like the rest of the Russian models Loch had seen over the years, spare and starving.

"I need you to witness a weigh-in." Harvey walked around his desk to the clinical scales set in the corner of the office and stood beside them. "Loch, whenever you're ready."

He watched her fold her jeans and flannel shirt and place them on the chair. At the last second, she remembered to pull off the beanie she usually kept pulled low on her head when she went out in public. She was seventeen the last time she'd had to weigh in; it was after Christmas, and she'd gained weight without realizing it. She didn't eat for six days, until the scale sank to the correct number. After that, she'd learned to keep her mouth shut at the table, holidays or not.

She stepped onto the scale, staring at the wall in front of her as he nudged it until the bar balanced and settled on a number. Then he pulled the tape measure from his shirt pocket and took her measurements, wrapping the tape around her waist, hips, breasts, and thighs. He noted all the numbers in his computer while she stood and stared out the window, then finally looked up and dismissed Christine. She slipped out and pulled the door shut behind her. Loch got dressed and waited. She knew what he was going to say.

"Loch, you're a professional. We haven't had this problem with you since you were a kid. What the hell were you thinking?"

Loch blinked away the tears she hoped didn't show and met his gaze. "Harvey, my aunt died, and I had to handle her estate. I've had a little more on my mind than my weight."

He sighed and shook his head, handing her a sheet of paper with a long list of dates. "We've worked together for a long time, so I'm going to be straight with you. Those are the bookings we've said yes to for next month, and the first one is in two weeks." He held her gaze. "Do you think you can get your shit together before then?"

"How much do I have to lose?"

"You're five eleven and up to a hundred twenty-one pounds at this point. That means you need to lose nine pounds before that first show." He cleared his throat and slid his glasses off his face, leaning back in his enormous leather office chair and scanning her body again. "You need to be one-twelve. If you miss that number, you can't do the show."

"That's not possible. I can't just stop eating for two weeks."

"Well, you can work," Harvey said, tapping his pen on the top of his desk. "Or you can eat. You decide."

"Can I skip that first show to give me more time?"

He sighed, taking the sheet of paper back and stacking it neatly on the desk. "Loch, that contract includes a spread in *Vogue Paris*, and it's worth over forty thousand dollars. Thirty percent of that is mine. I'll let you answer that question for yourself."

Loch stood, putting her bag back on her shoulder and met his gaze. "I'll take care of it."

"Good girl." Harvey turned back to his computer screen. "Call me when you've lost the weight."

Loch left the office, feeling the pointed stares of the staff as she walked past the front desk and waited in the silent lobby for the elevator to open.

❖

Amir looked across the table at Jason Turner, her lawyer. "Be straight with me." She glanced at her watch, then at the clock on the restaurant wall. "What are our chances in court today?"

Jason shut his laptop and slid it back into his leather bag. "It's the first day of the trial, so chances are it will be primarily jury instructions followed by opening statements, which tend to take a while."

"I know this will be down the line," Amir said. "But you told me to think about whether I wanted to take the stand, and I think I do. I want to be able to look the jury in the eye and tell them I didn't do it."

He shook his head, adjusting his jacket until he had the magazine-perfect ratio of jacket to shirt cuff at his wrist. A pair of sterling cufflinks glinted in the sun coming through the window beside them.

"You know I think you shouldn't testify. But if you decide to, you'll just need to go up there and tell the truth," he said, straightening his tie as he spoke. "And we're going to hope the jury believes you."

Jason Turner was one of the leading defense attorneys in Boston, and as a favor to Hamid, his fraternity brother, he'd agreed to represent Amir. He'd arrived in Bar Harbor the day before for the trial, and since then, he and Amir had been spending a late night preparing for every possible courtroom scenario.

He turned over his coffee cup for the waitress and met Amir's gaze. "I'm not going to lie to you, though. We've got our work cut out for us. I got word early this morning that both the surveillance tape and the photos of her alleged injuries will be allowed in as evidence, as well as your previous conviction. That's a loaded combination."

"Shit." Amir rubbed her temples and tried to stay calm. "That tanks us then, doesn't it? No one will believe me after that. It's like she's got a rock-solid case against me, and not one word of it is actually true. How is that even possible?"

"Listen," Jason said, moving aside his coffee cup to make room for the egg sandwich the waitress placed in front of him. "I've seen shit worse than this turn out okay. All we can do is get in there and kick some ass like we know we're going to win."

Amir shifted in her seat, uncomfortable in her dress shirt without a tie. Jason had suggested when he saw her that morning that she not wear it because it would "make her look too masculine for a woman," whatever that meant. She was a masculine woman. What the hell did that have to do with anything?

She'd asked the question, then wished she hadn't.

"Amir, it's my job to get you out of this situation, so if it were up to me, I'd have you in a dress. The more feminine you look, the less aggressive they'll assume you are." He dropped his voice then and leaned over the table. "Plus, and I realize that this is wrong on a few different levels, men love feminine lesbians, and there are nine men on that jury." He'd paused, looking her straight in the eye. "Lose the tie."

She'd gone back out to her truck and left the tie on the seat with her pride.

❖

But now it was three days into the trial, and Amir's defense was rapidly going downhill. The prosecutor had started her opening statements by saying, "Ladies and gentlemen, this is not the trial of a citizen accused of sexual assault." She'd paused then and turned slowly around to lock gazes with Amir. "This is the trial of a convicted rapist that has now attempted to rape *another* innocent girl. I can only hope you decide to send a message that predatory behavior like this is not acceptable in our community."

It was all Amir could do not to slump down in her chair, although apparently, there were more than a few legal issues at play with that statement, so she had a minute to collect her thoughts after a strenuous objection from Jason ended with discussion at the bench with both lawyers. The judge directed the jury to disregard that portion of the opening statement.

But it had already been said; every one of them looked at her as if they wished they could pull a gun and exact their own justice, and they weren't even past the first three minutes of the trial.

Amir turned around in her seat to see her father walking out of the courtroom and the door slam shut behind him. He hadn't been back. Charlotte's mother sat a few rows behind Amir's mother, stony faced, with her eyes focused straight ahead.

❖

Amir was late to the courthouse the fourth day of the trial, but fortunately, the jury hadn't filed in yet, and she slid into her seat beside Jason in the nick of time. "Sorry I'm late," she said. "I walked out to my truck this morning and someone had slashed my tires. I had to borrow a truck."

Jason only had time to nod in response before it was time for the jury to be ushered in, followed by the judge, who sat behind the bench and took several long moments to polish his glasses before he settled in and directed the prosecution to call its next witness.

"The prosecution calls Miss Charlotte Clancy to the stand, Your Honor."

Everyone turned as Charlotte walked through the doors in the back of the courtroom. She wore a modest white sundress with yellow patent flats and the front layers of her light blond hair pulled back in a gold barrette. She was tan, in subtle makeup, as if she'd stepped out of a Lifetime movie and into the Bar Harbor courtroom. She gave the jury a shy glance as she was sworn in and settled into the witness box, adjusting the microphone down to her level.

"Good morning, Miss Clancy."

The prosecutor, Teresa Grisholm, was a Texas transplant and tough as nails. Everyone in town knew she had a particular fondness for putting away sexual predators, and it was also well known that she'd been practicing law for twenty-three years and had lost only two cases in her entire career. One of those was later retried—she won it. Even Jason had just shaken his head and muttered something about hoping for the best when he'd found out she'd be trying the case.

"We appreciate you being here today, Charlotte," she said. "I know this can't be an easy time for you."

Charlotte looked down and didn't look up again until Ms. Grisholm asked her first question.

"Miss Clancy, can you tell us, in your own words," she paused as she stood and shuffled some papers on her desk. "what happened the day Ms. Farzaneh came over to your house?"

Charlotte shifted in her seat and looked past the prosecutor to her mother, sitting in the front row of the courtroom.

"Um…" Charlotte's voice cracked with her first word, and she took a sip of water with a trembling hand before she went on. "I'd only been home from boarding school for the summer for two weeks, and I was getting ready to go to my tennis lesson that morning."

"Were either of your parents home?"

"No, ma'am, they were both at work."

Ms. Grisholm walked to the front of the counsel desk and leaned back on it. "And were you aware that your father had scheduled Amira Farzaneh to come and fix the back step on your patio that day?"

Charlotte pressed her lips together and looked down. "Yes, ma'am, but I thought she would be working outside on the patio."

"When did you realize Ms. Farzaneh was inside the residence?"

Charlotte didn't answer, and when she finally looked up, it was because the judge had directed her to answer the question. "When she entered my bedroom as I was coming out of the shower."

"And what did you say when she came into your bedroom while you were naked?"

"Objection, Your Honor." Jason stood and looked at the judge. "What the witness was wearing has not been established on the record."

The judge looked at Grisholm and nodded. "Sustained."

"I'll rephrase the question. What were you wearing when the defendant entered your bedroom that morning?"

• 159 •

"I was wearing a towel with nothing underneath."

"Okay," Grisholm continued. "Please tell us what happened then."

"I asked Amira…" Charlotte faltered, glancing for the first time toward the defense table and hesitating before she went on. "Excuse me, I asked Ms. Farzaneh to please leave my room."

Grisholm walked to the jury box and laid one hand on it as she looked up at Charlotte.

"And what was her response?"

Charlotte hesitated, her face slowly turning red as she reached for a tissue from the box on the witness stand. She tangled it into her fist and leaned into the microphone, the first tear slipping down her cheek as she answered.

"She didn't say anything," Charlotte said, focused on the tissue in her hands. "She just pushed me back into the bathroom, locked the door behind her, and told me to drop the towel."

"And what happened next?" Ms. Grisholm looked at the jury as she asked the question, only glancing over at Charlotte when she failed to answer.

"I know this is hard," she said to Charlotte. "But we need to know what happened to you in that bathroom."

Amir had never felt so powerless in her life. She knew when Charlotte answered, the words she spoke would exist forever, and her life would never be the same. And all she could do was sit there and wait for her to say them.

"She walked up and pulled the towel to the floor, touched my breasts, then opened the door and told me to get on the bed."

Amir felt like she was falling, and her hearing faded slowly away. She didn't hear Charlotte tell the jury that she'd refused and Amir had thrown her on the bed, she didn't hear how Charlotte described being penetrated against her will, or the details of the physical attack that followed. All she heard was the static in her own mind, the surreal sound of her life being ripped away from her and shattered at her feet.

Jason leaned over and whispered in Amir's ear. "You're

gripping the table. Put your hands in your lap and keep your face neutral, no matter what she says."

Amir pried her white fingers off the edge of the table and forced them into her lap, but it didn't matter. Her entire world had just spun out of control and out of her reach. Nothing would ever be the same.

## Chapter Twelve

Loch turned up the speed on the treadmill and leaned into her run, sweat dripping into her eyes and blurring her vision. She'd just started her second hour of cardio, and she knew this one had to be more intense, with more incline, if she was going to be able to hit her numbers. She tried to focus on the music streaming through her headphones, and after a few minutes, she just tried to find a spot on the wall to stare at, anything to keep her focused enough to make it through the second hour. If she could get to the end of it, she could rest until her appointment with the trainer that evening.

She'd had seventy calories that morning for breakfast, a hard-boiled egg on her way to the gym, and that night after her training appointment, she'd eat one ounce of baked chicken breast and exactly one-quarter cup of steamed broccoli.

She knew what she had to do. No model with any real experience needed to be told how to uncover their bones. It wasn't discussed, especially not with the press, but her only choice was to have the discipline to hit her numbers. She had to eat no more than three hundred calories in a day and burn thirty-five hundred in the gym. It wasn't easy, but it was her job, and every other model she knew had done the same. She had two weeks to lose nine pounds, and Harvey would need to be able to see the hard lines of her bones before they'd let her step on that runway. The only good thing was that Skye was on a swim tour to several university meets. If she saw what Loch was doing, she'd raise hell, and Loch didn't need that on top of everything else.

The time she'd spent in Innis Harbor had started to seem like a dream. Amir had eventually stopped calling after a few weeks, begging her for the opportunity to explain. In her last call, she said she'd decided to give Loch space. There was a long pause, but when she spoke again, Loch could hear the tears in her voice.

*I miss you more with every breath, baby.* She paused, and Loch heard her take a breath. *Come back to me.*

Loch had listened to it twice, then slid down the wall to the floor. Her apartment turned dark around her as night fell, and she was still there the next morning when the sun rose through her windows in translucent, rose gold sheets. She felt as if someone had sliced the rope that connected her to an anchor she didn't know she had.

She kept waking up in the middle of the night, soaked in sweat from the same nightmare of being adrift on the black surface of the sea in a small wooden dinghy, the only light the undulating, silvered reflection of the moon on the dark water. Then a slowly spinning floodlight from a lighthouse illuminates three other boats, one by one. Her father in one, Samia in the next, and Amir in the third. Amir is calling to her, so she swims to her, but the water becomes harder and harder to move through, and she sinks slowly toward the bottom of the ocean, the wide beam of murky light from the lighthouse growing more and more faint as she sinks toward the darkness.

❖

Loch didn't sleep the night before the show. She hadn't eaten in four days and spent most of the day before in the sauna, sweating out any water weight possible before she had to weigh in. She felt she was right on the line of missing her goal, and she was due backstage at the House of Dior runway show to be weighed in with the other models in one hour. It didn't matter that she'd tried or that her vision had started to go blurry or that her heart had been racing for no reason. The scale didn't lie, and it was the only thing that mattered today.

She showered, then put on some jeans and an Adidas jacket

zipped up to her chin. She didn't bother wearing anything underneath it; once they were backstage, the models were constantly naked or in various stages of undress. Any form of underwear ruined the line of the clothing and how it moved on the body, so everyone wore a skin-tone thong at the very most, but often nothing at all. It was always the same, but even after all this time, sometimes the scene backstage at a show with the naked models holding glasses of champagne or racing from one outfit change to the next seemed surreal.

Loch caught a cab outside her apartment building and gave the driver the address. He managed to get her across town and within a block of the venue, but the deafening Manhattan traffic prevented him from edging any closer. Loch pulled her beanie low on her head and slid on her sunglasses before she got out and walked, using the service entrance at the back of the building to avoid the paparazzi starting to gather outside at the gates.

The show was getting closer to the start time, and the scene backstage was chaos. Someone from the agency recognized her and pushed her gently toward the hair and makeup area, and she sank down into one of the chairs and waited to be called for her weigh-in, her eyes suddenly too heavy to hold open.

❖

It felt as if the trial was dragging on forever. The prosecution called endless witnesses, trauma counselors describing the aftereffects of rape, Charlotte's friends and family describing the myriad ways she'd "changed" after the alleged assault, and law enforcement personnel doing their best to describe the scene they'd been called to.

Finally, after what seemed like weeks, the prosecution rested. It was a Friday afternoon, and the atmosphere in the courtroom was so icy it seemed to splinter with every whisper. Amir hugged her mother goodbye after court and told her she'd be over that night for dinner.

As Amir and Jason walked out into the glare of the sun, she stopped walking and turned to him.

"Tell me the truth." She bit the edge of her lip. "There's no way we can turn this around at this point, is there?"

Jason hesitated, watching the jury members as they filtered down the courthouse steps, squinting in the sun, and scattered.

"I'm going to do my best, but the fact that you have a previous conviction coupled with what's happened in the courtroom so far…" He paused, shrugging off his jacket and folding it over the briefcase in his hand. "I have to be honest. It doesn't look good."

They continued walking until they reached the truck that Amir had borrowed from Chris when she'd realized her truck tires had been slashed. She got in and turned back to face Jason through the open window.

Jason looked Amir in the eyes. "So, I need to tell you that I got a plea deal from the prosecutor today which, frankly, I'm surprised we got at all."

Amir gripped the steering wheel until her knuckles went white. "What is it?"

"Seven years in prison, with eligibility for parole after three, but you'd have to register as a sex offender for the rest of your life." He paused, choosing his words carefully. "At least think about it over the weekend. I'm not telling you to take the deal, but you're facing over twenty years for statutory rape and aggravated assault as it stands now. The judge isn't going to go easy on you with your previous conviction." Jason looked over his shoulder and dropped his voice. "And I wouldn't bet the farm on us coming out of this with an acquittal."

Amir started up the truck and slid on her sunglasses. "I don't need to think about it. I'm not doing time for something that didn't happen."

She started the truck, and Jason stepped back, watching her disappear around the corner toward the cliffs.

❖

Loch stepped onto the scale platform and closed her eyes while one of the model coordinators nudged the lever back and forth until it found a balance. When she opened her eyes, she had a hard time focusing on the tiny white numbers. The coordinator put a check by her name and looked up.

"One hundred and nine pounds," she said, already looking at the model behind her. "You're good, step off."

An assistant handed Loch a bottle of water as she stepped off, and she drank half of it before Anika, a model from Poland she'd worked with in the past, pulled it away.

"How long has it been since you drank anything?"

Loch tried to remember, but the last few days had run together. "A day or two."

"Then don't down that whole thing at once," she said. "You'll be sick."

Loch took it back and tried to sip slowly.

"That's better," Anika said. "It's Loch, right? I've never seen you have to weigh in."

"I've never had to weigh in before a show, but I took some time off and didn't make weight when I came back." Loch lowered the bottle and wiped her mouth, glancing at the set dresser waving her over to the fitting station. "I had to lose it all in about five minutes to stay in the show."

"Yeah, Dior is big. I'm lucky to even be here," Anika said in her clipped Slavic accent. "But eat something after, yeah? You don't look like yourself."

Loch squeezed Anika's sharp shoulder and edged through the increasingly frantic backstage crowd toward the set dresser with short black hair and glasses. She was standing on a stool, models and stylists swirling around her, holding the red silk dress Loch needed for the first pass down the runway. Loch stepped into place, and as it dropped over her head and down her body, it bagged around the hips.

"*Fuck* me," she spat out in a British accent tinged with panic. "I don't have the time to deal with this shit." She dug in her tool belt for her straight pins. "And they've moved you up in the bloody lineup, so you go on in two minutes."

She pulled the long skirt up, turned it inside out, and pinned it underneath to wrap Loch's hips more snugly. The dress was sheer sueded silk meant to flow around her body like water. It was cut to her waist and open in the front, so the sides fluttered open as she walked, revealing the ribs now more pronounced than her breasts. The second the dresser was satisfied, she pointed to the line forming at the back of the runway. She gave Loch's shoulder a shove. "Go, go, *go!*"

Loch ran to the line, where the runway assistant looked at her feet in panic. "Where the *fuck* are your heels?"

"I don't know," Loch said. "They didn't give me any."

"Then fuck it," she said, marking Loch's name off the clipboard in her hand. "Just go like that, and if anyone asks, we intended for you to walk the show barefoot."

She pushed her forward as Loch watched the models lined up in front of her climb the stage stairs and wait for their turn, shaking out their hands to keep them relaxed and dropping all expression from their faces. Loch stepped onto the bottom stair, trying to calm the heart that had started to flutter like a dying bird in the cage of her chest. She'd never let nerves affect her, but the chaos had started to rattle her.

She shook her head to clear it and narrowed her focus as she took the final step up and watched the model in front of her start to walk. When she turned at the end of the runway, Loch stepped onto the stage and focused her gaze at the wall in the back of the room. An explosion of flashbulbs and incessant clicking of cameras seemed to intensify to a blinding level, then fade to black. The last thing Loch heard was slow motion silence shattered by the sharp crack of her head on the runway.

❖

"Welcome back."

Loch opened her eyes and closed them again quickly, listening to the beeps and clicks of the machines around her. Judging by the number of machines she was hooked up to, she was fairly sure that this was not a casual hospital visit.

"How are you feeling?" Skye squeezed her hand and smoothed the hair out of her face. "It's about time you decided to come back."

Loch looked toward the distant skyscrapers visible outside the hospital window, an angular backdrop against the bright orange sunrise. "Why am I here?"

"Because you're an idiot." Skye smiled. "I don't know what the hell you did while I was on that swim tour, but you fell and cracked your head open on the runway at the Dior show."

"I don't even remember being there."

"Yeah," Skye said, stepping back as a nurse came in to check her vitals. "That's not surprising."

"How long have I been out?"

"Long enough for them to do some tests and figure out you've starved yourself so long that your heart muscle has been compromised. You had a heart attack on the runway."

Loch looked at the nurse changing out the bag on her IV stand, who glanced at Skye and nodded.

"When can I go home? I've got shows coming up that I've signed contracts for. I can't just not show up."

Skye looked at the ceiling and shook her head, and when she looked again at Loch, there were tears in her eyes.

"This bullshit stops now." A tear rolled down her cheek, and she brushed it away with her sleeve. "The doctor said you've done so much damage already that if you don't stop, you're in danger of your heart just giving out. You almost *died* out there."

"I know models have died of heart failure before, but they were way skinnier than me."

"No, they weren't." Skye took a deep breath and chose her words carefully. "I'm not saying you have an eating disorder. I've never thought that about you, and I don't now, but this business has twisted your sense of what's safe." She paused. "The doctor said your BMI is fourteen. It's supposed to be around twenty-three. And in case you don't know what that means, it's fucking dangerous. You've been in ICU since last night."

"I was in ICU?"

"Yeah." Skye pulled the scratchy white hospital blanket up to

Loch's shoulders. "They moved you to a regular room when your vitals evened out, but you're in for a shitload of tests in the next day or two to figure out where to go from here." She walked to the window and looked out into the hall. "Mom was on that trip to Napa Valley with her new boyfriend, but I called her this morning, so she'll be here soon."

Loch looked at the ceiling and let out all the air in her lungs. One of the Parisian models died of heart failure after a show last year, but all everyone talked about afterward was how to get around the token monitoring standards that were put in place in the aftermath.

Skye's phone pinged, and she looked at Loch. "I'm going to grab some coffee. It's been a long night. Can I get you anything while I'm down there?"

Loch shook her head and looked back out the window.

"And by 'anything,' I mean chocolate cake, pizza…maybe a burrito the size of your head?"

Loch smiled for the first time. "Don't you dare."

"Great," Skye said, giving her a thumbs-up. "Burrito it is."

Skye squeezed Loch's hand and went out the door. Loch was tired; she couldn't remember ever being this tired or even how to keep her eyes open. When she finally opened them again, the room was flooded with sunlight, and there was someone sitting beside her bed.

"Good morning, beautiful."

It was Amir. She looked worried, her face as creased as her clothes, like she'd been awake all night. Loch reached for her, and Amir held her without a word, then pulled away just enough to hold her face and kiss her gently, her tears falling on Loch's cheeks.

"How did you know?" Loch asked as Amir wiped a tear from her cheek with her thumb and kissed where it had been.

"Skye called me last night, and I got the next flight out. What did the doctor say this morning?"

"I haven't seen him yet, but the nurses told me at some point that my vital signs are almost normal. I'm supposed to be seeing a cardiac specialist today, I think."

"Well, that's something, I guess." Amir's brows pushed together, and Loch saw the stress lines on her face. "You nearly gave *me* a heart attack. I've never been so worried in my life."

Loch noticed the tie slung over the back of the chair Amir had been sitting in and her rumpled but obviously expensive dress shirt and pants. "Not that I don't appreciate the effort," she said, checking Amir out with the start of a smile. "But even in Manhattan, the dress code for most hospitals isn't quite this formal."

"Ahh, cracking jokes again, are we?" Amir kissed her forehead and winked. "I'm so happy to see you that I'm going to let you have that one."

Loch scooted over in bed and nodded toward the space. Amir sat carefully beside her and pulled her into her arms, or at least as much as she could with all the monitors Loch was hooked up to.

"So," Loch said. "You still haven't told me. What's with the butch prom dress?"

Amir laughed. "I was on my way home from court yesterday when I got the call from your sister. It took some string pulling, but the judge finally let me leave the state. I have to be back on Monday at nine a.m."

Loch shook her head. Her memories of everything seemed to be splintered since she'd woken up. "Why were you at court?"

Suddenly, it all came flooding back to Loch at once, the rape charges, the arrest, and the sudden crushing weight of the realization that the person she'd fallen in love with was not the woman she appeared to be.

She looked into Amir's eyes. "I'm in love with you, so I need to know the truth, Amir. All of it, even if it's ugly."

"I'm in love with you, too." Amir traced Loch's cheek with her thumb. "You've deserved to hear the truth about everything for a long time, and I'll tell you everything if you'll let me."

Skye suddenly threw open the hospital room door with her foot, balancing an enormous cinnamon roll and two giant coffees in her hands. A king size Snickers bar dangled from her front pocket for just a moment before it plunged to the floor with a thud.

"No...really." She shifted the cinnamon roll toward her body to keep it from sliding off the plate. "You two just sit there and keep canoodling. I've obviously got this." A second thud revealed the hidden packet of Skittles in her back pocket. Amir jumped up and grabbed the coffees, trying not to laugh, and set the cinnamon roll on a tray table beside Loch.

"I love cinnamon rolls," Loch said, swiping at some of the overflow frosting on the plate.

"Exactly my plan." Skye tossed the candy bar to Amir and tucked the Skittles back into her pocket. "And now that I see you're in capable hands, I'm going down to the cafeteria to meet my girlfriend for lunch."

"Hold up." Amir looked at Loch, wondering if she'd heard Skye wrong. "Girlfriend? How did that happen?"

Skye shook her head and looked at them with a slightly puzzled expression. "For a couple of gold star lesbians, you both seem to be fuzzy on the concept of how this stuff actually works." She smiled, leaning out the door and peering down the hall. "She's here, so I'm off. And I want to know what the doctor said when I get back, so pay attention!"

Loch laughed and just managed to get out a sentence before Skye disappeared out the door. "Tell her I want to meet her!"

Skye stopped in her tracks and stuck her head back in the door. "Fine, but I'm telling her I'm related to Amir. No offense, but this relationship is a little too new to introduce her to my supermodel sister."

"Hey!" Amir said as she disappeared down the hall. "I could totally be a supermodel!" They listened to Skye's laugh disappear down the hall, and Amir turned back to Loch.

"Okay." Amir squeezed Loch's hand. "Ask me anything."

Loch waited as a nurse came in at that moment, changed her IV bag, and checked the readings on the machines. She finally left the room quietly and shut the door behind her.

"I need to know the truth about your previous conviction for rape."

"First of all," Amir said, taking a deep breath and letting it out slowly. "I was charged with statutory rape, and it happened when I was in high school. I had no idea something like that even existed. It blew up my life completely."

"So, that was fourteen years ago?"

Amir nodded. "I was a junior in high school, and my girlfriend was a sophomore."

Loch let Amir's words sink in. The fact that the legal issue was age, not consent, hadn't occurred to her. The word "rape" was so horrible that she'd just tried not to think about it at all.

"I'm so sorry, Amir, that must have been awful for both of you," Loch said, tangling her fingers into Amir's. "What happened?"

"Her name was Elizabeth, and we'd been dating secretly for over a year. Her dad was a lawyer and active in Innis Harbor politics. They were super conservative, so coming out as a couple just wasn't an option."

Loch nodded and pulled at a corner of the tape holding the IV on the back of her hand until Amir put her hand over hers.

"I'm just loosening it," Loch said, her bottom lip making an appearance in a near pout. "It's itchy."

"Tough." Amir lifted her hand and kissed it. "We'll get them to look at it next time they come in, but leave it for now. You getting better is the only thing that matters, itchy tape or no itchy tape."

Loch smiled and smoothed the edges back down. "So, how did they find out?"

Amir sat back in her chair, rubbing the back of her neck with her hand. "Her father came home early from work one day and caught us in bed together. He shoved me out the door naked and threw my clothes on the lawn after me. The police came to my house later that night."

"Amir, I'm so sorry," Loch said. "Did you have any idea that law even existed? I wouldn't have when I was in high school."

"I didn't have a clue. Now they have what they call a Romeo and Juliet clause that provides an exception if the individuals are within five years of each other in age. We were just eighteen months apart. But back then, there was nothing like that. Elizabeth was technically underage in Maine, and I wasn't, so her father made sure I was arrested for statutory rape."

"Did you have to go to trial?"

"Somehow, I managed to just get probation, but I had to register as a sex offender for the next ten years. Elizabeth told everyone who'd listen that it was consensual, but after that, I barely graduated high school, and I got beat up like every other day. My dad didn't talk to me for over a year."

"I'm so sorry." Loch lay back against her pillow and stared at the ceiling. "Why didn't I just let you explain?"

"Loch," Amir said, "I don't blame you. Anyone would have thought the same thing. And if I had told you sooner, this wouldn't have happened at all."

❖

Later that morning, Loch's doctor came in to go over the results of her preliminary tests.

Loch had been a patient of Dr. Benidorm since she was a child. He was shaped like a beanbag, wore a white lab coat three sizes too big, and was constantly pushing up the sleeves to be able to write. His belly stuck out of the coat farther than his legs, but in fairness to his skills, he was the undisputed master of the comb-over.

"Loch," he said, pausing as he turned over the first page on his clipboard. "I've gotten the results back from the tests we've done so far, and it looks like you may have somehow dodged a bullet. Your heart muscle has been compromised because of your severe calorie restriction, but your heart attack was mild, and there doesn't seem to be anything at play here that can't be reversed."

"Great. How soon can I go back to work?"

"That said…" He drew out the words and peered at her over his glasses. "I need to talk to you about whether we need to get a psych evaluation here. We've talked about and monitored your BMI for years, but this is a new low, and you're on the way to doing some serious, irreversible damage to your organs if you don't knock it off."

Loch met his gaze. "I don't need a psych evaluation, Dr. Benidorm, I promise." His gaze didn't waver as he waited for her to go on.

"I hate having to be this skinny." She paused, balling up the edge of the sheet in her hand. "I hate what it takes to get this thin. I took some time off recently and gained weight, so I had a lot to lose in a short amount of time." She glanced up at Amir, who raised an eyebrow and said nothing. "I just took it too far without realizing it."

"I'll tell you what," he said, making a note on her chart. "I know your job requires you to be thin, but you're emaciated, and it's affecting your health. I'll let you off this time without calling in the shrinks, but I want you to come into the office and weigh in every month for six months. I need you to have a BMI of over nineteen in three months."

"I have to weigh in at work, too. They want to see under fifteen."

"Loch, I've known you and your family a long time." He paused and touched her hand. "You've been working yourself to death since you were a kid. Maybe it's time to slow down and breathe."

Loch's eyes filled with tears and she nodded.

"I'll leave it with you, but I'm going to call you personally if I don't get those monthly reports. I know you travel for work, but you can have any doctor's office call me with the results, okay?"

Dr. Benidorm's pager went off, and he quickly finished up with a promise to release her the next day and scurried out, leaving the room suddenly quiet.

"How do you feel about what he said?"

"I don't know," Loch replied. "I feel torn, I guess, like every choice I make is wrong for someone."

At the sound of a ringtone, Amir pulled Loch's phone from her pocket. "Your sister gave me this when you were still asleep."

"Great." Loch was instantly nervous and stared at the flashing screen. "It's Harvey Goldberg, my agent."

She hit the speaker phone icon and waited.

"Loch?" His voice was rushed, and Loch heard papers being shuffled on his desk as he spoke. "I heard what happened. How are you doing?"

"I'm still in the hospital." Loch picked at the tape on the back of her hand. "The doctor thinks I—"

"I've seen this before," Harvey said. "And you should be out in no time. You have that shoot for Lancôme coming up in three days. It was on that list I gave you when you were in the office the last time."

"I don't think I'm going to be able to do that, Harvey. I'm not even home yet, and I'm sure I'll have doctor's orders to rest."

There was a long pause, then Harvey spoke again, his words slow and deliberate. "I understand that you think you need to rest, but you have contracts going through the end of the year that you can't just pull out of like you did last time." He paused, letting his words sink in. "I'm not doing that for you again."

Amir shook her head and walked over to the window, trying to keep her composure and let Loch handle it.

"Actually, I don't have even one signed contract," Loch said, her neck painting itself with red splotches of anger. Her voice was low and controlled. "*You* have contracts. You were so concerned about weighing me when I came into your office that you never gave them to me to sign. I'm not legally obligated to do anything for anyone at this point."

There was a long silence on the other end of the line.

"Loch, you need to pull your head out of your ass. It's like you're *trying* to flush your career down the toilet."

Loch closed her eyes and took a breath, the red patches slowly rising from her neck to her face. Amir came back over and stood beside her, her gaze on the heart monitor that was suddenly beeping much more rapidly.

"Do they have you on an IV drip?" Harvey asked.

Loch paused, looking at Amir in confusion. "Yes…why?"

"What do you mean, 'why'?" He didn't try to hide the frustration in his voice. "Look at the writing on the bag, can you see it?"

"I can." She glanced above her head at the IV stand. "I think it just lists what's in it."

"Read it carefully. Take it down if you have to. Does it say it contains glucose or any other form of sugar?" He paused, then went on when she didn't answer. "If it does, take your IV out *now*. You can't afford the calories."

"Harvey," Loch said as she wove her fingers into Amir's, "go fuck yourself."

## Chapter Thirteen

Monday morning, Amir shifted in her seat behind the defense table, bracing herself for the next day of Charlotte's testimony. It was small comfort, but at least it was the defense's turn for rebuttal.

Jason started with some easy questions about school and Charlotte's plans for the summer. Charlotte looked cool and confident in white skinny jeans and a chambray shirt, her blond hair pulled back into a sleek ponytail and the courtroom lights glinting off her candy pink lip gloss.

"Is it true that your parents have known the Farzaneh family for several years?"

"Yes," Charlotte said, glancing over at the jury. "My dad and Amir's father have bought and sold a few houses together. I've known the Farzanehs since I was in middle school."

"And did you know that Amir Farzaneh was coming over to do some repairs on your family's home the morning that the alleged incident occurred?"

"Yes," Charlotte said. "My dad told me she would be working outside on the back deck, so I was surprised to see her in my room when I came out of the shower."

"Did she tell you what she was doing there?"

"She said she was there to fix something in the bathroom, but I asked her to leave so I could get dressed."

Jason walked to the front of the defense table and looked Charlotte in the eyes. "And what happened next?"

"Objection!" Charlotte's attorney stood and addressed the

judge. "Is it really necessary to make this young girl go through the details of this brutal attack again?"

The judge overruled, saying that the defense had the right to ask a witness about her previous testimony in detail, and Charlotte's attorney reluctantly sat back down, glaring at Jason from the prosecution table.

"I was afraid of her. She's as tall as a guy and bigger than me." Charlotte's voice shook as she visibly recalled the memory. "So, when she came into the bedroom and told me to get on the bed, I did."

Jason walked back around to the defense table and looked through the transcripts of her previous testimony.

"Let me make sure I have this right." He paused, highlighting a passage on the transcript before he looked back up at Charlotte. "Amir refused to leave your room, then told you to get on the bed where you say she attacked you?"

"That's right." Charlotte's voice was faint, and she pulled a tissue out of the box on the witness stand.

"Then why did you say Friday in court that she pushed you into the bathroom and locked the door behind her when she came into the room?"

"I didn't!" Charlotte faltered, then clarified when Jason showed her the highlighted passage. "That's right, I forgot. She did push me into the bathroom and rip my towel off me." She paused, her voice dropping to almost a whisper. "It just all happened so fast. It seems like this really horrible blur."

"But is it still your assertion today that the defendant forced herself on you that morning in your room?" Jason walked to the witness box and met Charlotte's gaze. "Or are those details fuzzy now, too?"

Charlotte straightened her shoulders and spoke clearly. "There is nothing fuzzy about my recollection of being attacked." Her voice cracked, and she looked toward the jury. "It's hard to forget something that ruined your life."

Jason walked over to the jury box and ran his hand over the railing, his face composed and thoughtful.

"One more thing," he said slowly. "You're the president of the drama club at your boarding school, are you not?"

The prosecutor objected, and Jason withdrew the question, giving Charlotte, then the jury a pointed look as the court broke for a recess.

"That was good, right?" Amir whispered as Jason stacked his files and put them back in the briefcase.

"That was a drop in the bucket." Jason met Amir's gaze and flipped the metal clasps shut on his briefcase with an audible snap. "What we need is an open tap."

❖

Amir was on her way to her truck that evening when she got a call from Hamid.

"Hey, brother, what's up?"

"What are you doing tonight?" Hamid said over the kids playing in the background. "We're grilling out if you want to come over. The little beasts have friends over, and they've already eaten, but Anna and I haven't had the chance."

He paused, and Amir held the phone away from her ear while he yelled for Hameen to stop running on the patio.

"Sorry about that," he said, coming back to the phone. "I have some of your grass dogs, so I can throw those on now. They take about an hour to grill, right? Just leave them on there till they're shriveled up and black?"

"Try three minutes, asshole," Amir said affectionately. "And turn them this time. I've got some news anyway, so that'd be great. I can head over now."

"Oh, and Kiran called this morning to ask if you were going to be there for some reason, so brace yourself. She's been acting squirrelly lately."

"What's wrong with her?"

"Nothing really, just being moody. She's not talking much lately, and I think she might be getting some flak about the trial at school."

"Shit, that's all she needs." Amir pulled out of the parking lot and headed toward Hamid's house. "Okay, I'll see you in a few minutes."

❖

An hour later, Amir had rescued her veggie dogs in the nick of time, and they sat to eat on the back patio, surrounded by beer, drippy bottles of mustard and ketchup, and the half-eaten strawberry cupcakes the kids had abandoned when the backyard sprinklers came on. The yard had just been mowed, so the scent of summer—fresh air and cut grass—drifted in with the late afternoon sun.

"So," Anna said, pouring a lake of ruffled barbecue chips onto Amir's plate. "How are you holding up? Anyone I need to beat up for you?"

"I'm hanging in there." Amir looked up and smiled, reaching over and finishing one of the abandoned strawberry cupcakes in one bite. "But it does make it easier that Loch and I are back together."

"What?" Hamid broke into a wide grin, and he shoved her playfully on the shoulder. "I knew it! When did that happen?"

"I'll let her tell you the whole story, but she had some stuff going on, so somehow Jason got the judge to sign off on letting me leave the state, and I flew to Manhattan over the weekend."

"It's about time you got your ass to New York." Anna pulled her into a hug and raised an eyebrow at Hamid. "Have you two learned nothing from romantic comedies we make you watch? I knew she'd understand if you just got the chance to explain."

Hamid shook his head as he counted the kids jumping through the sprinklers. "Anna, how many are we supposed to have out there?"

Anna looked over her shoulders at Hameen chasing his buddies with the garden hose. "Seven."

"Seriously? Because there's only five out there counting the ones we can't give back."

"That's close enough." Anna flashed a smile and rolled her

eyes in his direction. "I'm kidding. Yasmin and her friend went in to play house a few minutes ago."

"God, woman, sometimes I think you want me to die of a heart attack." He leaned over and pulled her to him on the bench, kissing her cheek.

"Anyway," Hamid said, picking up his beer, "what I can't figure out is why this Charlotte chick is lying about this." He dipped his chip into Anna's onion dip. "It just doesn't make any sense. Is she that desperate for attention?"

"I don't know, but I feel like the whole town looks at me differently." Amir reached out and caught a ball flying toward the table with one hand and tossed it back to Hameen. "I feel them staring me down everywhere I go, and I can't say I blame them."

Anna's phone pinged, and she picked it up and read a text, smacking Hamid's hand when he reached for her onion dip again. "Hey, Kiran and her girlfriend are on their way over. And evidently," she looked up at Amir, "you're not supposed to leave until they get here."

"Oh, good, I still haven't met her girlfriend." Amir finished the last of her beer and tossed the can into the recycling bin. "How do you like her?"

"She's a sweetheart," Anna said. "And she loves Kiran to bits. They're adorable."

A few minutes later, they heard the front door open, and Kiran and Amy came out to the back deck, holding hands. Anna introduced Amy to Amir and asked the girls if they wanted to stay for dinner.

"Yeah, you're gonna have to beat off the crowd trying to get to Amir's fake hot dogs, though," Hamid interrupted, talking around the huge bite of hot dog in his mouth. "Those things are just flyin' off the grill. Everybody wants 'em."

Kiran laughed, and she and Amy settled into chairs across the table from Amir, then Amy pulled her iPad out of her backpack and set it up in the middle of the table where everyone could see it. There was an undercurrent of nervous energy that Amir couldn't quite put her finger on.

"What's going on?" Anna popped open a couple of grape sodas and passed them down to the girls. "Please tell me this isn't another video of the kids stacking chairs on top of each other to reach the Oreos in the kitchen."

"No," Kiran said. "Those are gone, I ate those last week." She looked at Amir and smiled as she pressed play. "Trust me. This is way better than Oreos."

❖

Loch got out of the Bar Harbor taxi and crossed the street toward the courthouse in the blinding morning sun. She checked that her sunglasses were still on her face for the fifth time and scanned the courthouse steps for any sign of photographers, but she seemed to be in the clear for once. She wore pale blue skinny jeans, her black leather boots, a white button-up, and a shrunken blazer with the sleeves rolled up. She'd tried on several outfits that morning but had just taken a random guess in the end. With any luck, no one would know who she was anyway. The last thing Amir needed was more attention focused on the trial.

Once word had gotten out that she'd retired from modeling, Loch's phone had been ringing constantly with requests for interviews, the gossip blogs were ablaze with speculation about her health, and there always seemed to be paparazzi lurking outside her apartment building. It wasn't just that she'd decided to retire from modeling, it was the incident at the fashion show that had people in the industry insanely curious. Everyone wanted the scoop, but so far, Loch hadn't said a word about it to anyone, which only served to amp up the speculation.

Loch sat on the courthouse steps and pulled off her beanie, letting the warmth of the sun sink through the layers of her hair. Since the day people started to recognize her on the street, she'd worn a hat wherever she went, but it occurred to her now that outside of Manhattan, at least, she didn't need to bother. Soon people wouldn't care who she was anymore, and thankfully, it seemed that day had already come in Bar Harbor, Maine.

"Loch!"

Loch turned to see Amir striding up the courthouse steps toward her with a well-dressed man carrying a briefcase that Loch assumed must be her lawyer. Amir picked Loch up when she reached her and swung her around, breathing in the warm scent of her skin as she set her back down on the steps.

"Why didn't you tell me you were coming?" Amir smiled as she ran her fingers through Loch's bare layers of hair. "And you look like you're dressed for court. Why in the world would you want to go in there?"

"What, like I'd let you do this alone?" Loch said, smiling back. "No chance. They finally sprung me from the hospital, and I took the next flight out."

Amir suddenly remembered that Loch and Jason hadn't met.

"Jason, this is Loch Battersby, my girlfriend," she said. "And, Loch, this is my lawyer, Jason Turner."

Jason smiled and held out his hand. "I've heard a lot about you, Loch. It's great to meet you. My girlfriend is a photographer, so she's a big fan. I'll have to tell her I met you."

Loch offered to take a selfie for her, and Jason put his arm around her and pulled Amir into the picture, too.

"Thanks. That's going to be a huge deal to her." He slipped his phone back into his pocket and looked at his watch. "I'm going to go in and set up. We should be starting within five minutes or so. Take your time."

Amir assured him she'd be right in and turned back to Loch, tipping her chin up with a finger and kissing her.

"Thank you for coming, babe," Amir said. "Although I know this can't be a picnic for you. I wish it wasn't happening, but I'm so happy to see you."

"You look a little better," Loch said as she moved to the side to make room as a throng of people shuffled up the steps to the courthouse doors. "Did you get some sleep?"

"I should have, but I think I might have forgotten how to do that at this point."

Loch cocked her head and squinted up at Amir in the sunlight.

Her eyes were tired, and she still looked pale, as if she'd stayed up pacing the room all night.

Loch took her hand, and they hurried up the court steps and through the security check, then quietly through the double doors of the courtroom. Amir kissed Loch's cheek and made sure she had a seat before she slid into her chair behind the defense table.

As the jury filed in and the gallery rose for the judge to enter, Loch recognized Mrs. Farzaneh in the second row. She was sitting by herself. The courtroom seemed divided. Most of the spectators sat behind the prosecution table on the left side of the room, and just a handful were scattered in the rows behind Amir on the right. Mrs. Farzaneh was the only person in her row, and she looked smaller than Loch remembered, even with the sky blue headscarf covering her hair. Before she had a chance to talk herself out of it, Loch walked to the front and slipped into her row.

"Mrs. Farzaneh?" she whispered, settling into the seat beside her as the bailiff called the court to order. "Do you mind if I join you?"

Mrs. Farzaneh smiled, then squeezed Loch's hand and leaned into her shoulder. "I'd like nothing better." She let out a breath as her shoulders relaxed a bit.

After calling court into session, the judge asked the defense to call its witness.

Jason stood immediately and asked to approach the bench. Both lawyers spoke in hushed tones to the judge for so long that even the jury was whispering about the delay. Of course no one could hear what Jason was saying, but whatever it was, the judge thought for a few seconds when he was done before he nodded to Jason and spoke again to the two lawyers. When they both took their seats, the prosecutor instantly bent her head and conferred with the rest of her team at the table.

Jason stood, glancing behind him on the opposite side of the courtroom. "The defense calls Charlotte Clancy."

Loch knew this had to be the girl who had accused Amir of assaulting her, but it was the first time she'd gotten a look at her. Charlotte slid out of the row of people and walked confidently to the witness box. She looked like an affluent, entitled teenager, so no surprises there. Loch had met a few in her line of work.

"Ms. Clancy," Jason said after she had taken her seat. "Do you remember what we were talking about when we left off yesterday?"

"Yes," Charlotte said in a softer voice than Loch expected. "I was going over the details of my assault for you." She paused. "Again."

"Let's just recap for the jury," Jason said. "You testified that the defendant, Amir Farzaneh, entered your room uninvited on the morning of the incident and assaulted you on the bed, is that right?"

"Yes."

"Or was it that she first assaulted you in the bathroom?" Jason continued, tapping his pen lightly on the surface of the jury box. "You seemed confused on the specifics the last time we spoke."

The judge leaned over and said something to Jason that Loch didn't hear.

"I'll rephrase the question." Jason directed his attention back to Charlotte. "Is it your testimony that Amir Farzaneh held you against your will in the bathroom on the morning in question?"

Charlotte shifted in her seat. "Yes, it is."

"And is it also your testimony that she then forced you to submit to sexual activity on the bed even after you'd asked her repeatedly to stop?"

"Yes," Charlotte said, looking down at her hands. "And then she physically assaulted me when I resisted."

Jason walked back to the defense table and held up the eight-by-ten glossy photograph of Charlotte's injuries. "And is this the result of that attack?"

Charlotte's eyes filled with tears, and she turned her head away from the photo as it was passed from person to person on the jury.

Loch tensed in her seat. She knew Amir's lawyer must have a plan for this line of questioning, but two of the jurors winced when the photograph of Charlotte's injuries was shown again.

Jason nodded to the bailiff, who rolled in a TV screen and powered it up, plugging it into the laptop Jason handed him. It was a big enough screen for all the jury and some of the people in the gallery to see it clearly, and those who couldn't shifted in their seats to get the best view possible.

"Ms. Clancy, you're familiar with the security footage obtained from inside your home on the morning the alleged attack occurred?"

Charlotte looked confused, then shook her head.

"You weren't aware that we had obtained that footage?"

"I didn't even know that Dad's system still worked," Charlotte said, her voice even and calm. "I never thought about it. But if you do have that tape, you'll see Amir entering my room that morning."

"You're right, that's exactly what it shows." Jason walked back to the table and chose two more photos from a folder. "But it also shows you exiting the room a few minutes after Ms. Farzaneh left."

"So?" Charlotte said, her patience starting to thin. "Why is that important? Of course I left my room. I went downstairs to call my mother and tell her what had happened."

Jason pressed play on the laptop, and the black and white image of the empty hall outside Charlotte's bedroom filled the screen. Amir exited the room, and a few seconds later, Charlotte walked out and turned the corner toward the stairs. Jason stopped the tape.

"Now I know this tape is difficult to see in detail," he said to the jury. "So, we had an expert enhance some still images for you."

He walked over to the jury box and handed the first juror the set of two photos. He waited while each juror looked at them carefully, then handed the photos to the judge.

"Those photos side by side might raise some questions for you," Jason said. "I know they did for me when I first saw them."

Loch watched as three of the jurors nodded, and one more asked to see the first picture, as well as the last two, and held them side by side.

"In the first picture, we see the serious injuries that Ms. Clancy testified that she sustained as a result of resisting Ms. Farzaneh's advances." Jason looked away from the jury and into Charlotte's eyes as he continued. "The troubling part is that in the second pictures, pulled from the video of her exiting the room after the alleged incident occurred, there are no injuries."

Jason turned back to the jury. "The image, which Ms. Clancy

herself has told us was taken just after the alleged attack, shows no injuries." He paused for a moment and locked gazes with Charlotte. "There are no visible injuries because there was never an attack, isn't that right?"

The prosecution objected, which the judge reluctantly sustained, reminding Jason to let the jury draw its own conclusions.

Jason nodded. "I think we'll just let the next video take it from here."

Charlotte looked uncomfortable and looked at the prosecutor, who shook her head with a barely perceptible shrug.

"Before I start this tape, Ms. Clancy," Jason said, his gaze locked on the jury, "is there anything about the testimony you've provided under oath that's untruthful?"

"Of course not," Charlotte said. "I was assaulted by Amir Farzaneh." She turned and looked at the jury, tears shimmering in her eyes. "And it was the scariest experience of my life." The judge nodded to the bailiff to turn down the lights, and Jason pressed play.

The video started, and it was clear to Loch that it had been filmed in the diner at Innis Harbor. There was a lot of restaurant background noise, but when a blond girl leaned slightly into the frame, Loch recognized her as Kiran's girlfriend Amy from the picture she'd shown them that day in the high school parking lot. Amy leaned away from the camera and started to speak to someone else at the table.

"So," Amy said, her voice clear despite the background noise. "How much are you getting?"

"Not enough," another feminine voice out of range of the camera said. "This is becoming a huge pain in my ass. I never signed up to play Little Miss Innocent in court. It's, like, taking over my life or something."

Loch heard a sharp intake of breath from Mrs. Farzaneh, and there was a low murmur in the courtroom as the video played on.

"I know," Amy said, her voice tinged with the sarcastic knife edge only a teenage girl can wield. "You'd think they'd just arrest her and throw the book at her or something. How is she not still in jail?"

Loch's mouth dropped open, but she kept her gaze on the video that showed only half of Amy's face and the surface of a diner table at a slightly skewed angle. When she finally looked up, she saw Charlotte staring intensely at the prosecutor and mouthing, *That isn't me.*

"But whatever," Amy's voice continued off camera. "When you told me you made the whole thing up, I thought you were crazy, but if they're giving you enough money, who cares about a couple days in court?"

"Will you shut *up*?" the voice across the table from Amy hissed. "There's always somebody listening in this town, and I just have to pull this off before someone figures it out. I swear my mom already thinks something's up. I guess she and Amir's mom are friends or something."

The prosecutor sat back in her chair and shook her head, her jaw tense and set.

"Okay, sorry," Amy said as the video continued. She stirred sugar into her iced tea, the clink of the ice cubes in the audio magnified in the silent courtroom. She dropped her voice to ask the next question, but the words were still clear. "How do you know the guy is even going to pay you, though? When do you get the money?"

"I got half when I agreed to do it and smashed that step out back. I knew Dad would call her to come over and fix it. And I'm supposed to get the rest when it's all over, but I don't know if I'm actually going to see it. The guy hasn't been returning my calls for a week."

Charlotte stood and started to leave the witness stand.

"Ms. Clancy," the judge said after the video had been stopped. "You'll stay on the witness stand until I excuse you."

"I don't have to listen to these lies," Charlotte said, her words tense and staccato, with an edge like torn metal. "I don't know who that girl in the video hired to make this up and pretend to be me, but I never said any of this."

The judge cut her off. "Young lady, sit down. Now."

Charlotte reluctantly took her seat.

When the video started again, there was another exchange between the girls that was drowned out by what sounded like a truck passing by a window, then Amy's voice was suddenly audible again.

"How did this person even ask you to do this?" she said. "I mean, you don't just walk up to random people and ask them to frame someone for trying to rape you or whatever."

"It doesn't matter," Charlotte said, her voice low and annoyed. "The only thing that matters is that I wrap this the fuck up and get back to the pool. I'm getting seriously pale from all this drama."

There was an audible gasp from the courtroom, and Loch felt Mrs. Farzaneh's hand over hers.

The sound on the tape was muddled for a few seconds as Amy unexpectedly picked it up and angled the camera at Charlotte's face.

"Just checking to see if my mom finally stopped texting," Amy said as she put the phone back down and Charlotte disappeared from the screen. "She's such a bitch sometimes."

The courtroom fell silent as the girls gossiped about other people for a few minutes on the video until Amy finally turned the subject back to Amir.

"At least your face looks better finally," she said to Charlotte. "How did you manage to make it look like that, anyway? Beat yourself up?"

There was a pause, then Charlotte's voice dropped to a whisper. "It's amazing what you can do when you're thinking about all the stilettos five thousand dollars will buy."

## Chapter Fourteen

After the video clicked off, it didn't take the prosecutor long to decide to drop the charges against Amir, and the judge even apologized to Amir on the court's behalf before he told her she was free to go.

Amir had known before court that morning that the charges would probably be dropped given the video, but it was still surreal to think that if that video hadn't been filmed, she could have been hours away from prison. The person who framed her had to have known about her conviction for statutory rape; without that knowledge, the accusation would have been too flimsy to stick. She'd stayed up nights sifting through the people she knew who might have a motive to ruin her life but hadn't come up with even one possibility. She knew now she'd have to find a way to let this whole experience go, but without knowing why it had happened, she couldn't shake the feeling that it might happen again.

Later that evening, everyone gathered on the dock behind Amir's house to celebrate. When Hamid pulled up with his family, Hameen got out of the truck proudly carrying a stack of pizza boxes taller than his sister, and they ate at the end of the dock, their feet dangling in the water while they watched the sun sift through the clouds and slowly sink behind the cliffs. Amy and Kiran supervised the younger kids with the sparklers Anna had brought, then they joined the adults as the sky shifted from blue to fiery oranges and pink as the sun sank behind the cliffs in the distance.

Loch looked over at Amy. "I've been wanting to ask you this since I saw the video. Did you pick up your phone near the end just to get Charlotte's face on camera?"

"Yep," Amy said with a slow smile. "I didn't want her to be able to say later that it wasn't her."

"Smart," Loch said. "She tried to say that before the tape was even finished."

Amir smiled, flipping the top off a beer and handing it to Hamid. "We didn't hear much from her once the camera showed her face, though."

Loch shook her head. "Well, I think Amy's a genius. I wouldn't have even thought about that."

"What I want to know," Hamid said, folding an entire slice of pizza into his mouth, "is who paid Charlotte to accuse Amir in the first place."

"That's what I was saying the other day. I can't think of anyone in town that has ever even disliked you," Anna said, handing Hamid a napkin. "Why would someone go to all that trouble and expense? It just doesn't make sense."

"I guess we'll never know now," Amir said. "Unless they can pry it out of Charlotte."

"Did Jason say they're bringing charges against her?" Loch asked.

"He said they're getting the charges together now, and there's a list." Amir raised an eyebrow and looked at Amy. "She won't be getting to the pool anytime soon, let's just put it like that."

There was a pause in the conversation while Anna opened more juice boxes for the kids, and Amir tried again to think of a way to thank Amy and Kiran, but she knew if she even tried to say something now, she might tear up.

Anna looked at Amir, then back at the girls. "I know you're staying with us this weekend, Kiran," she said. "But what's Amy's curfew on Friday nights?"

"Midnight." They said it together, then Amy added, "We've come close a few times, so we try to keep track better now."

"Well," Anna said. "This Friday night, we're buying you guys dinner, anywhere you want to go, and Hamid has volunteered to be your personal chauffeur until midnight."

"I'll happily drive your little bad asses around all damn night," he said with a wide smile. "You just saved my sister's ass. I'm at your service. I'll even wear a little hat and everything."

He made an exaggerated bow, and the girls giggled while Amir got up and came around the table, pulling both of them into a hug.

"Thank you doesn't seem like enough," Amir said, trying to talk around the lump in her throat.

"Whose idea was this, anyway?" Hamid asked.

"It was Kiran's, actually," Amy said. "I never would have thought to even ask Charlotte about it without her suggesting it. She said she owed someone a favor or something."

Loch smiled and locked gazes with Kiran for a long moment before she silently bumped Kiran's fist with hers.

❖

The next day, Loch walked back to Samia's house for the first time while Amir was fielding calls from clients trying to get their projects back on her schedule. Word that Amir had been cleared had gotten around Innis Harbor pretty quickly, and it seemed like the whole town suddenly had something they needed done.

As Loch climbed the hill toward the house, she noticed right away that something was different. The dangling shutter on the second level had been replaced, the graying cedar shingles had been freshly stained, and the door had even been painted a brilliant cherry red with a shiny brass door knocker in the center. The trim was a sunny, bright white, and even the lawn had been shaped and freshly mowed. She paused before she turned the key in the door and remembered the same moment a few weeks before when she'd done the same thing after arriving in Innis Harbor. It seemed like a lifetime ago now. This time, she didn't hesitate. She took a deep breath and stepped in.

The scent of fresh paint lingered in the air, and as she walked around the house, she realized that every room had been painted exactly how Loch and Skye had described to the crew the day Amir was arrested. Soft tones of earth and sky blended into one another as she walked from room to room, melding into a calming, serene palette. The wood trim on the doorframes and windows had been sanded and varnished to a high gloss; even the baseboards looked perfect. Loch walked through the upstairs, peering into the rooms that she remembered playing in as a child but now also looked brand new and full of possibilities, like a color picture superimposed on black and white.

When she got to her bedroom, she pulled the dust cover off the only piece of furniture left in the house, Samia's cherrywood sleigh bed that had once belonged to Loch's great-grandmother. She'd always loved this room. Expansive bay windows looked out over the sea, and a bathroom with an old clawfoot tub and wooden floors connected it to the bedroom and the walk-in closet. As she turned around in it now, she realized how much her heart had healed. She felt balance now, between her memories and her future. It would always be Samia's house, but now it felt like hers, too.

She'd assumed that when she flew back to New York, Amir would pull her crew and leave the house the way it was, but she'd done the opposite. She'd made sure everything was finished exactly how Loch had described and had even gone beyond that to refinish the hardwood floors, update the light fixtures, and replace the hardware on the cabinets and drawers to a more modern silver tone with a brushed satin finish.

Loch came back downstairs and tried to imagine the furniture still in her Manhattan apartment in the house as it was now, and it blended seamlessly in her mind. She pictured her red velvet chaise lounge under the sunny window in the living room, with her linen-covered sofa in the center of the room and one of her aunt's paintings on the wall above the mantel. She looked around again and pulled her phone out of her pocket.

Skye picked up on the first ring. "Hey, stranger. I was about to hop on a plane if I didn't hear from you soon," she said. "How did everything turn out with the trial?"

"It's a long story, and I'll tell you every detail later," Loch said.

"But the short version is that they dropped the charges, and Amir was cleared. Even the judge apologized."

Loch held the phone away from her ear and waited for Skye's cheering to stop.

"I *knew* it!" Skye said finally, when she came back to the phone. "How is she after all that?"

"Tired, but happy." Loch paused. "So, I think I'm going to stay out here for a while."

Skye laughed. "There's a shock. Do you want me to send you some clothes?"

"Actually..." Loch smiled as she drew back the curtains on the kitchen window to let the sunlight in. "I know living with your mom is every twenty-year-old's dream, but how do you feel about living in my apartment for the next year or so until I decide what to do with it?"

"Are you kidding?" Skye's words tumbled over one another with excitement. "I'd love that!"

Loch smiled. "And if you pack up all my shit and oversee the movers I send out there, you can live there rent-free."

"Are you serious? Then I have to find some boxes, like, today. Mom has taken up singing in some old people's choir, and they practice in the house." She paused for dramatic effect. "Every night."

"Oh, God, seriously? Well, you have the key, so if you can get Georgia boi to help you pack my stuff up, the movers should be there by next week and you can start moving in."

"This is amazing, thank you." Loch heard the emotion in Skye's voice. "I can't wait to come out there and see you. I forgot how much I love Innis Harbor."

"Anytime," Loch said. "How's it going with the new girlfriend, anyway?"

There was a pause while Skye searched for the words. "I've seriously never been this happy in my life. She's amazing. You'll love her."

"Definitely bring her with you when you come out here to visit. I have a feeling she'll love it, too."

They talked for a few more minutes about a swim meet Skye

had coming up, then Loch got off the phone with a promise to send pictures of how the new paint colors looked on the walls while the house was still empty.

Loch clicked the phone off and put it back in her pocket, then walked to the door of Samia's studio. It was the only room in the house Loch had left untouched, and she felt Samia's energy hovering in the sun-warmed air the second she turned the doorknob and heard the familiar creak as the door swung open. A domed skylight filled the circular room with light, and dust-covered paintings were stacked up against the walls in organized chaos, some with splatters of paint on the exposed sides. Sensuous nudes in velvet shades of scarlet and graphite hung high on the wall next to vivid sea landscapes in unexpected colors and textures. Samia's art covered every inch of the studio, and the tops of the highest frames even butted up against the bottom of the skylight, as if vying with the sky for more space.

Loch walked around the studio, trailing her fingers over the edges of the frames, her memory warmed by seeing the canvases she'd watched Samia paint during her summers in Innis Harbor. Most of the art looked familiar, but there was one painting of her and Skye when they were little that she'd never seen before. She picked it up, running her fingers over the driftwood frame. In the picture, they were playing in the sand on an Innis Harbor beach. She recognized the local landscape and cliffs in the distance, but she knew Samia never painted outside the studio. But then the black leather sketchbook Samia always carried in her back pocket caught her eye. It was lying on the edge of a paint-splattered easel across the room. She must have sketched them playing on the beach, then used it to paint the scene later. Loch turned the painting over and read Samia's tiny script across the brown paper that covered the back of the canvas and frame.

*My Heart, March 14, 2019.*

Loch looked for any paintings with a more recent date but found none; it was the last painting that Samia had completed before she died. Loch picked it up and carried it into the sunny living room where she placed it on the mantel, leaning it lightly against the wall and stepping back to admire it.

The doorbell rang, and Loch stepped backward, taking a last look at the painting before she went to get the door. It was Amir, holding white takeout bags stamped with the market's sandwich shop logo.

Loch took them and pulled Amir inside, holding her close in the empty room and drawing in a deep, soft breath.

"What are you thinking, beautiful girl?" Amir tucked a stray lock of hair behind Loch's ear when she finally let her go.

Loch smiled up at her. "I'm thinking how good it is to be home."

❖

Later that afternoon, Amir was at the hardware store when she got a text from Cara.

*Can you meet me at the diner? It's important.*

Amir furrowed her brow and tried to think of any reason Cara would need to see her. They'd always remained friendly, but even back when they were seeing each other, they didn't really talk about their day-to-day lives. The diner was only two stores down on Main Street, so she paid for the bolts she'd chosen from the hardware sale bin and walked into the café.

"Hey," Cara said when she looked up from the register. "What did you do, teleport down here?"

"Yes," Amir said, choosing a bar stool and turning her coffee cup over. "Are you impressed?"

"Always," Cara said as she poured Amir's coffee. She went to the fridge and slid the cream down the counter to her, pouring herself a cup and meeting Amir's gaze. "You're not going to believe who was just in here."

"Why do I have a feeling I'm not going to like this?"

"Yeah," Cara said, glancing through the glass doors as if she was expecting whoever it was to walk back in. "That's pretty much guaranteed. It was Charlotte."

"Her parents sprung her out of jail, huh?"

"For now. From what she said, they pretty much threw the book at her, but she's still a minor, so it won't be on her permanent record."

"What did she want?"

"She wanted to tell you something, but I told her it might be better coming from me."

"That's an understatement." Amir smiled and tried to ignore the feeling of dread building in her chest. "What is it?"

"I don't know how to tell you this, so I'm just going to say it." Cara paused, leaning closer so no one would be able to hear her voice. "The person that hired her to frame you"—she hesitated—"was your dad."

"What? That makes no sense at all." Amir shook her head, trying to process what Cara was saying. "Why should I believe her?"

"I know. I didn't, either, but she showed me the texts on her phone." She paused. "They came from your dad's number, Amir. You gave it to me once when I was looking at renting that house on the beach."

"Do the police know that?"

"No. Believe it or not, she was savvy enough to switch SIM cards before the trial started." She looked around and dropped her voice again. "Only you and I know, and I told her I'd kill her myself if she ever told anyone about it."

Amir thought for a few long seconds, staring into her coffee, then looked up at Cara. "Thanks for handling her. I owe you one."

She was almost out the door when Cara gestured for her to come back and pressed something into her hand.

"What is this?"

Cara smiled. "You didn't think I was going to let her walk out of here with the SIM card, did you?"

❖

Amir pulled up to her parents' house a few minutes later. Only her dad's work van was sitting in the driveway; she knew her mom would still be putting in her volunteer hours at the library. She walked in and up the stairs, stopping at the door of her father's study. He was working on paperwork at the desk, humming and tapping his pen on the surface.

She knocked lightly on the door but didn't go in when he turned around in his chair to face her.

"Amira, what are you doing here?" He paused, confused. "Were we supposed to look at a house or something?"

He turned the page in his datebook, then looked back to Amir.

"Dad." Amir ignored the tear she felt drop onto her cheek. "I know."

Mr. Farzaneh leaned back in his chair, covering his face with his hands for a moment before he looked back at Amir, his jaw set, his face expressionless.

"Amira," he said. "What I did for you, I did out of love." He looked her in the eyes. "I don't want you to waste your life. You should be thinking about your future."

"So you thought it would be better if I spent the next twenty years in jail?"

He shook his head, and his face fell for just an instant. "I never intended it to get that far. I never told her to report it to the police, I only wanted her to start a rumor in town."

"Dad, why would you do that to me?" Amir sank into the tweed chair beside her father's leather-topped desk. "What good could possibly come of that?"

"I've tried to steer you in the right direction, Amira," he said, his knuckles white as he gripped the arms of his desk chair. "But you are so stubborn. You don't know what you're giving up to be…" His voice faltered, and he looked down.

"Be what, Dad?" Amir tried to control the anger starting to simmer in her mind like a distant tornado. "To be gay?"

Her father said nothing, just looked down.

"So, that was the point of all this?" she asked. "To punish me for being who I am?" He looked up at her finally, and Amir saw the emotion in his eyes.

"I knew people would hear about it, and I thought if your business slowed down, you might finally think about getting married and starting a family."

"You've got to be kidding me." Amir struggled to keep her voice at a respectful level. "You wanted to shame me into marrying some man I'd never love?"

Mr. Farzaneh slammed his fist on the desktop. "You don't know you'd never love him!" Tears shimmered in his eyes. "I didn't even know your mother when I married her, and we have a wonderful life and two beautiful children. I want that for you."

A few long seconds passed before he spoke again, his voice tinged with a softness Amir hadn't heard since before she came out. "I want you to be happy, to have someone who loves you in this world when your mother and I are gone."

"Dad, is that really what you think? That I'll be alone?"

Mr. Farzaneh turned and wiped his eyes with his arm.

"I'm in love with someone now that I hope to be with the rest of my life. She's amazing, and frankly, I don't deserve her."

"Is that Samia's niece?"

Amir nodded.

"I'm…" His voice faltered, and he stopped and started twice before he got the words out. "I am sorry I brought that boy over to meet you. Your mother is still angry at me." He paused. "I just didn't know what else to do."

Amira leaned forward. "I'm not angry anymore. I didn't know what was happening then, but I think I'm starting to understand." She hesitated. "But I need you to tell me the truth. Do you hate me because I'm gay, or were you just worried I'd never have what you and Mom have?"

"Amira." This time, he didn't bother to wipe the tears falling down his cheeks. "I've loved you from the moment I first held you in my arms. I could never hate you. I just wanted to be sure you'll be happy in life, and I didn't know how that would happen with"—his words faltered—"the gayness."

Amir smiled, then laughed, and finally even her father's face cracked into a smile.

"Really?" She tried to stop laughing, but it was just too good to pass up without a comment. "*The gayness*? Really?"

They laughed together until Mr. Farzaneh got up and poured Amir a short glass from his secret stash of bourbon, then one for himself.

"Does Mom know you drink?"

"I don't drink. I'm a Muslim," he said with a straight face. "There are certain things wives never need to know. Like the fact that your mother has also always been too good for me."

Father and daughter clinked glasses and took the first sip just as Amir's mother rounded the corner and stood in the doorway.

"I thought you were at the library," Mr. Farzaneh said, sliding the bottle back into his desk drawer.

"Don't bother hiding it, darling. I've known about your little stash for thirty years." She rolled her eyes, then looked at Amir. "Are you staying for dinner?"

"I can't, I have somewhere I need to be, but I'll come down and hug you before I leave."

"Fair enough." She paused, her voice suddenly soft. "It's good to see you two getting into trouble together again."

She left, and Amir waited until she heard her go down the stairs before she pulled a tiny metal square out of her pocket and put it in her dad's hand.

"What's this?"

"That's the SIM card from Charlotte's phone. The only proof that you ever had anything to do with this."

"Why are you giving this to me?"

"Because this secret stays with us." She squeezed his hand. "No one else needs to know."

❖

Later that evening, Loch was hunting for her lighter. Again. She'd looked in every drawer twice and had started to think about walking downtown to the hardware store before it closed. She picked up her phone to check the time, and it rang in her hand.

"Want to come over?" Amir asked. Loch heard the evening sounds of gulls flying over the water in the background. "I have a fire."

Loch smiled. "You know I can't resist a fire."

"Get ready, I'll pick you up in fifteen."

Loch clicked the phone off and jumped in the shower, then into the only pair of jeans she packed in her carry-on bag before the mad rush to the Manhattan airport. She pulled on a long-sleeved T-shirt and her down vest, grabbed her toothbrush, and dropped it into her bag on the way out to the porch.

A few minutes later she hopped in the passenger's side of the truck just as Amir was taking the keys out of the ignition.

"What?" Loch said. "I thought we were going to your house."

"We are." Amir wrapped her hand around the back of Loch's neck and pulled her into a kiss, letting her go reluctantly with a soft bite on her lower lip. "But we're taking your truck."

Loch looked confused for a second until she remembered Samia's antique Chevy that was hers as soon as she learned to drive it.

"You're kidding, right?"

"No, ma'am." Amir's gaze dropped to Loch's lips. "But you're going to need to be far less hot if I'm going to concentrate on backing that thing out of your garage."

In the end, Amir did manage to get the bright yellow Chevy out of the garage and onto the road, then pulled up behind her own truck and shifted the Chevy into neutral.

"Ready?"

"I'm not sure I'm ready to do this." Loch's lower lip made an appearance, and she looked up at Amir for a long second. "Will you drive it for me and let me watch you shift?"

Amir slid her hand up Loch's leg and raised an eyebrow. "I'm actually dying to drive this thing," she said. "But you're going to have to learn to drive it eventually, okay?" She looked around the white leather interior. "I know you can do it, and everything about it just looks like you."

"Deal."

Loch settled back as Amir put the truck into gear and pulled out onto the road to her cabin. The sun was setting quickly as they drove, and Loch rolled down her window to let the wind slide over her palm in the soft evening light. She didn't know what she wanted to do with her life from that point, and just that single thought made her feel lighter than she had in years. An idea had started to take shape in the back of her mind, pieced together from her past and whispering to her, but she wasn't sure she wanted to know yet.

As they pulled into the long, winding driveway of Amir's house, the path from her cabin to the dock was illuminated by candles flickering in iron lanterns. There were dozens of them, lining the length of the dock, illuminating the hardwood and the shimmering dark water on either side. The stars beginning to show in the night sky glittered above, as if reflecting the candlelight in the lanterns, but it was something ten yards or so out from the end of Amir's dock that caught Loch's eye. Mostly because it was on fire.

"Amir?" Loch got out of the truck and peered past the dock. "I think there's something burning out there."

Amir laughed and slipped the truck keys in Loch's pocket, taking her hand and leading her down to the dock. "I told you I had a fire."

They walked down to the end of the dock, and Amir pushed a button on one of the support beams at the outer edge. As the fire drew closer, Loch realized it was actually a copper firepit on a large square of hardwood dock.

"How is it getting closer?" She squealed, grabbing Amir's arm. "That's so beautiful. I love it!"

"I love that you're so easy to impress." Amir laughed, putting out a hand to stop the large square of floating dock and hook it onto the end of the main dock. "It's not magic, it's actually attached to the side of this dock by a steel wire that winds itself onto a motorized pulley when I press this button. That way, you don't drift out to sea or have to swim back."

Big pillows in bright prints lined the sitting space around the firepit, which had split logs stacked underneath. Dripping candles glowed at all four corners, and a stack of soft wool blankets waited at the edge.

"This is gorgeous," Loch said as she took off her shoes and let Amir help her onto the dock, which seemed surprisingly stable given that it was only attached to the main dock by two silver hooks. "I can't believe you did this for me."

Amir stepped onto the square after her and unhooked it, pushing out from the dock into open water. Gentle currents moved them away from shore, and night sky draped the floating square in navy velvet from every side. Loch closed her eyes and inhaled the scent of the cold seawater as a flock of white birds glided low over the surface, their chatter growing more and more distant as the last of the light faded.

When she opened her eyes, Loch noticed the scarred chrome toolbox on the other side of the firepit. "What's in that?"

Amir smiled. "I realize it's not the most romantic container," she said, lifting the lid. "But I didn't have anything else to put the chili dog stuff in."

"Are you serious?" she said. "That sounds amazing. I feel like I'm always starving now."

"I love that you eat now." Amir slid a hot dog on a metal stick and handed it over to her. "I worried about you all the time."

"I did, too, to be honest," Loch said. "I'm just going to eat like a normal person now and see where my body wants to settle. I think I'll end up similar to my sister. She weighs about twenty pounds more than me."

"What did the doc say you should weigh?"

"I'm just over five ten, so about a hundred thirty-five pounds at the lowest." Loch turned the stick so the flames started to bronze the other sides of her veggie dog. "I don't know if I'll quite get there, but I'll give it a shot."

Amir leaned over and handed her a bun. "Well, I have three aunts at a Persian restaurant in Bar Harbor that will be delighted to fix that little problem for you in an hour or less."

Loch laughed and opened the veggie chili container she found in the toolbox that was still surprisingly warm, and they ate under the stars, drifting in the seawater that lapped at the side of the dock. Loch decided to pile several logs on the fire at once while Amir was distracted, insisting as they roared to life that it must be safe since they were surrounded by water. Amir laughed and pulled her closer, handing her the hot dog stick to poke it with.

"I don't think I've said this yet." Loch leaned back against Amir's chest as they both watched the fire flare against the inky backdrop of the water. "But no one has ever done something for me like you did while I was gone."

"What do you mean?"

"The house." She settled back into Amir's arms as she wrapped them around Loch's shoulders. "I can't believe you finished everything. I got tears in my eyes the second I opened the door. It's perfect for me."

"Actually," Amir said, "you can thank Chris for that. When I got to your house the morning after Hamid bailed my sorry ass out of jail, Chris had already been there for four hours and had the kitchen painted in that warm yellow you picked out."

"He just showed up on his own and got to work?"

"He did." Amir smiled. "I tried to tell him that you'd gone back to Manhattan, but he just looked at me like I was stupid and handed me a paintbrush."

"That sounds like him," Loch said, smiling at the thought of Chris patiently teaching Graham how to two-step for his wedding. "What did he say?"

"To pull my head out of my ass."

"Is that a quote?"

Amir laughed, the sound echoing off the glass like surface of the water. "Yes, ma'am."

She pulled a blanket over Loch's legs and wrapped her arms around her shoulders as Loch poked the fire with the metal stick, sending blue and gold sparks swirling into the night sky.

"He said I had two choices," Amir said. "I could mope around like a chump or make you a home to come back to. Then he just stood there staring at me until I took the paintbrush, and we got on with it. It took us two solid weeks. He never even let me pay him."

Loch sat silent, looking into the fire for a few moments before she turned to Amir.

"I love you for making the house so beautiful for me." She watched the fire in the backlit amber of Amir's eyes. "But you're my home."

# Epilogue

*One year later*

Skye edged through the door laughing, carrying a flat wooden box piled with rustic bouquets of French lavender, fresh rosemary, and delicate purple and yellow freesia, each tied with a butter yellow strip of raw edged silk.

"I swear," Skye said. "If one more person mistakes me for the bride, I'm going to wear a name tag walking down the aisle."

Cara looked up from across the room where she was attempting to get some last-minute practice walking in heels. When Loch had asked her to be a bridesmaid, she'd neglected to mention that she'd be walking on stilts.

"Is it Amir's family?"

"No." Skye laughed. "This time, it was our great-aunt Jordy on Mom's side. You'd think she'd recognize her own family, but that pre-wedding cocktail hour was a huge hit with the over-seventy crowd. When I walked past just now, she was being seated by Hamid, holding her enormous purse in one hand and a martini glass in the other."

Anna laughed around the makeup brush in her mouth as she leaned in to do a last-minute touch-up on Loch's brows. "I know who I'm sitting by at the reception. She sounds like my kind of lady."

"She only sloshed on a couple of the guests as she went down the row," Skye said, handing Amy the last of the bridesmaid's bouquets. "And she made Hamid promise to bring her a refill before she let him go back up the aisle. Twice."

Loch smiled and laid a hand on her chest, realizing suddenly she was more nervous than she'd ever been in her life.

"Hey," Cara said, managing to totter over to Loch without falling over. "Are you okay?"

"I'm so nervous," Loch said. "I know this is silly, but what if Amir changes her mind? Do we know if she's even here?" She paused, closing her eyes against the thought. "Wait, don't tell me if she isn't."

Skye smiled at Loch and looked down into the garden from where she stood at the second-story window. The house belonged to one of Amir's aunts in Bar Harbor, and she'd invited them to use it for the wedding. It was a classic Maine home converted in the fifties from a rambling barn overlooking the sea, and dozens of white wood folding chairs dotted the vivid green lawn below. At the end of the aisle, there was a white wooden altar platform with two antique cathedral doors at the center, partially open to frame the view of the blue sea beyond.

"Hey, Loch," Skye said, looking down at the lawn below. "Come here."

Loch stood beside her, following her gaze below the window to the lawn. Amir looked up at her with soft eyes, touched her heart with her hand, then blew her a kiss before walking over to join Hamid, Chris, and Kiran at the altar.

Loch turned back toward her bridesmaids, nerves replaced by a beautiful smile. Anna put the finishing touches on Loch's makeup, then walked downstairs with the other girls to take their places and make sure the flower girl was ready for her trip down the aisle.

Loch took a final look in the mirror. Beautiful mehndi henna covered the back of her hands and extended past her wrists. Amir's mother applied the designs herself and included some of the same intricate patterns she'd worn when she married Amir's father. Her dress was antique ivory silk with clean, simple lines that fit her new healthier frame beautifully, and her sapphire engagement ring sparkled in the light from the window. It had belonged to Loch's great-great-grandmother, and Loch's mother had given it to Amir when she'd asked her permission to marry her. Amir had proposed with it a week later, and now it was her something blue.

"How do I look?" Loch turned to Skye.

"Happy," Skye said, tears shimmering in her eyes as she hugged Loch. "You look happy."

Minutes later, Loch and her bridesmaids watched from a hidden window as Yasmin started down the aisle with her basket of rose petals. Anna had practiced with her the night before on how to scatter them as she walked down the aisle, but Yasmin was so delighted by all the attention that she just passed out the rose petals to the guests in the aisle seats, giving a tiny handful to each, then paused for a moment at the front as she considered what to do with the rest. In the end, she dumped them all in a pile on the altar and handed Amir the sparkly white basket before she did a little bow and took her seat.

After every bridesmaid had taken her place at the altar, Loch slipped her hand around the arm beside her.

"Thank you for walking me down the aisle," she whispered. "It means the world to me."

"You're my daughter, too, now," Mr. Farzaneh whispered as the doors opened and Loch saw Amir waiting for her at the altar and blue sea beyond. "Where else would I be?"

## About the Author

Patricia Evans is currently writing your new favorite novel in her hand-built tiny house, nestled deep in the forest, where she's surrounded by a bevy of raccoons and a sleepy brown bear named Waddles.

She travels to Ireland and Scotland several times a year in search of the perfect whiskey and cigar combination and spends most of her time trying to ignore the characters from her books that boss her around as she writes by the fire.

Follow her adventures:
www.tomboyinkslinger.com
@tomboyinkslinger on Instagram
patricia@tomboyinkslinger.com

# Books Available From Bold Strokes Books

**Close to Home** by Allisa Bahney. Eli Thomas has to decide if avoiding her hometown forever is worth losing the people who used to mean the most to her, especially Aracely Hernandez, the girl who got away. (978-1-63679-661-1)

**Innis Harbor** by Patricia Evans. When Amir Farzaneh meets and falls in love with Loch, a dark secret lurking in her past reappears, threatening the happiness she'd just started to believe could be hers. (978-1-63679-781-6)

**The Blessed** by Anne Shade. Layla and Suri are brought together by fate to defeat the darkness threatening to tear their world apart. What they don't expect to discover is a love that might set them free. (978-1-63679-715-1)

**The Guardians** by Sheri Lewis Wohl. Dogs, devotion, and determination are all that stand between darkness and light. (978-1-63679-681-9)

**The Mogul Meets Her Match** by Julia Underwood. When CEO Claire Beauchamp goes undercover as a customer of Abby Pita's café to help seal a deal that will solidify her career, she doesn't expect to be so drawn to her. When the truth is revealed, will she break Abby's heart? (978-1-63679-784-7)

**Trial Run** by Carsen Taite. When Reggie Knoll and Brooke Dawson wind up serving on a jury together, their one task—reaching a unanimous verdict—is derailed by the fiery clash of their personalities, the intensity of their attraction, and a secret that could threaten Brooke's life. (978-1-63555-865-4)

**Waterlogged** by Nance Sparks. When conservation warden Jordan Pearce discovers a body floating in the flowage, the serenity of the Northwoods is rocked. (978-1-63679-699-4)

**Accidentally in Love** by Kimberly Cooper Griffin. Nic and Lee have good reasons for keeping their distance. So why does their growing attraction seem more like a love-hate relationship? (978-1-63679-759-5)

**Frosted by the Girl Next Door** by Aurora Rey and Jaime Clevenger. When heartbroken Casey Stevens opens a sex shop next door to uptight cupcake baker Tara McCoy, things get a little frosty. (978-1-63679-723-6)

**Ghost of the Heart** by Catherine Friend. Being possessed by a ghost was not on Gwen's bucket list, but she must admit that ghosts might be real, and one is obviously trying to send her a message. (978-1-63555-112-9)

**Hot Honey Love** by Nan Campbell. When chef Stef Lombardozzi puts her cooking career into the hands of filmmaker Mallory Radowski—the pickiest eater alive—she doesn't anticipate how hard she'll fall for her. (978-1-63679-743-4)

**London** by Patricia Evans. Jaq's and Bronwyn's lives become entwined as dangerous secrets emerge and Bronwyn's seemingly perfect life starts to unravel. (978 1 63679 778 6)

**This Christmas** by Georgia Beers. When Sam's grandmother rigs the Christmas parade to make Sam and Keegan queen and queen, sparks fly, but they can't forget the Big Embarrassing Thing that makes romance a total nope. (978-1-63679-729-8)

**Unwrapped** by D. Jackson Leigh. Asia du Muir is not going to let some party-girl actress ruin her best chance to get noticed by a Broadway critic. Everyone knows you should never mix business and pleasure. (978-1-63679-667-3)

**Language Lessons** by Sage Donnell. Grace and Lenka never expected to fall in love. Is home really where the heart is if it means giving up your dreams? (978-1-63679-725-0)

**New Horizons** by Shia Woods. When Quinn Collins meets Alex Anders, Horizon Theater's enigmatic managing director, a passionate connection ignites, but amidst the complex backdrop of theater politics, their budding romance faces a formidable challenge. (978-1-63679-683-3)

**Scrambled: A Tuesday Night Book Club Mystery** by Jaime Maddox. Avery Hutchins makes a discovery about her father's death that will force her to face an impossible choice between doing what is right and finally finding a way to regain a part of herself she had lost. (978-1-63679-703-8)

**BOLDSTROKESBOOKS.COM**

Looking for your next great read?

Visit BOLDSTROKESBOOKS.COM
to browse our entire catalog of paperbacks, ebooks,
and audiobooks.

**Want the first word on what's new?
Visit our website for event info,
author interviews, and blogs.**

Subscribe to our free newsletter for sneak peeks,
new releases, plus first notice of promos
and daily bargains.

**SIGN UP AT**
BOLDSTROKESBOOKS.COM/signup

# Bold Strokes Books
Quality and Diversity in LGBTQ Literature

*Bold Strokes Books is an award-winning publisher
committed to quality and diversity in LGBTQ fiction.*